CW00485195

THE Changing ROOM

JANE TURLEY

Sweet and Salty Books

Sweet and Salty Books
www.sweetandsaltybooks.net

Copyright © Jane Turley 2014
The right of the above author has been assigned in accordance
with the Copyright, Designs and Patents Act 1988. All rights
reserved. No part of this publication may be reproduced, stored
in a retrieval system, or transmitted in any form or by any means
electronic, mechanical, photocopying, recording or otherwise,
without prior permission of the publisher.

All characters and events in this book, other than those clearly in
the public domain, are entirely fictitious and any resemblance to
anyone, either living or dead, is purely coincidental.

A catalogue record of this book is available from the British
Library.

ISBN 978-0-9928754-4-2

Cover designed by Gracie Klumpp
www.gracieklumpp.com
Formatting by Polgarus Studio
www.polgarusstudio.com

Also by Jane Turley

A Modern Life
sweet and salty short stories

Discover more of Jane's writing on her blog, The Witty
Ways of a Wayward Wife at www.janeturley.net.
Connect with her via Facebook at
www.facebook.com/janeturleywriter
or on Twitter @turleytalks

In Memory

of

John & Christina Dempsey

&

Raymond & Audrey Turley

1

"You're fat," says Mum.

"I'm not fat! I'm just a little overweight," I say, turning pink as I try to slide the sassy pinstripe dress off and it sticks around my waist.

"Would you like to try a bigger size?" says the sales assistant.

"Not whilst I'm still breathing," I reply, sucking in my stomach with the sharp intake of breath I normally save for pictures of Daniel Craig's chest. The dress still won't budge so reluctantly I pull it carefully off over my head.

"I hate Sarah Jessica Parker," I mutter.

"When I was your age I didn't have a spare tyre. We couldn't afford luxury food. It was just the basics," says Mum in a reproachful voice from her seat in the corner of the changing room.

"I hardly eat anything!"

Mum snorts and gestures at my stomach with her walking stick. "She'll try a sixteen."

"Mum!"

The assistant looks pityingly at me. I'm not sure whether it's because I need a bigger size or because Mum is being a complete pain in the arse. Come to think about it, it *is* because Mum is being a pain in the arse. We've been in Trés Chic for about twenty minutes while I look for a new suit for work which I'm also planning to wear for the PTA meeting later this week and so far Mum's had a cup of tea, a visit to the loo, knocked over a display of hats and broken a string of fake pearls. If she wasn't my mum I would have disowned her. Although, to be honest, I haven't ruled that out yet.

The assistant slips out of the changing room to fulfil Mum's request as I grimace and study myself in the full length mirror. I hate these group changing rooms. It's bad enough seeing your own thighs up close and personal without everyone else doing so too. And if the whole process of clothes shopping isn't soul destroying enough when you're over forty why on earth did I think bringing Mum with me was a sensible idea? I must be going insane. By the end of this shopping expedition we could both be bonkers. I had this stupid idea that, despite her Alzheimer's, Mum could cope with a couple of dress shops and a coffee before rounding it off with a visit to M&S's twinset and pearl section to buy the replacement clothes she so badly needs. That would be about two hours at most with a good thirty minutes sitting down in a cafe. As it stands, this outing is proving to be the longest two hours of my life.

"I've brought the next size up," says the assistant, tactfully not mentioning my size as she slips back inside the changing room with several dresses draped over her arm. "And I've brought some other dresses too. I know the blue one is not what you're looking for but it would really suit you. It's a perfect match for your eyes."

"I might as well try anything you've got that fits," I say, prompted to take a closer look at my eyes in the mirror. The good news is that I can still see them; the bad news is that my mascara has run and I look like Joan Rivers on speed. I groan out loud.

"It's no good feeling sorry for yourself," says Mum, waving her stick at me again. "You'll have to get off your backside and shift that fat. When I was a girl…"

Oh. Please. God. Not another "when I was a girl" story.

"…I would walk three miles to school and three miles back again and then when I got home I would scrub the floors and sweep the backyard. You young people don't get enough exercise. You drive everywhere, fly abroad for holidays and have no idea what a hard day's work is. That's the problem!"

The assistant turns away to hide her amusement. She pulls out a tissue from a nearby box and without saying a word turns back and hands me a tissue to blot away my mascara, a look of sympathy and understanding in her eyes.

"Mum, life isn't like it was years ago," I say. "It's different now. The pace of life is much faster. We have different problems to contend with and I have a full-time job, a self-employed husband for whom I also do a lot of work, three kids and a host of other commitments."

"That's no excuse for being fat."

"Maybe not. But we all have our weaknesses, Mum. I don't drink too much, I don't smoke and I don't have time to go to the gym or pamper myself."

"It shows," snorts Mum.

The assistant zips up the side seam of the size sixteen whilst I decide to ignore Mum's last remark. Instead I watch her reflection in the mirror as she sticks her head inside the enormous bag she insists on taking everywhere.

"That's a much better fit," says the assistant.

"I still look like a beached whale," I say with resignation.

"No comment," says Mum trying to get the lid off a jar of Vicks nasal rub.

"Try on the matching jacket," says the assistant with an encouraging smile. "They're wonderful for covering all those bits we'd rather not see."

I slip the jacket on, turn around and view my backside in the mirror.

"That's not so bad," I say, knowing that while it does the job the outfit is not as flattering as I'd hoped.

"My lips feel strange," says Mum, pulling a face like she's bitten into some overly ripe Stilton.

"Mum, that's nasal rub not lip salve!" I say, turning around and grabbing the pot of Vicks out of her hand.

The assistant quickly hands me another tissue and I wipe the Vicks off Mum's lips the same way I used to wipe the kids' bottoms.

"Don't lick your lips," I say in my authoritative voice as Mum and I switch roles and I'm the carer again. "We'd better get you to the bathroom and get this off properly."

My shoulders sag as I imagine Mum in casualty with camphor poisoning whilst I'm investigated by social services for being an unfit daughter. What was turning out to be a bad morning could turn out to be a hideously bad morning.

"Let me do it," says the assistant, calmly.

"Are you sure?" I reply, my resistance slipping away. The assistant's offer is beyond the call of duty and Mum's definitely going to be more difficult than your average customer but sometimes...sometimes I just need some help.

"Don't worry. It'll be fine," says the assistant. "You try on your outfits and I'll sort it."

"Thanks," I say, complying with the assistant without the polite refusal one should normally give in these circumstances. I step back and let her take over, a wave of relief flowing over me.

"You have a few moments to yourself," says the assistant, taking hold of Mum's hand and guiding her out of the changing room.

I take off the suit and try on the other dresses, saving the blue one to last. The first two dresses look much better than I expected. I'm tempted to have both of them as well as the suit but that would be a huge extravagance, which with Dave's business as it is at the moment, I simply cannot justify. I look sternly at my reflection in the mirror. I must be very selective; I can afford one outfit, two at a stretch.

I put the suit to one side to contemplate further and reluctantly hang the other two dresses on a rail to be returned to the showroom. That leaves the blue dress which has caught my eye. I take it off the hanger and hold it up against my body. Thankfully, it's long enough to cover up the top of my tan coloured pop socks. The dress is the colour of the Caribbean Sea, the material is soft and flowing and ripples in waves under my touch and it is, as the assistant said, the perfect match for my eyes. I've never thought of my eyes as like the sea before but somehow this dress seems to bring out the blueness in them. I slip it over my head and it slides effortlessly over my pear shaped hips. I zip up the small seam under my arm and as if by magic the dress comes alive on me. I twirl around in it and look at it from all angles. It has long flowing sleeves with a low cut top which accentuates my breasts and it gathers at the waist to make it look like I've actually got one before falling smoothly over my hips and swirling around my calves. Now I look less like Joan Rivers and more like…me. The me I used to be.

"Now that looks stunning on you," says the assistant reappearing with Mum at her side. "I knew it would."

"Yes. Very nice," says Mum. "I wish my daughter would buy a dress like that. It would cover her bottom."

"I *am* your daughter."

"Well, you must buy it, my dear," says Mum, momentarily disconcerted before a brief flicker of recognition crosses her face.

"I think I will," I say, knowing Mum is still not totally sure who I am because she always calls me "my dear" when she can't remember my name.

"Have you got any shoes to go with that outfit?" says Mum to the assistant, pointing with her stick at my dirty trainers which are pushed up against the wall. "Some of these modern trends are quite disgusting. In my day, everyone wanted to look like Audrey Hepburn. Nowadays everyone wants to look like… like…"

"P. Diddy," I say as Mum struggles for a name.

"Yes. That's right, P. Diddy," says Mum, knowledgably. Even though I know she doesn't have a clue who P. Diddy is.

"Actually, I think I've got something that will be perfect and will suit your present circumstances," laughs the assistant and looks down at my swollen toe which is why I've been wearing the trainers I use to walk Mutley. "What happened?"

"A boy ran over it with his bike."

"You have been in the wars," says the assistant, leaving the room again with another pitying smile.

You know, the assistant is right. I do feel like I've been in the wars. It's been such a struggle lately, especially the last few years as Mum's mental health has declined. I need to do something about it. But I'm not exactly sure what or even where to start.

"Who's P. Diddy?" says Mum, interrupting my thoughts.

"A rapper."

"What's a rapper?" says Mum.

"Well, rapping is a type of modern music where they do a lot of rhythmic talking. A rapper is someone who does it," I reply.

"A bit like the vicar when he sings the Eucharist?"

"Um…sort of…only with more backing music."

"Try these," says the assistant, presenting me with a pair of strappy blue sandals with big decorative white daisies on the front.

"Oh, they're gorgeous!" I exclaim and slip them on, seeing at once that the daisies distract from my swollen toe and black toenail.

I gaze at myself in the mirror again in the beautiful blue dress and sexy sandals. They make me look taller and less like a hobbit. A wave of optimism washes over me; I look and feel refreshed even though inside I'm totally frazzled. Maybe I'm having one of those moments when you're rejuvenated by a new hair style; one of those occasions when you're inspired to change things and make life better. Perhaps this is one of those moments. Maybe I *can* change my life.

"Sold," I say, running my fingers over the fine fabric again. "And the sandals."

"If you slip them off I'll pop them in a bag for you," says the assistant, smiling. "What about the suit?"

"I think I'm going to leave it for the moment," I say. "I need to lose a few pounds first for that one."

Mum snorts again as if to say a few pounds is not quite enough.

* * * * *

"These look comfy," says Mum as I return from the cash desk where I've been keeping a watchful eye on her progress around M&S.

Mum holds up a pair of extra-large Christmas novelty pants emblazoned with reindeers.

"They're men's pants," I say, trying to keep my exasperation under control.

"Are they? They're very nice. I had no idea men's pants were so attractive these days. Perhaps we could get some anyway?"

"I've just bought you some underwear," I say, raising my arm so Mum can see the plastic carriers weighing me down. "We also chose a coat, a roll neck jumper and two cardigans. Remember?"

"Oh yes, of course, dear," says Mum. "Splendid."

"I think we should make a move now," I say, beginning to break out in a sweat with the cumbersome bags and the heat of the store. "I'll take you back home and we'll have lunch."

I bend down and rearrange my shopping bags so they're easier to hold, taking my eyes off Mum for a moment. When I look up Mum has wandered off to admire the men's dressing gowns.

"Mum," I say, loudly. "Let's go."

"I'm coming, dear."

We head towards the exit. I struggle along with the bags whilst Mum points at products with her cane and almost decapitates a woman carrying a poinsettia. A security guard spots us, and realising I'm fully occupied keeping my shopping and Mum under control, politely holds the doors open.

"What a lovely young man," says Mum as the security guard gives us a warm smile.

"Y…es," I say, my voice trailing away as I notice some black material with a reindeer on it sticking out of Mum's right hip pocket.

The fine film of moisture that was already on my forehead turns into a tidal wave of sweat as I realise Mum is in the process of shoplifting men's underwear from M&S. What's more, it's too late to do anything about it without elongated explanations and acute embarrassment.

"Are you alright, madam?" says the guard.

"Hot flush," I say, waving a hand of dangling carriers in front of my face which fortuitously blocks his view of Mum.

"Never a good time for one of those," he replies with a jovial wink.

"No," I say with a false smile. "Thanks for your help."

We walk a few steps out into the shopping mall where I omit an almighty sigh of relief that Mum has not been caught shoplifting. I let out an even bigger sigh of relief that I have not been caught colluding with her. I immediately decide I'll buy an M&S gift voucher at a later date and rip it up to ease my conscience.

"Are you alright, dear?" says Mum.

"Yes, fine, Mum. Let's go home."

We walk into the adjacent multi-storey car park and wait for the lift. The doors slide open and we step in.

"What floor, dear?" says Mum as I struggle with the bags and she hovers her finger over the control panel.

My mind goes blank; I have absolutely no recollection of where I parked my car. Except it was in a corner somewhere. Maybe. I search the far recesses of my mind.

"I think it's Level Four," I say, hoping that my memory will kick in the same way it does at the supermarket checkouts after that moment of initial terror when I think I've forgotten my PIN number.

We arrive at Level Four. The doors open, we leave the foyer and walk into the dimly lit car park. I scan the nearby rows of cars and realise with absolute certainty I have no idea where I parked the car and, even if I did know at the time we arrived, the stress of the last two hours has been more than enough to wipe my entire memory of the event.

I stare vacantly into space whilst I think over a course of action. One thing's for sure, I cannot drag Mum all over a huge multi-storey car park.

"I can't remember where the car is," I say.

"Oh dear," says Mum. "Are you sure we didn't come by train?"

"No, it was definitely by car," I say. "Let's go down to the ground floor and see security. You can stay with them whilst I look for it."

"Fish is good for memory loss," says Mum. "You need to eat more of it. When I was a girl we had fish every Friday."

I clamp the retort on the tip of my tongue and escort Mum back to the lift. When we step out on the ground floor I see the security guard is preoccupied with two police officers whose squad car is pulled up in a nearby parking bay. My heart begins to palpitate. I turn around with my back to the officers, pull out the reindeer pants from Mum's pocket and shove them into one of the M&S bags.

"What are you doing?" says Mum in bewilderment.

"Just making sure you don't get banged up, Mother."

I lead Mum over to where the security guard and officers are chatting. It sounds like there's been a theft in the car park. For a moment I pray it's my car that's been stolen and I'll be saved the humiliation of not knowing where my car is, but it soon becomes apparent that someone had left their Christmas shopping on the back seat of their car and an opportunist thief has nabbed it.

"Excuse me, officers," I say. "I'm sorry to interrupt. But could I have a quick word with security?"

The three men stop talking and look at me with interest. I imagine I appear pretty distressed and dangerously volatile. I certainly feel that way.

"Go ahead," says the older of the two officers.

"I'm terribly sorry," I say, addressing the security guard. "I've been a complete idiot and totally forgotten where I've parked my car. Would it be possible if my mother could sit in your office with my bags whilst I look for it?"

I'm standing in front of Mum so I whisper, "She's got Alzheimer's," so the guard understands my predicament.

"I know you've forgotten where the car is, dear," pipes up Mum. "But I don't think you've got Alzheimer's. Are you absolutely sure we didn't come by train?"

I give the security guard my best pleading look.

"I tell you what, love," says the older police officer before the security guard can say anything. "Why don't you and your mum jump in our car and we'll drive you around."

"Thanks, but there's no need for that," I say even more flustered; I don't want the help of the police force when I'm harbouring a stolen pair of underpants.

"It's no trouble," says the officer and takes my bags.

I've no choice but to comply so Mum and I follow the two officers to their car and climb into the rear seats. The young officer is driving and reverses out of the bay and pulls up ready for instructions.

"I think this is an emergency," says the older officer.

The young officer turns on the blue lights and siren and the two of them burst out laughing.

"Which one of you has Alzheimer's?" says the young officer, looking at me in the rear view mirror.

I force a smile and wonder why I thought buying a new dress could change my fortunes.

2

"These pants look a little too big," says Mum as I enter the lounge where she's seated with her back to me in her favourite flowery high-backed chair which has prime position in front of her digital, all singing and dancing television, her only real acknowledgement of the technological advancements of the last forty years. The rest of the house pays homage to the 1970s - and not exactly in a way that makes you feel nostalgic.

"They're the same size you always have," I reply.

"Really?" says Mum holding up the stolen men's boxer shorts, not her new ladies' pants, as I move to her side and place her cup of tea on her coffee table. "I had no idea I'd gained weight. It must have crept up on me without me noticing."

"You're right, they do look on the large side," I say, remembering Mum's recent lambast of me in the dress shop and rather enjoying her discomfort at the thought of putting on weight, even though the truth is she resembles a stick insect. I've always wished I'd had a physique more like Mum's rather than my Dad's which was more rotund and, no doubt, led to his fatal heart attack ten years ago. That fear alone should be reason enough for me to lose weight – never mind the fact my thighs haven't seen the inside of size ten jeans for twenty years.

"Age does terrible things to your body," says Mum still aghast at the size of the pants and shaking her head in disbelief. "The next thing I know I'll be losing my mind."

"I think you're already there," I mutter under my breath.

"Where am I?" says Mum.

"At home," I sigh. "And those are the men's underpants you stole from M&S."

"I stole them?"

"Yes. You put them in your pocket and *stole* them."

"Oh dear," says Mum, her eyes filling with tears.

"No, no. I'm only kidding," I say, regretting my words and pulling another fake smile. "We bought them as your Christmas present for Dave. Remember? He'll love them."

"Oh yes, of course we did," says Mum, eager to dismiss the thought of her stealing. "For a moment, I thought you were being serious."

"Don't be daft, Mum. Besides, Dave will love the reindeer pattern. They're the sort of fun but really useful Christmas present he likes."

Mum beams and starts to fold the boxer shorts into a neat little package.

"What would like in your sandwich?" I say as Mum smooths out the creases in the fabric and peels off a sticker. I imagine Dave's reaction as he unwraps his gift; I should probably forewarn him so he doesn't swear in front of the kids.

"What have we got?" says Mum as my phone vibrates in my jeans' pocket.

"Chicken, tuna or cheese. Have a think whilst I get this call. It's probably Dave trying to get out of parents' evening tonight."

I pull out my phone and straight away see it's not Dave. I let out a long, arduous groan.

"Who is it, dear?" says Mum.

"Mr Frost, my boss at the store. I'll leave it," I say, terminating the call and replacing the phone in my pocket.

"You shouldn't have done that. It could have been urgent."

"Unlikely," I say as the phone starts vibrating again.

"You see; it is urgent. No one would ring back that quickly unless it was an emergency," says Mum.

"Frosty's emergencies aren't like other people's emergencies, Mum. To most people an emergency is a broken leg or a sudden death. To Frosty it's when he can't find a marker pen for his whiteboard."

Mum frowns so, reluctantly, I accept the call.

"Mr Frost," I say, deadpan.

"Sandy?"

"That's me."

"I have a crisis."

"You've lost your whiteboard marker?"

There's a brief pause whilst Frosty digests what I've said and then let's out one of his stilted nasal laughs.

"Yes, good one, Sandy. By God, I wish you'd been in the army with me. I could have done with you as my adjutant. It helps to have someone around with a sense of humour when there's a crisis. Keeps the morale up amongst the workers. Now, can you come in today? Mrs M's sprained her ankle and Guy's rung in sick. I need someone to help cover the lunch breaks."

"I'm spending the day with my mother. My *elderly* mother," I exaggerate so hopefully he gets the message that I don't want to go in.

"I'm sure she won't mind if you explain."

"I've given her carer the day off."

"Could you bring her with you?" says Frosty after a brief pause.

"Are you serious?"

"There wasn't too much damage last time."

I walk back out to Mum's kitchen so she can't hear what I'm saying; I don't want to upset her again.

"Last time was the *last* time, Mr Frost."

"Please, Sandy. I need you. There's no one at all to cover soft furnishings. I could have the television wheeled up from the staffroom to accounts – that way Margery can keep an eye on her so we don't have a repeat of last time. It was only a small flood anyway. We didn't even have to call a plumber."

"Mr Frost, I am not…"

"Please, Sandy. You know you're my most prolific salesperson; I have the highest regard for you. I can pay you double time."

"Mr Frost…"

"If you can make it for 12.30 pm that would be first class."

"Mr Frost…" I say with resignation, as I know Frosty isn't going to give up without a fight. "This has to be the last time. The *very* last time."

"I won't ask again"

"Is that a promise?"

"12.30 pm then?" says Frosty, conveniently ignoring my question.

"Alright," I say sullenly and cut him off.

"Mum?" I say going back into the lounge.

"Yes, dear?"

"I've got to go into work. You'll have to come too."

"Now? I was just going to try on these new pants. Aren't they lovely?"

Mum holds up the reindeer boxer shorts. Again.

* * * * *

I hold open the door to Hendersons and wave Mum through into the furniture store where I spend most of my weekdays, weekends and the occasional evening. Hendersons is like a second home: only it's neater, cleaner and generally quieter than my actual home. Perhaps that's no surprise when I've got two kids leaving a trail of devastation wherever they go, another who drops in from university with mounds of stinking washing on a frequent basis, a dog, a cat and my husband, Dave, who trudges in and out of the house in his work gear dropping grains of cement and sand and wood shavings everywhere. To put it bluntly, my home resembles the inside of a launderette that has had a close encounter with some Semtex explosives. Hendersons, whilst cleaner and tidier than my home does, however, have its own set of unique problems. Today, the problem is a customer complaint because as I lead Mum across the showroom towards the offices a vitriolic voice rises above the soft background music.

"I know it's fucking broken! Why do you think I'm here?" says a stocky muscular man, waving a broken table leg in the air.

"Yes, sorry. I didn't mean for it to come out that way," stutters Harvey, our fast track management trainee. Harvey, twenty two and skinny as a rake, is the epitome of the spotty student fresh out of college who didn't see daylight between the ages of thirteen and twenty one. Flustered and red-faced, he shuffles from one foot to another as the customer continues to shout at him about his broken table.

"I want a new table!" shouts the burly man still gesticulating with the table leg as we pass him and his even burlier son, neither of whom would look out of place in a rugby scrum.

"Put that down, before you hurt someone," I say, as Mum flinches.

The man turns to me and gives me a long, hard stare. "Push off, you nosey cow. It's none of your business."

Harvey shoots me a pleading look for help but since I'm with Mum, it's my day off and he gets paid more than me as a graduate, I decide it's time he took the fast track customer complaints course.

"What a horrid man, he looks like a Rottweiler" says Mum looking back at the complaining customer. "I wonder if he's a Nazi?"

There's a momentary silence behind us.

"I doubt it, Mum," I say, "although there's more than a passing resemblance to Hermann Goering."

"Bitches," says the man.

"Take no notice, my dear," says Mum, patting me reassuringly on the arm. "He's obviously very inarticulate."

"Mr Frost will have to take over; Harvey is completely out of his depth," I say as "I want to see the manager" rings in our ears as we exit the showroom.

"Thank goodness you're here, Sandy," says Margery as Mum and I turn into the accounts office.

Margery is our hyper-efficient accounts manager in her early sixties. She's superb with numbers but she starts to panic when things, other than numbers, start to go wrong.

"We're having crisis after crisis this morning. You're exactly the person we need. I've just heard from head office that the MD is passing through on a fleeting visit. He'll be here in less than an hour."

"Does Frosty know?" I reply.

"Not yet," says Margery, taking a gulp of air. "I can't get hold of him."

"What do you mean - you can't get hold of him?"

"He had a phone call about thirty minutes ago. Apparently it was an emergency and he said he needed to leave straight away. He said to tell you that you're in charge until he gets back."

"What? This is supposed to be my day off. I only agreed to cover lunch breaks not run the store!"

Margery pulls open her desk drawer, takes a puff of her inhaler and forces an encouraging smile. Unfortunately, just then Harvey appears dishevelled and breathless in the doorway. His jacket is falling off to one side of his bony shoulders, his tie is askew and his cheeks are blotchy as if he's about to burst into tears. Margery takes a second puff of her inhaler as she senses another imminent crisis.

"Sandy, please can you help me with this customer? He's going ballistic," pleads Harvey. "Nothing I say is helping and now he wants to see the manager. You're the most experienced senior member of staff here."

"The most *underpaid* senior member of staff," I reply.

"Please, Sandy," says Harvey. "I don't know what to do. He's a nutter."

"You're the only hope we've got," says Margery, backing up Harvey. "We need you."

"This is not the Titanic, Margery," I say. "It's a furniture store."

"Pleassssse," says Harvey.

I pull a DVD out of my handbag knowing that I've no choice but to get on with the job before Harvey and Margery both have nervous breakdowns. Why they are both working in retail I have no idea; Margery is more suited to the antiquities department of the British Museum and Harvey is more suited to something else – I'm not sure what but probably something a long, long way away. In Iceland, maybe.

"Mum will watch this," I say and hand Margery the DVD.

"The Great Escape?" says Margery.

"Don't ask," I say, steering Mum towards Margery, "Just take care of her." I turn back to Harvey and give him instructions whilst I take off my coat.

"Put the word out the MD is on his way and tell anyone on lunch break to cut it short and make it up to the showroom by 12.45. They can have extended lunch breaks and cream cakes later in the week. Don't forget to say "Please." Then get back to the showroom and make sure the front doors are completely clean and free of smears - first impressions count."

I leave the room, picking up my walkie-talkie off the holding rack in the corridor and call Derek, our security guard.

"We've a nutter in the showroom," I say.

"Yes, I'm monitoring it."

"Give me five minutes with him and then come on down. I don't want you to antagonise him but if it escalates further be ready to step in."

"Will do, Sandy."

I re-enter the showroom and head over to the customer who is now pacing up and down like a trapped animal. His son looks twitchy and nervous and I wonder if it's because his dad's public meltdown is embarrassing him or whether it's because he knows something more about the table.

"Good afternoon," I say, using my most professional demeanour and deciding the way forward is to pretend we've not encountered each other before. "I understand you have a problem with your dining room table."

"You!" shouts the man. "I don't believe it. You're the manager?"

"No, I'm not the manager," I reply. "The manager is off duty and I am the senior staff on the premises."

"I'm not talking to you. You insulted me. And you're a…*woman.*"

"Dad…" interjects the boy, who's now completely red-faced.

"I can make an appointment for you to come back and see the manager at a later date. Would that help?" I say, ignoring the chauvinistic comment.

"I haven't come in here to be told I have to come back another day," says the man, the veins on his neck standing proud. "My son sat on the table and it collapsed underneath him. He's trialling for the England rugby team next month and your fucking table nearly killed him. I want a new table and compensation!"

The young lad now has guilt written all over his face. I suspect he didn't sit on the table but his whole rugby team jumped up and down on it during some crazed booze-up, probably whilst his dad was topping up his tan in Tenerife or on the golf course swigging back gin and tonics.

"Well, it does sound like we need to get to the bottom of this as clearly we cannot have our customers and their children's lives put at risk by our tables," I say. "Perhaps you'd like to take a seat and we can discuss what we can do to help?"

"Just get me the manager."

"As I said, he's not here. I can help you - if you'll allow me to."

"Fuck off."

"As you wish," I say and turn around and head off to the central administration area.

"Hey, where do you think you're going?" calls the man. "Don't you walk away from me when I'm talking to you."

"You're not talking to me," I say, turning around to face him. "You're yelling at me. You're being rude and objectionable to me and my staff. And neither they, nor I, are paid enough to stand here and listen to your ravings. This is actually my day off; I've been asked to come in to help because of staff shortages and I'm not going to take any crap from you or anyone else."

The man stares back at me for a moment, undecided what course of action he should take. I carry on talking whilst I've got the chance.

"So if you want me to sort this problem, I can. But first we have to return to some sort of civility. I'm going to make a coffee and fetch my notepad whilst you take a moment to calm down. If you decide you don't want to talk in a reasonable manner then please leave - or I will have you ejected from the premises."

The man screws his neck even further into his shoulders so that he looks like an angry rhinoceros. At any moment I expect him to impale me to the nearest wall.

"What's your father's name?" I say to the boy.

"Rob… Mr Knight," he replies.

"Please take a seat, Mr Knight" I say. "I'm going to get the coffee."

I walk over to the central administration podium and rummage through the CDs whilst I sense Mr Knight's eyes burning into me like the sights of a telescopic rifle.

"What are you doing?" says Harvey, appearing at my side still clutching a cleaning cloth and glass spray.

"I'm giving him some chill time to think about what a complete arsehole he's been whilst I put on some therapeutic music. Hopefully, it'll be something he'll recognise and empathise with. This should do," I say, holding up a Carpenters' CD.

"Who are The Carpenters?" says Harvey.

"You've a lot to learn, Harvey" I say.

I put the disk in the CD player and set the track to Close To You and turn up the volume slightly. Karen Carpenter's melodic voice fills the showroom. I make a coffee using the filter machine, as I do when I'm schmoozing customers on the verge of opening their wallets, when I notice that Mr Knight has finally sat down on one of the leather suites. I lower the volume down on the loud speakers and switch on the tannoy.

"Mr Knight," my voice echoes around showroom, "one sugar or two?"

Mr Knight looks over and raises two fingers in a deliberate manner. I wave a finger at him like he's a naughty school boy and slowly he turns his fingers around the other way into a Churchill victory sign. I smile sarcastically at him and, as I stir his coffee, I decide to serenade him (with the help of Karen Carpenter) during the last chorus and closing refrain. He stares at me in total disbelief, as do the sprinkling of other customers who have been eagerly watching the unfolding events. Harvey looks at me as if he has no idea what I'm doing because singing to customers isn't in any of the training manuals. Which it isn't. However, I decide that if Mr Knight wants a new table out of me, he's going to have to suck up my (dubious) musical talents. When the song ends, I make my way over to where Mr Knight is seated and put down his coffee on the mahogany display table in front of him.

"Shall we talk?" I say.

* * * * *

I fling open the door to my car and stick the keys in the ignition as Mum settles herself in the passenger seat and opens her bag to start ferreting again.

"Seat belt, Mum," I prompt.

"Oh yes, of course," says Mum and closes her bag and turns to put on her seat belt.

"Right, we have twenty minutes to get to school to meet Tabby for parents' evening. I managed to get a 4.30 pm appointment so she's staying on in the library. I'll have to take you home afterwards. Is that okay?"

"Whatever you say, dear," says Mum.

"Right, let's go," I say starting up the engine. "Next time I see Frosty I'm going to kill him for dumping me in it."

I drive as fast as I can, braking sharply for the speed cameras on route, whilst I imagine nailing Frosty's nipples to the staffroom door. Not only did I have to spend almost an hour placating Mr Knight but I had to do thirty minutes kissing arse with the MD before Mr Frost returned and dismissed me with a cursory, if somewhat embarrassed, nod.

Mum and I pull into the solitary place left in the school car park and Tabby runs out from the school foyer towards us. Her socks, which were white this morning, are now grey, her hair is a tangled mess and there's a stain on her blouse that suggests school dinner was spaghetti bolognese.

"Mum, you're five minutes late," says Tabby in her *my mother is an idiot* voice.

"It won't matter, they're always behind schedule," I reply. "Is your father here?"

"No, he's late too," says Tabby, as if Dave and I are the naughty ones when she's the one who's always in trouble. Needless to say, I don't generally enjoy parents' evenings.

"Oh well, I'm sure he'll be along any minute. Why don't you help Nan out of the car and bring her in whilst I go and get in the queue?"

I make my way to the corridor outside Mrs Frampton's class where a number of parents and children are already waiting.

"How long is she behind?" I say to Tim Lewis, a father of one of the boys in Tabby's class, who is the nearest parent.

"Twenty minutes," he replies after a dejected glimpse at his watch.

"So that means that by 8.00 pm she'll be about three weeks, sixteen hours and ten minutes behind," I say. "Thank God I got an early appointment."

Tim grins whilst his wife, Dawn, seated next to him, meticulously studies the pile of her daughter's books stacked on her lap.

"I see you've got the only decent chair," I say to Tim, who is obviously bored but, luckily for him, seated on the only normal-sized chair which at least makes his boredom more comfortable. All the other parents, including Dawn with her stack of books, are either trying to balance their bottoms on midget-sized chairs drafted in from the reception class or lolling up against the wall wearing faces like they're waiting to be executed.

"I flipped a coin for it with Sean," says Tim gesturing over to one of the other dads leaning up against a book case. Sean looks up from staring at his feet at the mention of his name and shifts from one foot to another which prompts a whole load of books to slip off one of the shelves and onto the floor.

The classroom door opens and out walks Tricia Marshall, chair of the PTA, with her son, Oliver, obediently at her side.

"You're next, Mr and Mrs Lewis," she says. Tim and Dawn rise to their feet and head towards the classroom whilst I plop my bottom on Tim's chair with undignified haste. Sean rolls his eyes.

"Hi, Sandy, are you coming to the PTA meeting next week?" says Tricia when she sees me.

"Ah…yes, I think I can make it," I reply, not wanting to sound overly eager as I know that the plan is to oust her and, worse, I'm the unfortunate soul who's been volunteered to do it.

"Great, I'll see you there. We're going to take a vote on the playground subsidy."

"Oh, that's wonderful news," I say, trying to sound interested when, in reality, I'm as enthusiastic about the subsidy as I am about cleaning up the dog muck in the garden. Yes, I know, I know, the subsidy is a great idea. However, I've more important things to think about - like how much longer I can cope with Mum and, on cue, Mum and Tabby turn into the corridor to remind me of my responsibilities. As they amble down the corridor, arms linked and giggling, I notice that Tabby is growing more like Mum with her fine cheekbones and slender legs. I have another pang of regret that I don't look more like Mum.

I give my seat to Mum and Tricia leaves with Oliver at her heels when she sees I'm now fully occupied with Mum. For the next ten minutes, Tabby and I answer Mum's questions about where she is, who everyone is, why we are here and where her Vicks nasal rub is, which (perhaps unsurprisingly) I have removed from her handbag. Tabby takes it all in her stride and doesn't seem to be bothered by the repetition; I want to put a paper bag over my head. Eventually, Tim and Dawn come out from the classroom. They both look at Tabby with undisguised curiosity.

"Your turn, Sandy," says Tim, smirking. "I hope you've got your bullet-proof vest."

"I think you'd better come with me," I say to Tabby.

"I can't leave Nan by herself," says Tabby, trying to wriggle out of accompanying me.

"Well, she'll have to come in too," I say. "Whatever you've done, you're not leaving me to take the brunt of it alone, young lady."

Mrs Frampton has launched into her speech about how "different" Tabby is to her two older brothers, whom she also taught, when the door opens and in rushes Dave wearing his fluorescent workman's jacket and jeans plastered with mud.

"Sorry I'm late. Crisis on the building site."

Dave smiles apologetically at Mrs Frampton before pulling up a chair next to me so that the four of us - Mum, Dave, Tabby and I - are now sitting in front of Mrs Frampton's desk like a row of upright (soon to be chastised) pegs.

I lean towards Dave as Mrs Frampton frowns and studies her notes before launching into another spiel about how Tabby's behaviour is a distraction to the rest of the class.

"You can take off your hard hat," I whisper.

Dave gives me a sheepish grin and removes his yellow plastic helmet.

"So now, I have come to the subject of Tabatha's latest escapade. Would you like to tell your parents, Tabitha, or shall I?" says Mrs Frampton who is clearly asking a rhetorical question and wants to break the news herself.

Tabby ignores her and gazes out the window. I can tell she is trying to play down whatever it is that she's done.

"Tabitha has been selling tickets in the school playground," announces Mrs Frampton with Shakespearian drama.

Tabby's gaze turns away from the window and switches to her shoes, as she realises that she's not going to get away with her crimes. Mum rustles in her bag again and Dave and I exchange wary glances. Mrs Frampton milks another dramatic pause before hitting us with the full force of Tabby's misdemeanours.

"Yes," continues Mrs Frampton, "Tabitha has been selling tickets, at the cost of fifty pence a time, to the other girls so that they may participate in...beauty pageants."

"I made twenty-five pounds," mumbles Tabby, her head still lowered.

"The parents of the other girls are furious," says Mrs Frampton, "that their children are being exploited. And rightly so."

I'm about to open my mouth to protest about the use of the word "exploited" (as I don't think I can find much else to protest about) when Mum leans forwards and puts two pounds on Mrs Frampton's desk.

"I'll have four tickets, please. I love raffles," says Mum, delightedly. "I won a lawnmower once."

* * * * *

Dave helps Mum into the car whilst I throw my handbag into the back and climb wearily into the driver's seat. Tabby's money-making scheme has been a disastrous end to a day I'd like to wipe entirely from my memory.

"I'll go with Dad in the van," says Tabby, edging closer to her father.

"Good idea," says Dave. "Mum has to take Nan home anyway."

I glance from Tabby's mischievous face to Dave's gullible one and know that by the time I get home Dave will have succumbed to some sob story Tabby's invented about needing the money from the beauty pageants to help the poor in Africa.

"We'll talk about your behaviour later, Tabitha," I say. "Meanwhile, you're grounded."

"Mum!"

"Don't say a word, Tabby," I say, sternly. "I've had a long, stressful day and I'm not going to talk about this now. Your father and I will discuss it later and decide what punishment is necessary. You make sure you've done your homework and you're in bed by the time I get home."

Dave pulls a face suggesting I'm being too hard on Tabby and puts an arm around her shoulders as I wind up the window and drive out of the car park. I look in the rear view mirror and watch him lift up Tabby and heave her onto his shoulders for a piggy-back across the car park. He's such a soft touch. A loveable one, of course, but definitely a soft touch. No wonder his business doesn't make enough profit.

"What an enjoyable day!" says Mum, as we drive back to her house. "We must do this more often."

"Yes, it's been lovely," I reply, knowing that Mum has already forgotten most of the events as "enjoyable" is certainly not a word I'd use to describe our day. "I'll drop you home now and Lori should be there to keep you company till bed time."

"Lori?"

"Your carer."

"Oh yes, wonderful girl. Reminds me of my maths teacher at school, Mrs Cartwright. She married a jockey.

They had three children before he fell at the fences and broke his neck."

"Yes, I know," I say. The Mrs Cartwright story is one of Mum's favourites. I've heard it several hundred times. The next instalment is about how Mrs Cartwright later married a church warden who turned out to be gay. Luckily, before Mum can continue, a text comes through on my phone which provides an opportune moment for distraction.

"Will you see who that is, Mum? Press "Messages" and the message should pop up."

Mum picks up my phone off the dashboard and follows my instructions.

"What does it say?" I prompt.

Mum puts her glasses on which are hanging around her neck on a gilded chain; it's the only way she'd find them in less than an hour. She studies the text for a minute and then reads it out slowly and deliberately like she's reading for the first time.

"U were supposed to pick me up at 6. Still here. Waiting. Wots 4 tea?"

"Shit," I exclaim. "It's Max. I've forgotten to collect him from football."

"Who's Max?" says Mum.

"Your grandson."

I turn the car around and head back into town to collect Max. I didn't think today could get any worse but forgetting my own son is quite an achievement. I don't think it's likely I'll ever win a prize as Mum of the Year. I glance at Mum who seems oblivious to my distress and is happily reading through all my texts. I realise that whilst I may not look like her, I've probably inherited a few of her other traits.

Life is so unfair sometimes.

3

A week later, I arrive at Mum's house to find it dark, unnaturally so. At this time on a winter's evening Mum's bungalow is usually lit up like the spaceship in Close Encounters of the Third Kind but tonight it's shrouded in darkness, an ideal setting for a teenage horror flick. I scuttle up the garden path, shying away from the overhanging shrubs, as a sheet of rain whips around my legs. A shiver runs through me as I pull off the soaking wet hood of my coat and huddle into the confines of Mum's porch, fumbling in the outside pocket of my bag for the house keys. I'm cold, tired and I've had another stressful day at work and now I'm faced with the prospect of an evening of yet more problems with Mum.

I put the key in the lock, my heart pounding as a host of scenarios run through my mind, all of which feature Mum dying or, very possibly, dead. The door swings open and the familiar musty odour weaves its way into my nostrils. I close my eyes for a moment, my pulse slowing as the memories of long winter evenings curled up at my father's feet come flooding back. On those nights, Mum would be across the other side of the room knitting scarves and mittens, her needles clicking with ruthless precision, whilst Dad moaned about whatever was on the television. I was just happy being with my family, even though the telly was black and white and I was curious how Marc Bolan looked in colour. My childhood seems so long ago now I have my own family. Life was a lot simpler back then. Before I grew up.

I force my eyes open and back into the present and run my hands along the wall, searching for the light switch. Finding Mum having peacefully passed away would, in some ways, be a quiet relief and yet I know that, despite all the complications, all the madness of her senility, I'm not ready to lose my mother. Maybe there's never a right time for the death of someone you love, but there's a time for acceptance of the inevitable. I suppose I haven't reached that stage yet. I'm still hoping for miracles. I might be a mother myself but I still don't want to be an orphan. Not just yet.

I find the light switch and flick it on. Nothing happens. I flick it up and down several more times in frustration and still nothing happens. Another sharp gust of wind whips around my legs and I realise that if the lights have fused, it's more likely Mum is lying injured somewhere. I close the door which eliminates the last rays of light from the roadside and kick off my wet shoes and strip off my damp tights. I'm tempted to use my phone as a torch but the battery is low and I may need that later. For the moment, I decide I'll have to negotiate my way around in the dark.

"Mum?" I say.

All is quiet.

"Mum?"

There's still no reply.

"Mum, where are you?" I say louder.

The answering silence is unnerving. I clear my throat and lick my lips as fear takes hold again. Mum's usually transfixed by The Great Escape or The Guns of Navarone or one of her other favourite war films in the evenings. When I arrive after work, the first sounds I normally hear are either Richard Attenborough's clipped RAF tones or Gregory Peck's deep timbre resonating through the walls. But tonight there's no sound at all, apart from my own faint breath and the rhythmic beating of the grandfather clock.

I edge cautiously down the hallway, my hands outstretched in front of me, trying to avoid the table I know is about halfway down on the right, until I reach the far wall. I splay my hands across the bumpy, patterned wallpaper until I locate the kitchen door, press down its handle and push it open. An acrid smell of burning plastic immediately assaults my senses and a warm glow from the cooker throws out a soft light, making shadows dance and flicker upon the walls; Mum has left a gas ring alight on the hob and the handle of the pan on the ring behind is melting and beginning to burn. I rush over, remove the washing up bowl from the sink, turn on the taps, grab some tea towels and pick up the hot pan by its rim and dump it in the sink, stepping back as the water sizzles and spits.

"Bloody hell, that was close," I mutter.

The action of dealing with something tangible, rather than imaginary, forces me into practical, multi-tasking mode. I know I need to get to the fuse box which is high up on the wall in the cloakroom and negotiate the coats, brooms and other paraphernalia that have gathered there over the last fifty years. So I leave the gas cooker on and rummage under the kitchen sink for a torch, removing the heavy blue one that was Dad's favourite from amongst the cloths and cleaning fluids. I replace the battery every year but even so when I switch it on the light is feeble. Hopefully, it might last a few minutes till I sort out the fuse box.

I leave the kitchen by the other door and make my way to the cloakroom. As I walk past the dining room I hear a faint rustle. I freeze for a moment. There's another rustle and a muffled throaty cough. Yes, I know it's probably Mum and she's obviously alive so I don't know why I should be scared. It's just I get nervous at times in the dark - maybe it's because I've always found this house a little spooky and my imagination can be a bit far-fetched. Peter, my brother, used to say I was a scaredy-cat because Dad's mother died in the room which became my bedroom. But the truth is it has more to do with being addicted to horror movies when I was a teenager; an axe wielding madman hiding behind a door pushes all my girlie buttons. Besides, I can scream better than Jamie Lee Curtis just looking at my own reflection on a Sunday morning.

"Stop being an idiot, Sandy. It's only your mother," I whisper to myself, my hand lingering over the door-knob. "Get on with it. Mum could be in trouble." I turn the cold brass handle. "Oh – and stop whispering to yourself. People will think you're nuts."

I push open the door with a cautious fingertip and shine the torch slowly around the room, across the sideboard, the large mahogany dresser, past the dining table and chairs and finally sweep the light up and down the curtains looking for a slim bulge which might be Mum or the ominous blade of an axe. But there's no sign of either. I hear another little cough and I swing the light to the source of the sound which appears to be…underneath the dining room table. I notice something odd; one of Mum's large embroidered tablecloths has been draped over it so you can't see anything below the table top. What's more, there's a tiny red light coming from behind it.

"Mum?" I whisper.

No answer.

"Mum?"

"Is that you, Denise?" Mum replies softly.

I let out a small sigh of relief, even though tonight I'm Denise.

"Yes, it's me," I whisper in return, playing along that I'm Denise in whichever madcap world Mum has invented tonight.

I inch forwards and lift up the tablecloth to discover Mum sitting on the floor surrounded by cushions. There's a tiny stub of a lit candle in front of her which looks like it's about to expire at any moment.

"What on earth are you doing, Mum?"

"Sssh," whispers Mum, putting her finger up to her mouth. "They might hear you."

"Who might hear us?" I say, imagining the axe murderer again. "Is there someone else in the house?"

I squat down, put my torch on the floor and squash myself underneath the table next to Mum.

"The invasion. It's started," whispers Mum.

"The invasion?"

I don't have a clue what Mum is on about. And I've told the carer never to put on any science fiction films as I can't handle the subsequent questions about little green men.

"The Hun, Denise, the Hun. It's the invasion. It's happening like Churchill said it would."

"Mum, the war ended over sixty years ago."

"You'd better get out your father's pitchfork."

I take Mum by the hand and look her straight in the eye. "Mum, the war is over and Churchill died in 1965."

"But the Luftwaffe has been flying over all night!"

"We're on the flight path to Luton Airport." I stare deep into Mum's eyes and squeeze her hand. "The...war...is...over," I say.

I see a flicker of recognition in her eyes. We stare at each other for a long time. I can almost hear her brain clunking into gear as her eyes search my face.

"I'm going mad, aren't I?" says Mum.

"You're just getting old, Mum. It happens to us all."

"I never thought it would come to this, Denise," says Mum, her mouth drooping.

I make a small, tight smile. She still thinks I'm Denise even though part of her brain has switched back on. I won't contradict her though. These days I accept that I'm whoever she wants me to be; it's easier this way. In the early stages of the Alzheimer's I sometimes corrected her but it was like breaking her heart over and over again. It's pointless reminding her of her anguish - that Denise died in a car crash over thirty years ago. Denise was only seventeen. Her boyfriend had just passed his driving test. Same old story, I suppose. A new driver, a wet road and then it's all over. I was ten at the time. Mum was devastated. I don't think she has ever truly accepted my sister's death.

Anyway, it's all part of the Alzheimer's. Being stuck in the past. Mum rarely remembers who I am although I'm the one that supported her and Dad all these years. I've spent more time with her than anyone else, especially since Dad died. I'm not jealous or angry or anything like that – I guess it hurts that Mum can't remember me so much as my older siblings and often doesn't know who I am at all. I wish I could share more with her in these last few years but, in a sense, it's just not possible anymore.

43

"I need to go and fix the fuse box," I say. "You stay here. Promise me you won't move. Not one inch."

The last glow of the candle fizzles out.

"I promise," says Mum. "Don't be long. My arthritis is starting to hurt."

"I'll try," I say, holding back a retort about being stuck unnecessarily underneath a table when there isn't a war on, Churchill is dead and my tea is probably getting cold underneath the grill.

"Hitler has a lot to answer for," I mutter under my breath.

"What's that? Hitler? Are the Germans coming?" says Mum, beginning to panic. "Have you got the pitchfork yet?"

I look at Mum with despair. She's already fallen back into her other world.

"No," I say, "I need to take the torch with me to get it. So don't move. Stay *exactly* where you are. We can't risk discovery. Remember - we are the resistance."

"Whatever you say, Denise. Be careful now. Those Hun are devious. Mr Churchill was right all along, you know."

"I'm going now," I say, picking up the torch before we fall into full scale role playing.

I get up from underneath the table as the light from the torch goes out. Immersed in the total darkness, I knock my head loudly on the edge of the table.

"Fuck!" I cry.

"Sandy, what have I told you about swearing?" says Mum. "Just because I'm old it doesn't mean I'm deaf."

"Sorry," I wince, rubbing my head furiously.

Mum always remembers who I am when I'm in the wrong. How annoying is that?

* * * * *

The lights are back on, the radiators are on maximum and Mum and I are sitting at her dining room table playing cards. I shuffle the pack one more time, deal, and place the remainder of the pack in the centre of the table on top of the tablecloth whose bright psychedelic sixties' swirls have faded to pale imitations with years of washing. I look at the hideous green flowerpot I made at school that still sits on the mantelpiece alongside a photograph of Denise on her sixteenth birthday and know that I can't leave Mum tonight, not while she's so unstable, not while she needs me. I'll have to stay over again. Dave will understand, as he always does, but it can't go on forever. I just can't do it all anymore, not even with the part-time help from a carer. I'll have to make a decision soon.

I look over the top of her cards at Mum's grey thinning hair, her lined face and wrinkled eyes and search for any signs she remembers me. But her eyes are screwed up, her expression studious as she manoeuvres the cards into groups. I pick up my cards knowing I've already got the jack of hearts, which has two creased corners, and the three of clubs which has six holes in it where Peter skewered it with his school compass in 1981. The cards, which have Buckingham Place on the back, are the same ones we've used since I was a small child. Denise bought them in 1977 during the Queen's silver jubilee celebrations and even though I've bought Mum numerous other packs she still insists on using these ones. I've accepted that as much as the cards were initially part of Mum's grief they've also become part of her need for familiarity and certainty as she's aged. I sometimes wonder when that point will be for me: when I'll be happy knowing that you can still buy Marmite and PG Tips and that the No 77 bus still stops outside the Post Office.

"You've got the jack of hearts," says Mum.

I slide my cards closer together, hoping Mum won't see the pinpricks on the three of clubs. It's pathetic to want to win against an eighty-three-year-old woman with Alzheimer's but Mum never gave us any leeway at cards when we were kids so I don't see why I should now she's old. Besides, she has a photographic memory for cards. It's nigh impossible to beat her. I try my best but, to be honest, the only card game where I stand half a chance is snap.

Mum's penchant for card games goes back to when she was a child. She learnt how to play during the Blitz, squashed up with her neighbours and family in the corrugated shelters buried at the bottom of their gardens. Later, when she was evacuated, she played with her hosts, Mr and Mrs Swanson, in the parlour of their country house whilst other children played in the fields. Mum can remember it all in precise detail. From the colour of Mrs Swanson's parlour curtains to the hand of cards she was holding when Churchill announced peace. By the time Mum went home she was hooked for life on cards.

"Last game before bed," I say, placing my jack of hearts on the table and retrieving the upturned seven of diamonds off the top of the discard pile. I've also got the king of hearts but, now Mum is on to me, I decide to ditch the idea of sticking with hearts. Immediately, I regret my decision as Mum picks up the jack and discards the two of spades. I search her face for clues as to whether she needs the jack or if she's bluffing. But as usual, I don't have any idea as she doesn't betray the tiniest expression. God knows I've looked for a nervous tic or sweaty brow over the years but, when it comes to cards, Mum is David Blaine.

I refill our liqueur glasses with Mum's favourite, crème de menthe, grateful she didn't chose advocaat tonight. I'd prefer a whiskey but I'd probably get a lecture about hard core drinking so, as usual, I stick with her choice. I glance at the clock on the mantelpiece as we rotate our turns. It's 9.15 pm; I'd better ring Dave soon and tell him I'm staying over again. In the meantime, it's time to break open the orange Matchmakers which have been sitting on the sideboard, beckoning me.

"Did I tell you I used to play cards during the war?" says Mum, repositioning her cards as I pick up a new one and discard the six of diamonds.

"Yes, you did," I say, trying to disguise the weariness in my voice.

"We played for hours in the shelter. I learnt poker, bridge, crib and rummy. They called me The Whizz Card Kid. When I got evacuated I lived with Mr and Mrs Swanson. They had a big house near Bletchley Park."

Mum leans forward conspiratorially and taps the side of her nose. "Mr Swanson did something top secret."

"Really?" I say, trying my best to sound interested, even though I've heard this story numerous times. I stir my crème de menthe with my orange Matchmaker and suck it luxuriously to alleviate the boredom.

"Yes. He was a code breaker. Only we didn't know back then. It was all very hush-hush."

Mum picks up another card, studies her hand intensely, and puts down the three of spades. This seems odd as she's only recently put down the two of spades.

"Hmm, curious," I say, smoking my Matchmaker like Sherlock Holmes and deducing that Mum's hand is probably better than I'd anticipated. I take another puff of my Matchmaker and rue the fact that Dr Watson is not here to assist me – or indeed *anyone* with some new conversation. Evenings can be very, very long with Mum.

"Of course, even though Mr Swanson was a code breaker, he couldn't beat me at cards," says Mum. "Not even when I drank some of their home brew cider and got tipsy."

"Well, I'm not surprised you beat him," I say. "You've always had an excellent memory."

And don't I know it, I groan inwardly. I could repeat all of Mum's stories in my sleep. In fact, I could repeat all of Mum's stories in my sleep, whilst inebriated. I've read a lot about memory recently and how the brain works, so I now know more about it than I do about baking (which isn't a vast amount) but nevertheless a lot more than I learnt in Biology at school. Mostly, we studied reproductive organs and sprouting beans.

"I was the best in the class at tables," boasts Mum, interrupting my train of thought. "Ask me any and I'll know the answer!"

Mum's eyes light up with excitement at the thought of a maths challenge. I decide to go with the flow. "What's seven times seven?"

"Forty nine!"

"Six times eight?"

"Forty eight!"

"Nine times seven?"

"Sixty three!"

"What's nine times three, multiplied by two, minus thirteen?"

"Forty one!" exclaims Mum, striking the table.

Mum beams with satisfaction, I smile spontaneously and she resumes examining her cards with added enthusiasm. It's good to see her happy. If only the Alzheimer's wasn't so frustrating, so bloody exhausting. Day in, day out, it's the same old stories and maths challenges. It wears me down. And now there's the confusion between fantasy and reality. It's becoming tougher to deal with it all, especially when I'm tired.

But Mum is tired too. Lately, her lines look deeper, her complexion greyer. I know the illness is draining her, eating away at her body and mind, and there's nothing she or I can do about it. The frustration inside me is mingled with sadness and defeat as I watch her sweep a loose strand of her hair over her ear like a flirtatious young woman. But she's not flirtatious or young anymore, she's frail and old and death is edging closer. I glance at the picture of her and Dad on their wedding day framed on the wall. Even though the picture is in black and white, I see how beautiful and vibrant she was, her youth and exuberance exuding life as she tosses her rose bouquet in the air, her vivacity captured for eternity in a single photograph.

We take several more turns, sucking our Matchmakers and sipping the sticky green liqueur in silence, absorbed in our own thoughts. Mum must be getting close to winning by now but, as I peruse my cards I realise my random duds, selected under the influence of alcohol, might disrupt the flow of the game. Mum will be expecting me to behave rationally whereas I've actually been getting slowly sozzled. I decide to concentrate and see if I can pip her at the post. I pick up from the discard pile and see if I can match anything; it's the queen of hearts. I kick myself for having disposed of both the jack and king earlier. I put it straight back down and, as Mum picks it up, my mobile breaks the silence.

"Oh cripes, I forgot to ring Dave," I say, jumping up and retrieving my phone from my coat pocket. Dave has left a text for me: *Where r u? Dinner burnt. Kids in bed. I am horny. XXX.*

I text back: *At Mum's. Long story. Will ring later. Have to stay over so no sex tonight. Sorry. Kiss. Kiss. Kiss.*

"Well, it would be a long way to go just for sex," says Mum.

I realise I've read my message aloud. It's an embarrassing habit that I really need to stop.

"It's not that far home," I say, defensively.

"Why Peter had to move to Melbourne, I'll never know."

Oh God. Now Mum thinks I'm Lucy, Peter's wife.

"I mean, why would anyone want to go to Australia? They haven't had a decent cricketer since Donald Bradman."

"Well, there's been Shane Warne," I say, thankful we aren't in public where Mum's political incorrectness might have repercussions.

"Shane who?"

"Shane Warne. He was an excellent cricketer. He dated Liz Hurley for a while."

"Liz who?"

"Liz Hurley. The actress who also used to go out with Hugh Grant - the actor who was in Four Weddings and a Funeral. You've seen it lots of times."

"Four weddings and a funeral? Now that does ring a bell," says Mum, thoughtfully.

I make a satisfied smile that Mum that has remembered something post 1990 that isn't about Countdown or Carol Vorderman.

"Yes, I remember now," says Mum. "Four weddings and a funeral - that was the year Aunt Lil and Aunt Elsa both got married, my best friend's stepmother eloped to Singapore and Vera, who lived at the bottom of the street, ran off with the deputy bank manager. Oh yes, and the vicar died during Christmas service. It was 1959, if I remember correctly."

My mouth falls open. An orange Matchmaker falls out.

"I was talking about the *film,* Four Weddings and a Funeral," I protest.

"We have a film of them?" says Mum, a huge smile spreading across her face. "Why don't we get out the projector? I remember Aunt Lil and Aunt Elsa looked like twins, even though they weren't."

Oh God. Not the projector, anything but the projector.

"It's late," I reply, hastily. "Maybe we could do that tomorrow?"

"I shall look forward to that," says Mum, spreading out her cards for me to see. "I win."

"Well done," I say, grateful the game is over and we can go to bed.

"Let's see your cards." Mum leans forward to examine them. Reluctantly, I spread them on the table. Mum looks at them, readjusts her glasses and takes a second look.

"I can't make head or tail of those. Not even a pair after all this time!" says Mum, pulling a despairing face. "I shall have to teach you. You can't let the family down not being able to play cards properly. Now Sandy, she can play cards ever so well. She almost beat me once."

"Really?" I say, delighted at the inadvertent mention of me in an almost flattering light.

"Yes, but I was having a bad day. The cat had died."

"Oh." I pack up the cards and put the stopper in the crème de menthe. "Time for bed. Can you manage in the bathroom whilst I lock up?"

"Yes, dear. I've still got my marbles, you know."

Mum totters off to the bathroom and I quickly check the locks and phone Dave. He answers straight away.

"My God, what's happened now? Is Mum unwell?" says Dave, who's obviously been worrying whilst I've been getting sloshed on an empty stomach.

"No, no, darling. It's just when I came round earlier I found her hiding under the dining room table, the lights out and a pan burning in the kitchen. She thought the Germans were invading."

"Jesus Christ! She's gone completely bonkers!" blurts Dave before he can stop himself.

"Dave!"

"Oh sorry, love," says Dave. "I know she's your Mum but you have to make a decision soon. You can't stay there every night. It's not good for us or the kids."

"I know. I'll make a decision soon, I promise," I say, despondently.

"The sooner the better, love. It can't go on like this for much longer. You're wearing yourself out."

"I know."

"You alright, love?"

"Yes," I reply, tears welling.

"She'll be fine whatever you decide to do. She might be bonkers but she's a tough old bird. You'll see."

"I've got to go; Mum's almost done in the bathroom," I say, grateful that my Dave is always so kind-hearted and optimistic.

"Bye then, love."

"Dave?"

"Yes?"

"Do I talk in my sleep?"

"You bet."

"Oh. What do I say?"

"I'll tell you tomorrow night when you get home," Dave says in a knowing voice. "It can't be repeated over the airwaves."

I giggle and make kissing noises and end the call as Mum comes out of the bathroom.

"My husband used to do that," says Mum.

"Do what?"

"Purse his lips when he lost at cards."

I tuck Mum up in bed and she rolls over on to her side. I'm too tired to make up the spare bed so I strip down to my underwear and take one of Mum's old flannelette nighties from the top drawer of her dresser. I pull it over my head, lift up the bedding and slip underneath the sheets next to Mum and switch off the bedside light. I'm worn out after the long day and a bit woozy from the drink so I start to doze off in the warmth.

"Thank you for staying tonight," Mum says through the dark.

"That's okay," I mumble. "That's what daughters are for."

"You're a good girl, Sandy. A good girl."

A tear runs down my cheek and drips onto the pillow.

4

I stare at the feet of the PTA committee members in their various poses underneath the table on the school stage. Every one of them is wearing Ugg boots except Tricia Marshall who is wearing long shiny black boots circa Germany 1939. I look down at my new flowery white and blue sandals and decide that, even though they are totally inappropriate for winter, at least I don't look like I'm about to break out in a traditional Himalayan dance.

You see, I had a moment of madness and decided to wear my lovely blue dress and sandals. In the privacy of my bedroom, it didn't seem such a bad idea. In fact, it felt just right. But now, with the curious stares from the other mums, I feel like I'm dressed for a disco and not for a PTA meeting where I'm supposed to be proposing a motion of no confidence in the tyrannical Tricia. So I've been telling everyone I'm going on to a party with work colleagues to counteract any potential playground rumours about me turning into a hippy fruitcake with a penchant for feng shui. The thing is, whilst I may be in disco gear, everyone else is looking smart tonight; the committee are dressed to kill, the working mums are suited and booted and there's even an absence of velour tracksuits amongst the mumsy contingent. I suppose it's because everyone's expecting a heated debate and women always dress smartly when they expect fireworks: it gives them confidence. Well, that's what Mum always used to tell me when I was a girl in her usual direct way: "Always look smart, Sandy, it doesn't pay to be caught with your knickers round your ankles." It was one of her better pieces of advice - even though it meant I was paranoid about my knicker elastic for years.

The committee shuffle their papers in preparation as I contemplate why Mum seems to have more opinions than most mothers. As the proceedings begin, and before I can come to any sensible conclusions, Deidre makes a late appearance, slinks through the doorway and skims down the row of chairs, taking off her trademark Bluetooth headset and squeezing into the empty seat beside me. Tricia looks up from her introductory welcome and gives Deidre one of her disapproving looks, which is the same one she used to give her Oliver when he peed his pants in reception.

"You're looking radiant tonight, Sandy," whispers Deidre, placing her headset delicately on top of her handbag. "Love the dress."

I mouth "Thank you" whilst trying to stay out of Tricia's line of vision.

Deidre Walker is my best friend at the school gates. She collects her grandchildren, Lily and Hugh, from school almost every day. Jen, Deidre's daughter, is a big shot city lawyer who doesn't know how lucky she is to have Deidre to look after her kids. Jen doesn't have to worry about after school clubs, sick days or carol concerts accompanied by squeaky recorders that make you want to stick a pitchfork through your head, because Deidre does it all for her. Deidre and I have been friends for a few years now, since I apologised for the rumour I'd unintentionally started about her selling telephone sex. As I said, you have to be careful about playground rumours.

"You look fabulous. Maybe you should come and work for me," winks Deidre.

"Now there's an offer worth considering," I giggle, sliding down in my seat behind Tina Simpson who is diligently taking notes.

"Seriously, Sandy. You look a different woman tonight. What's up?"

"I'm done working full-time," I whisper, impetuously. "Mum needs more help and with the costs of Tabby's after-school club I might as well call it quits."

"Probably not before time. You can only do so much," says Deidre, smoothing her silver-grey hair and unfastening the buttons on her smart tweed jacket.

"I've had enough," I say as the thoughts that have been spinning round in my head pour out. "It won't be long before Mum doesn't recognise me at all. Her moments of lucidity are getting fewer. Today, she thought I was

Florence Nightingale. Besides, I'm fed up of wearing black and grey and looking like a nun all day."

"I keep saying you need more fashionable clothes."

"I'm making a start," I say, glancing down at my silky dress which seems to be having a positive effect on me again.

"You're doing the right thing, Sandy," says Deidre, patting my knee in a motherly way. "You've only got one mum and you need to do right by her. I intend to get my own back on Jen for all this free childcare by living until I'm a hundred."

"Can I have a vote on the subsidy for the new playground equipment?" barks Tricia.

Almost everyone raises an arm, including Deidre and I. Tricia surveys her support and starts counting.

"You know, I really might have a job for you," says Deidre out of the corner of her mouth.

"I don't come cheap, you know," I reply in a similar fashion. "And I won't do anyone over seventy, any S & M and I may charge extra for foreplay that takes over a minute."

Deidre snorts like a pig trying to suppress her laughter.

"And I'll want my own stationery."

Deidre snorts even louder.

"Any objections?" says Tricia, ferociously.

I raise two hands. A few other arms wave above the melange of heads. Tricia sighs with impatience and does a quick scan of the hall. "That's seven against and sixty-four in favour. I declare the motion passed!"

Tricia turns back to the committee table, her voice unintentionally catching the microphone. "I thought there were sixty-nine of us tonight? How come that amounts to seventy-one? I'm sure I counted correctly."

Maggie, the secretary, shrugs and begins to methodically count the register.

"Oh, it doesn't matter," snaps Tricia. "It's a clear win anyway."

"See, I said she was as blind as a bat," I say to Deidre as Tricia moves onto the next item on the agenda. "I wonder if she sleeps hanging upside down?"

"She's probably a vampire bat. You'd better close your windows at night."

"You could be right. I'm going to buy a stake."

"Whoever it is who keeps talking will they please stop. I am trying to conduct a meeting!" shouts Tricia in her loudest, most pompous voice.

A few people turn round and look towards us. I duck down pretending to pick up something from the floor. Deidre taps me on the leg and I pull myself upright, grinning like a naughty schoolgirl.

"She's sounds like Mrs Thatcher," whispers Deidre.

"Don't insult Mrs T," I say. "She was a mere pussy compared to our Tricia."

"Look, whoever is talking, will they please be quiet or just leave!" screeches Tricia.

There are a few murmurs, a rustle of feet and Tina turns round and glares at me, her eyes bulging. I shrug and look behind me, as if to suggest the noise is coming from another row. Unfortunately, I've forgotten that Deidre and I are right at the very back so when I turn back Tina is looking as smug as it's possible to look with Botox implants – which is a bit like a puffer fish, only with dentures.

After Tina's reprimand we sit quietly listening to the proceedings: the summer fair raised £4,500, masses of home-made cakes are needed for the Christmas bazaar and the PTA is funding a trip to the panto. Would anyone like to volunteer for the stalls and to assist on the trip? My hand stays rigidly fixed to my side, knowing that I'll get the stall with the electric buzzer that constantly rings anyway. No one else will agree to it. The thought of another three hour migraine makes me wonder if maybe, this year, I should tell Tricia I'm too busy.

If I think about it - and I've been doing a lot of thinking this evening since I put on this dress - I am too busy. Mum needs me more than the school bazaar. Maybe Dave could take the kids and I could spend another morning with Mum? I have this feeling that Mum won't be around much longer and, whilst she may be as mad as a hatter, she's still my mum and I love her.

Another nudge from Deidre jerks me out of my thoughts. She passes me a message written on the back of an old utility bill.

20 hrs a week, 16 hours from home, 4 hrs in office. Extra hrs to cover hols etc. £12 per hr + commission on leads you find yrself. Selling advertising space, chasing up enquiries etc.

for The Herald - should be a doddle with yr retail background.

I read the note several times. Telephone sales? It can't be any more frustrating than selling soft furnishings. The worst that could happen is that someone might put the phone down on me. But at least no one will set fire to the sofas or let their kids throw up on the divans. What's more, with a phone and a laptop, I could do this job anywhere. I could see Mum almost every day.

I scribble my reply, *offer accepted,* and pass back the bill, feeling an overwhelming relief. My days filling out interest free credit agreements are numbered.

"Are there any other matters before we wrap up?" says Tricia, tidying her papers.

The coughing and feet shuffling begin in earnest. Some of the girls turn towards me: Dawn, Rachel, Mandy, Lesley, Sharon, Heidi. I know they expect me to call a vote of no confidence. Slowly, amidst prolonged murmuring, I rise to my feet. Sometimes, I wish my old proactive student days didn't follow me around. These days I can barely find time to wash my hair, let alone think about politics and sit-ins at the library. In fact, the last time I was supposed to be involved in a strike, instead of warming my hands around a brazier, I went to a restaurant; it was a lot warmer there and I particularly enjoyed the garlic mushrooms.

"Yes?" says Tricia with a hint of impatience. "What is it, Sandy?"

The hall falls quiet, a prelude for war.

"Well…" I say, wishing I was Sigourney Weaver. I'd rather take on an alien any day rather than our Tricia. "Well…I've been talking to a lot of people and…"

"And what?" snaps Tricia.

I look around at the girls and see their faces stuck somewhere between fear and ecstasy, like the expression you get when you spot a chocolate at the bottom of the box only to discover it's a strawberry cream. You see, I know how they feel about Tricia; she's a small town bully who runs everything to her own agenda. A woman who ruthlessly corners people in the playground and squeezes them till they excrete two hundred hand-decorated cupcakes and a dozen table decorations made out of plastic holly, potatoes and tinfoil. A woman whose boots are so shiny you could see your facial hairs in them. Yet, I also know there isn't anyone in the hall who wants Tricia's role. Tricia's only got one child, her parents live abroad and her husband has a wallet the size of a sperm whale. Tricia has the time, energy and finances to devote to the PTA, whereas most of us don't. We're too busy struggling to pay the bills, or coping with aged parents, or exhausted from trying to be all things to everyone.

"I'd just like to say on behalf of everyone here…"

Tricia flushes a deep red, a quiver of doubt flickers across her pale features as she adjusts her delicate gold rim glasses. I know she's a bit of a dictator but I also know that underneath her hardened veneer is a kind, loving woman. She means well. She really does. But she doesn't know how to communicate. What Tricia needs is a proper job to learn about equality and diversity and all the kind of bullshit that most people get thrown at them in their jobs every day. In a way, it's a godsend she doesn't suffer all that politically correct mumbo jumbo that bogs everything down but, on the other hand, it means that she rules the PTA with a rod of iron. Her idea of democracy is sort of – Stalinesque.

There's a lump in my throat. Somehow, I know I've got to do the right thing for all of us. Tricia is the obvious person for the chairperson's role but sometimes people can't see it because her demeanour rubs them up the wrong way. How do I reconcile the differences? This is the trickiest situation I've been in since Dave and I got caught on the new CCTV at Hendersons' Christmas party five years ago. I had my knickers round my ankles.

I clear my throat and take a deep breath as the muttering increases. I take a glance at Deidre who gives me an encouraging nod.

"I'd like to say a few words," I say, raising my voice so everyone can hear.

Tricia's face changes from anxious to fearful. I can't help but admire her for being so earnest, so dedicated. She genuinely wants to contribute, whereas most of the other mums, including myself, contribute to the numerous fund-raising schemes through guilt or a sense of duty.

"There's been a lot of talk lately which has been getting out of hand. So I wanted to say, I think you're doing a marvellous job, Tricia. I'm sure everyone here thinks the same. I'm also sure that, deep down, everyone knows that there is not *one* amongst us that could do your job as well or with as much dedication."

There are some muted whisperings of discontent so I raise my voice even louder.

"Look, I know that sometimes there's backbiting and whinging amongst us but that's true of any organisation. It's been the same wherever I've worked. I think we shouldn't let petty jealousies or silly talk get in the way of what's best for this school and what's best for our children. This PTA committee, managed by Tricia, has been the most effective, resourceful and productive PTA in all the time I've had children at this school. And, as some of you know, that's been a long, long time."

There are a few stifled giggles.

"So I would personally like to say a big thank you to Tricia on behalf of myself, and everyone here, for the huge effort and contribution Tricia makes to the welfare of this school."

I look over to Tricia who's sitting, astonished, on the platform. "Well done, Tricia. And thank you for all your hard work!"

There's a moment's silence before Deidre begins to clap. A ripple of applause begins to spread out across the room until everyone is clapping. As it reaches a crescendo there's a universal gasp as a tear slips down Tricia's cheek. She wipes it away with an embroidered handkerchief retrieved from her stylish handbag.

"I would like to propose a vote of confidence in our chairwoman," I say.

"Hear, hear," shouts Deidre.

"I second that," says Tina.

"All those in support of the chairwoman, please raise your hands," I say.

A sea of hands rises like a tidal wave across the hall.

"I declare the motion passed!" I say triumphantly and sit down with a thump as Tricia moves to the microphone.

"Well done," says Deidre, grinning.

"Do you think I can get away with not doing the buzzer stall this year?" I whisper.

"Fat chance," says Deidre.

"Thank you, thank you," says Tricia, choking back sobs. "I can't tell you how much that means to me. Thank you so much. Thank you, Sandy. Thank you, *everyone*. I know I'm not the easiest person to get along with but I do want to help. I really do."

The applause starts again.

"Sandy, where did you get that dress?" says Tina, leaning back in her seat, still clapping. "I love it. I could do with something similar for a party I'm going to."

After more tears and thanks Tricia finally closes the meeting. It's the first time a PTA meeting has finished where everyone looks genuinely happy and not ready to stab each other in the back. Tricia's smiling face says it all. I'm glad I didn't buy some dull grey suit in which I might have been a bitch and taken the hard line and ousted her as we planned. Even though Tricia annoys the hell out of me at times, it would have been the wrong decision. Although Tricia's a dictator, it's only in the loosest sense of the word. People like her run PTAs, clubs, societies and scout groups all over the country refusing to be bogged down by a wealth of senseless government red tape. They're the backbone of the voluntary organisations in this country that make up for governments which are weak in morals and short in common sense. Frankly, sometimes I could fire a cannon up the backsides of those idiots in Whitehall. I wonder if any of them have any idea what happens at grass roots level? I doubt it.

Deidre and I walk across the car park, discussing a potential start date for me once all the formalities are done. I wave goodbye as she hops into her car and heads off into town to see her boyfriend. She's sixty-two, single and sexy and I'm forty-five, fat and frumpy. Well perhaps not so frumpy anymore. But I feel put to shame by Deidre; I probably need to make some changes. Deidre would be the first to say it's hard raising a family, working and doing all the stuff we parents do but, nevertheless, I've been asking myself questions for a long time. And I don't have all the answers. But, then again, who does? But tonight, in fact ever since I put on this dress, it's as if suddenly all my constraints are falling away. And even though it's the middle of winter it feels like spring.

5

"I'm home!" I shout as I close the door behind me and drop my bags on the floor.

There's no reply from Dave, the kids or even a solitary woof from Mutley, whose duties as a guard dog are already up for review. Only Stallone, who strolls out of the lounge and proceeds to wind himself around my legs in a self-congratulatory way, acknowledges my presence.

"Have you dumped in the bathroom again?" I say, bending down to stroke his thick, luxurious fur.

"Meow," meows Stallone, looking up at me with his evil eyes.

"Hmm," I say, trying to assess the level of his boastfulness. "We could be in mouse territory here. I don't expect to find one on my pillow, okay?"

"Meow," meows Stallone and casually saunters off and up the stairs towards my bedroom.

I pull off my scarf, throw it over the bannister and wander into the kitchen as a ping goes on the microwave.

Dave is mixing up tuna and sweetcorn in some low fat mayonnaise.

"I thought I'd step up to the mark and make you an exotic dinner," says Dave as he sees me and gives one of his big welcoming smiles.

I eye up the steaming baked potato and the packet salad on the side and then the bin overflowing with tinfoil and wrappers.

"And what did you and the kids have?" I say as I wander over and plant a kiss on his cheek.

"Um…a takeaway," says Dave, rolling his big brown eyes, trying to make himself appear innocent.

"I knew it. You're a traitor, Lovett. What happened to our pact to eat more healthily?" I say, picking up a piece of uninspiring lettuce and nibbling it.

"It's a Friday night?" grins Dave, slicing open the potato and dumping a huge spoonful of tuna on the top.

"A fat lot of good you are," I say. "I'm out for one night and you're already cheating."

"How did the meeting go?" says Dave, trying to distract me from the topic of his guilty curry.

"We gave Tricia a vote of confidence."

"I thought you were going to give her the push."

"Well, we didn't," I say, shaking the contents of the packet salad around trying to find something that looks remotely tempting.

"What happened to my racy political firebrand? I thought you said Tricia had to go because she was alienating everyone."

"It's not what Tricia does, it's her manner. She deserved a second chance. Besides, I didn't want to do it," I say, giving up on the salad bag and taking in the aroma of sweet curry. My futile attempt to quit eating takeaways on the back of Mum's criticism isn't going to last long in this household. "It got foisted on me."

I slip off my coat and eye up the healthy, but mildly disappointing, tuna and mayo baked potato.

"Bloody hell, where did you get that dress?" says Dave as I wonder if I can sneak a packet of crisps past him.

Dave's tongue is practically hanging out as he admires my appearance. The last time he did that was three years ago - although he was actually mimicking the dog.

"You like it?" I say giving him one of my flirty, come hither looks.

"Baby, you look so hot I almost want to shag you."

"Almost? What the hell does that mean?" I say in my most indignant voice.

"I'm afraid the duel anticipation of getting my leg over and discovering the exorbitant price of your dress will give me a coronary."

I giggle, hitch up my dress and pose like a ballroom dancer in an attempt to delay telling Dave the price of my new outfit. It's something he doesn't need to know.

"Your feet are blue!" exclaims Dave. "I can't shag a corpse. Go and warm them up by the fire. Why the hell are you wearing sandals anyway? It's the middle of winter."

"I like them and my toe's broken. As you know."

"Well, *if* you hadn't filled those Ugg boots I bought you last Christmas with sand and used them as a doorstopper, and *if* Stallone hadn't pissed on them, you'd have had the perfect footwear for your current circumstances."

"And *if* you'd thought to ask me first, and *if* you'd thought to keep the receipt, I could have swapped them for something that didn't make me look like Neil Fucking Armstrong!"

"God, you're so bloody difficult at times," grins Dave, handing me my dinner. "Now go and warm up so I can get my hands down your knickers before I lose the will to live."

I spoon up some of the tuna into my mouth. Dave watches closely as if I'm testing some celebrity chef masterpiece.

"Mmm…delicious, delicious," I say between mouthfuls. "I taste hints of aromatic spices, sweet tangy lemon and smooth creamy luxurious mayo…"

"Oh for goodness sake, Sandy. Stop taking the piss. Be grateful I made you anything at all."

"Thank you, sweetheart," I grin. "Your diligence is duly noted."

"Does that mean I can get your knickers off?"

"Are the kids in bed?"

Before Dave can reply, a shout echoes through the ceiling.

"Nooooooooooooooooooooooooooo! You cannot shoot from there! Get back behind the wall before you get your brains blown out!"

I look up towards Max's bedroom. Dave picks up the broom and bangs it several times on the ceiling, giving me a shamefaced look.

"I'll take that as a no then," I say, putting my plate down on the table and pouring myself a glass of wine.

"Oh my God, he's got me!" says Max, his voice reverberating through the house. "The bastards have got me with a sniper! Retreat! Retreat!"

"Get to bed!" yells Dave, pounding on the ceiling again with the broom.

There's some low pitched muttering, which sounds rather unaffectionate. That's as much as I'm prepared to say about my own son who, in every other way, is a charming young man. Well, that's what Mrs Templeman, his school tutor, tells me. I believe she suffers from anosmia though.

"Is Tabby in bed?"

"She went about an hour ago with Harry Potter," says Dave putting the broom down and selecting a beer from the fridge.

"I suppose we have to be grateful for small mercies. It could have been Justin Bieber."

I pick up my plate and wine and trot off to the lounge with Dave close at my heels. The fire is burning nicely but, unfortunately, Mutley has taken up prime position, spread-eagled in front of it with his snout only a few inches from the woodstove.

"Why does Mutley always get the best seat in the house?" I say, carefully lowering myself down onto the floor so not to snag my new dress and wedging myself between Mutley's big furry brown torso and the fireside chair. "I don't know how he manages to sit that close. I keep expecting his eyes to explode like popcorn."

"Pity they don't. That would be one less mouth to feed."

"Dave! How could you say that about Mutley? He's a very special dog," I say, tickling Mutley behind his ears.

"He has a very special wind problem, that's for sure. No one but you will sit within ten metres of him."

Dave sits down in his favourite armchair and flicks on the TV with the remote. "By the way, Andy called. He's run out of cash."

"What again?" I say, spitting out my wine over Mutley, who opens a woeful eye. "How can that boy get through so much cash? I transferred him two hundred pounds only last month."

"Two hundred doesn't last long. You know that," replies Dave, flicking from channel to channel.

"He'll have to get some extra bar work. We can't finance his beer consumption."

"Give him a break. University is all about beer consumption."

"He'll have a huge loan to pay back, even with our contribution. He needs to cut back or work some extra hours at the bar. Besides, I've decided to leave Hendersons."

Dave tears his eyes away from the bikini-clad blonde on the television, gives me one of his serious look and flicks off the television.

"Do I get a say in this?"

I polish off my last mouthful of baked potato and put my plate down on the grate. Mutley's nose instantaneously begins to twitch as his food detecting radar kicks in.

"Of course," I reply, knowing that my powers of persuasion are usually Dave's undoing. Frankly, the man will concede to anything for a blow job. Still, I suppose we'd better discuss it like adults first and then, if necessary, I'll fall back on Plan B.

"It sounded like a statement," says Dave challengingly, "rather than an open ended question."

"Oh sorry, darling. It's just I've been thinking what a hassle it is working on the weekends and late nights. I don't think it's worth it anymore, especially now Mum's getting even more unpredictable. I'm exhausted."

"I know. I suppose the big career drive is over then?" says Dave, levering the foot rest closer with his toes so he can sprawl out.

"It's never going to happen," I say, finally acknowledging what I know to be true. "Hendersons are happy to let me top the sales figures but they're always going to promote the young graduates over me because it costs them less. And now they've switched from individual to group commission, it doesn't even seem worth it for the money. I could work part-time with not a vast amount of difference in pay bearing in mind how much we'd save in childcare and fuel costs."

"Exactly how much are we talking about?" says Dave. "Now's a bad time to be dropping our income. This recession is a killer."

"I know. But I'm thinking – maybe a hundred and fifty to two hundred pounds a month? I think it's manageable if we tighten our belts and cut back on the luxuries."

"Would that be little luxuries like new dresses?" says Dave with enough hint of irony to get his point across.

"It was a bargain and cost far less than a new work suit!"

"But you still need a new work suit too?"

"Oh you're so logical," I protest. "Well, if I'm leaving, I won't need one!"

Dave always has an answer to everything although he also says that about me. The difference is Dave's answers are always rational and mine are irrational - or maybe impulsive - depending which way you look at it. However, since I have women's hormones I think that's only fair. The trouble is women often get defined by their emotions. For example (no disrespect to the male species) but I think it's tougher in the workplace being a woman. You've only got to have one bad day and burst into tears and nobody forgets it. There's been a few times at Hendersons I've wanted to cry but, at my age, I know better than to show the slightest weakness so I either lock myself in the loo or, if the staffroom is empty, I beat the hell out of one of the sofas. I know, I know, beating the hell out of a sofa is not very feminine but, in my defence, it limits the damage on the mascara front and the pink and yellow striped sofa in the staffroom is particularly hideous and deserves everything it gets.

"So what kind of job do you want? That is, if you intend to get one?" says Dave.

"Of course I intend to get one," I retort. "What do you think I intend to do? Slope around the house all day watching day-time television?"

"Just checking, my love," grins Dave. "With you anything's possible."

You know, Dave can be very annoying at times, even when he's joking. I swear to God, he has no idea of the concept of multi-tasking even though he runs his own business. By the way, he also collects butterflies, Hornby train sets and is rebuilding a 1973 Saab Sonett. I think he may be autistic.

"I've already got a job. Bar the formalities," I say, proudly.

"Aha! Now we're getting to the bottom of it," says Dave. "Somebody's offered you a nice cushy number and you've decided to throw in the towel at Hendersons rather than reduce your hours there."

"It's not like that at all," I say. "I've been thinking about it for a while. I can't work full-time in that kind of job with those irregular hours anymore. I happened to mention it to Deidre at the PTA meeting and she offered me a job."

"I thought you said Deidre was a madam? I'm not sure I like the idea of my wife cavorting on street corners," says Dave, grinning. "Especially if you're wearing that dress. I can't believe you wore it to the PTA meeting. Your boobs look almost twice their normal size."

I look down at my breasts which, I have to admit, look a lot bigger than usual. It's amazing what good quality clothing can do for a woman's appearance and ego. I feel like a sex vamp. If Dave is amenable and hasn't overdosed on beer by the time we go to bed, there's a good chance we might indulge before one of us starts snoring. Yes, I know it might be shocking but occasionally people over forty still have sex, even Maggie and Ken next door who are in their sixties. What's more, now that Ken's retired, they even have sex in the afternoons. I'll admit I was shocked the first time I heard them at it; I thought Maggie's vacuum cleaner had developed a high pitched squeak. It was only when Ken pitched in with his impression of a steam engine that I realised what was going on. By the time they'd finished, it sounded like La Traviata.

"Stop looking at your breasts," says Dave. "It's turning me on."

I look up, suddenly aware that I've been studying my own breasts whilst thinking about Ken and Maggie shagging. That's probably not normal. It might be a good idea to get some action before I do the vacuuming tomorrow.

"Oh right," I reply, flushing and getting back on topic. "Deidre isn't a madam as you know only too well. She's in charge of sales and advertising at The Herald. There's a vacancy and the job's as good as mine, so long as I don't stuff up a formal interview."

"Telesales?" says Dave, raising a sceptical eyebrow. "You mean you'll spend even longer on the phone than you already do?"

"Uh-huh," I nod, pulling my plate away from Mutley's tongue which somehow he's managed to manoeuvre out of the side of his mouth to lick my plate clean without even moving his head.

"Dear God, have mercy on me!" says Dave, clasping his hands in prayer either side of his beer can. "What have I done to deserve this?"

"Oh stop it," I counterattack. "I'm not on the phone half as much as you watch football on the telly!"

"Yes, but watching football winds me down," replies Dave. "When you come off the phone you're usually about to spontaneously combust because Tricia Marshall has tried to coerce you into dressing up as a reindeer, or Hendersons want you to do overtime, or your mother has been found wandering around M&S with tights over her head trying to hold up the cashier. If I were you, I'd bury the bloody thing in the garden."

"A tempting thought," I say, pretending to consider the option seriously. "But that would mean I wouldn't get to read all those hot little messages you've been sending me lately."

"What messages?" says Dave, instantly bristling.

"Now don't pretend it's not you trying to get me all steamed up," I say, pointing my finger at Dave like a school mistress. "The other day, I felt so fruity I had to go and take a cold shower."

"But I haven't left you any messages!"

"Oh don't deny it, Dave. Who else would leave me a message that says, "Your arse is so sweet I could kiss it." No one else but you would say that."

"What? I don't believe it! Where's your phone? I want to see this for myself!"

Dave leaps to his feet, storms out to the hallway, retrieves my handbag and starts to ferret through the contents. "What the hell are these?" says Dave, holding up a large pair of granny knickers as if they were a belligerent lobster.

"Oh they're Mum's. In case she has an accident."

"Is this what I've got to look forward to?" groans Dave, tossing the knickers onto the sofa with disgust. "Now where's this phone?"

The Mission Impossible theme tune starts to ring out from the depths of my handbag.

"Ah ha!" says Dave, zooming in on the sound and pulling out my phone and touching the screen. "It's Andy."

"I know. Who did you think it was? Tom Cruise?"

Dave tosses me the phone and I accept the call.

"Hello, Andy."

"Hi, Mum."

"It's not like you to phone this time of night. I thought you'd be down at the student bar. What's up?"

"I'm skint."

"Have you eaten today?"

"Yes…um…is there any chance I could have some more cash, Mum?"

"No." I end the call and toss the phone back to Dave. "Well that's sorted," I say.

"You're too hard," says Dave.

"And you're too soft. He's got to learn to manage his money."

"He's a kid."

"He's twenty one. You were out working on building sites at nineteen. It won't do him any harm to grovel a bit more."

The Mission Impossible theme tune rings again. Dave tosses me my phone back.

"Mum?"

"Yes?"

"Pleeeeeeeeeeeease."

"No."

"You're the best mum in the whole wide world."

"Go on."

"You're the best mum in the whole wide world and you only look half your age?"

"And?"

"I feel really safe when I'm in your car and not at all at risk?"

"Hmm. That's more like it. Anything else?"

"I love you?"

"Now that's better. Exactly how much do you love me?"

"More than my iPhone, my laptop and my Xbox 360?"

"Good. Now let's be clear here, Lovett Junior, I'll transfer you some cash tomorrow but you've got to tighten up your spending. Your father and I aren't made of money and in a few weeks I'm going part-time so I can spend more time with your Nan. There'll be less cash around so you've either got to rein in your spending or find some extra work in the new year."

There's a momentary silence at the other end of the phone. "Is Nan okay?"

"Yes, she's fine, Andy. But she's not going to be here forever and I need to spend more time with her. And now you need to be more responsible too."

There's another pause. "Okay, Mum. I'll tell them down at the bar that I'm available for extra hours if they come up and I'll cut back on the beer."

"Good. Neither your father nor I expect you to be working more than you're studying. Your studies take top priority. But don't go overboard on the spending. You don't want to be crippled with a massive debt when you leave uni."

"Yeah, I know."

"Good. Everything else okay?"

"Yes."

"Okay. I'll send you a text when I've transferred the money."

"Thanks, Mum."

"Nighty night, Andy. Don't let the bed bugs bite."

"Love you, Mum."

"Love you, too."

I end the call and toss the phone back to Dave again.

"So it looks like you're definitely leaving Hendersons since you've told Andy," says Dave.

"I guess so," I say, smiling sweetly.

"I think that rash decision means you'll have to make it up to me," grins Dave with a lecherous face. "But first I want to see those text messages. If someone's been flirting with my wife, I want to know about it."

"Oh, don't be daft," I say. "I'm winding you up."

"Ah ha!" says Dave, triumphantly. "I thought so. You'll have to be even more attentive to me now for being such a tease."

Dave throws the phone on the sofa, offers his hand to me and pulls me up so we are a few inches apart.

"If you insist," I say demurely and undo the buttons on Dave's shirt and slip my hands around his waist. Dave's still a very handsome and athletic man. His hair has only a few streaks of grey and his body is still trim and muscular through years of hard labour. I'm a lucky woman.

"But first, my good wife," Dave whispers in my ear, "I'm going to get my hand down your knickers."

"Oh, sir, you're so naughty!" I reply as Dave hitches up my dress and his hand wanders up my thigh.

"Let's get this dress off." Dave lifts the dress over my head when there's a loud ripping noise.

"My dress!" I exclaim.

"I was very careful," says Dave grimacing. "Maybe it's not a big tear."

Dave peels the rest of my dress off and lays it across his arm so I can inspect the seams. Inwardly, I feel distraught that my dress is probably ruined but I don't want Dave to see me upset. It was an accident; another in a long line of mishaps that seem to follow me around. I'm probably a walking disaster area.

"Oh my God, what's that hideous smell?" chokes Dave as I peer at the fabric through blurred eyes.

"What smell?"

"That smell!"

"I can't find a tear and I can't smell anything either," I say, keeping my head down and wiping away a tear.

"How can you *not* smell that?" says Dave.

I look up and sniff the air; a vile, stinking odour reminiscent of rotting vegetables, maggot invested meat and Max's underpants is permeating the room.

"It's Mutley," I say. "Obviously, tuna and mayo disagrees with him."

"So it was Mutley and not your dress ripping," says Dave with undisguised relief. "Thank God."

"Mutley, that is utterly, utterly disgusting," I gag as the smell worsens. "Even I, your loyal supporter, cannot abide such an assault upon my senses. I'm rationing your portions as of tomorrow morning!"

Dave and I stare vehemently at Mutley who opens one eye and looks at us, as if he has no idea what we're talking about.

"And don't pretend you're innocent," I say, pointing my finger at him.

"Shall we go upstairs now?" says Dave. "I can't make love in the same room as Mutley. He's a passion killer."

"Good idea," I reply, delighted that my lovely dress is still in one piece and that Dave is not at fault. "There's only so much even my nostrils can take in one evening."

"Can I still get my hand down your knickers?" says Dave.

"It'll cost you," I say.

"Don't I know it," grins Dave.

6

I sign my name at the bottom of the letter with a flourish and relax back on the garish yellow and pink sofa in the staff canteen. It's a cosy sofa but we have a love/hate relationship which is mainly hate because it's such an eyesore but, on the other hand, it takes all my punches without answering back so I sort of love it too. I can't believe the company paid some celebrity designer to conceive it though. It's like something a seven-year-old would draw; it even has heart shaped cushions with lace frills. We only sold one in the entire company and that was in the Aberdeen store to a crazy woman who brought it at seventy percent off for her stray cats to sleep on.

I wriggle my toes in my high heeled sandals, lift up my feet and rest them on the sofa. Everyone else is back on the shop floor and I'm on a late lunch. We've been exceptionally busy during the main lunch hours, with a last surge of customers taking up our offer on pre-Christmas delivery on the sofas. Since I can fill out twice as many interest free credit arrangements, at twice the speed as everyone else, this is the way it normally works when it's hectic. There used to be a few grumbles from new staff when we were on individual commission but, sooner or later, they would acknowledge that an unhappy customer kept waiting does no one any good. And if you've ever been on the receiving end of a customer who's got out of bed on the wrong side, has two screaming kids and a wife with mastitis, you'll know what I mean.

I take a final proofread, fold up my letter of resignation and pop it into an envelope whilst taking a satisfied slurp of my coffee. It was my third attempt at crafting a suitable letter. I preferred my first version which read, "Dear Mr Frost, I quit, Yours Sincerely, Sandy Lovett," but I was even more enamoured with my second which read "Dear Frosty, It is with overriding joy and abundant glee that I quit this motherfucker of a job, Yours delightedly, Sandy Lovett." However, after considering that such honesty might affect the quality of my leaving present, I decided to be less blunt. So instead, I've written a long emotional letter about how I needed to care for mum (which is true) but also how much I enjoy my job and how desperately sad I will be to leave etc. etc. etc.

Anyway, on the basis that even Frosty will weep buckets when he reads my letter, I'm now expecting a whopper of a leaving prezzie. And, if I have any luck, I'll also get a male stripper. I've always wanted one of those. Just out of academic interest, of course. Dave makes a good attempt at stripping when he's drunk but the fact is his moves are not as good as John Travolta's, which is a bit of a sore point. Yep, you've probably guessed it; this is not the first time I've had a broken toe.

I suppose you'd probably like to know less about my toes and a little bit more about my job? Actually, I do enjoy it. Well, some of the time. I love meeting people so long as they're not grumpy, they don't smell, their children are fully under control, they have no pets with them and they can use words with more than one syllable. I'm not fussy, obviously. The truth is, in retail, you have to be fairly open-minded and hold very few prejudices. You should also preferably own a can of air spray, have easy access to a dishcloth, possess a relatively thick skin and be prepared to work some hellish hours.

Anyway, I'm pretty good at what I do which is, fundamentally, selling. I can sell almost anything. For the last five years or so, it's been home furnishings but I've sold just about everything in the past including electrics, jewellery, houses and garden ponds. This means I know a lot of stuff about stuff. I'll never be a brain surgeon but if you need some advice on a replacement microwave, or how many carp you should have in your pond, I'm your woman. It doesn't matter what you sell, there are three overriding principles to being successful in retail: be efficient, know your product and smile, smile, smile. You see, smiling is the ultimate weapon in sales unless you have yellow teeth in which case you're better off working in a funeral directors. I've also worked in one of those by the way; I quit after six months though as I like talking and you don't get a lot of conversation with a corpse.

Surprisingly perhaps, as smiling is so important in retail, Mr Frost, the shop manager, is not a smiler. In fact, he's barely amenable at times. Sometimes, I think names reflect who we are, a bit like dogs which look like their owners. Frosty is not cut out for sales at all. He's terribly efficient with the admin side of things, but getting a smile out of him is like a doctor squeezing out a diagnosis of terminal illness. Frosty used to be a Lieutenant Colonel in the army and he runs Hendersons with absolute military precision. "Shoot to kill, Sandy," he says when he sees a customer walk through the door and, every Tuesday morning at staff training, he elaborates on the principle of the "Seven Ps" he learnt in the army: "Prior Planning and Preparation Prevents a Pretty Poor Performance" which, theoretically, should be great motivation. However, hearing it explained in conjunction with the Battle of Waterloo, Culloden and Operation Overlord is a bit wearing, especially with Mum banging on about the war all the time.

I swing my legs off the sofa and make my way over to the internal phone and ring Mr Frost's extension. He picks it up almost immediately.

"Frost," he snaps.

"Hello, Mr Frost. It's Sandy."

"Hello," says Frosty, his voice softening a little. (I am, after all, his number one sales consultant.)

"I'm on my lunch break. Can I come up and see you?"

"Yes, of course," replies Frosty, warily.

"Great. Thanks."

"See you in five. Over and out."

"Roger."

I replace the phone on the receiver, click my heels together and wander back to the sofa wondering why I play along with Frosty. I suppose it amuses me. Mum's delusions are different to Frosty's quirks though. I try to see the funny side of them but, ultimately, it's just sad that most of the time Mum doesn't know who I am.

I put the letter in my bag, sling it over my shoulder and make my way upstairs to Frosty's office. Knowing how he is (he's a man and ex-army, so it's not difficult to work out) he's probably already got my personnel record and sales figures and is scanning them trying to second guess me.

I tap gently on Frosty's door.

"Come in!"

I open the door, pull my shoulders back and straighten my back like a squaddie.

"Ah Sandy, there you are," says Frosty, closing the cover of what is obviously my personnel file.

You see, I was right.

I look around the room in awe, as I always do. I can't believe anyone can be so methodically neat. If this is what being in the army does to you, I'm glad I never married a soldier. The stress of having to be a house-proud forces wife would probably have made me take a gun to my head.

I lower myself into the chair opposite Frosty's desk and continue examining his office. There isn't even a paperclip out of place. However, what draws my attention most is the map laid out on his desk. It has the entire store planned out on it and figurines, representing the staff, are placed on it like those little flags they used at Bomber Command. Not for the first time, I wish Frosty was twenty or thirty years older so that he and Mum could entertain each other. At the moment though, Frosty is still compos mentis. Only just though.

"So, what did you want to see me about, Sandy?"

"Oh…umm," I reluctantly pull my gaze off the map upon which I've noticed that Derek has been relocated from his security office to the rear of the building. This means we're having a body search tonight. I make a mental note to warn the other staff not to steal a three piece suite. Theft can be a big loss in retail but, frankly, it's pretty hard to nip out with a dining room table and six chairs in your back pocket. Unluckily, Frosty, as an ex-army man, takes his security measures very seriously indeed, but luckily, Derek, as an ex-policeman, doesn't. The checks never affect me that much anyway as Derek usually lets me waltz through his barrier with a wink and a "No need to check you, Sandy. I've seen everything you've got!"- which is a reference to the knickers round the ankles incident.

"I wanted to give this to you personally," I say, handing over my letter.

"And what's this?" say Frosty.

"My resignation."

Frosty looks me in the eye and says nothing, picks up a silver paperknife, slits the letter open and begins to read. He glances up only when he reaches the third page.

"I'll say one thing for you, Sandy, you know how to make a convincing argument. It's no wonder you have the best sales figures."

I study Frosty as he continues reading. He's over six foot with an upright military bearing. His hair is silver-grey, as are his glasses, and his eyes are a piercing blue. If you were the enemy and came face-to-face with him you probably wouldn't fancy your chances. He has that look of calm ruthlessness that puts the fear of God in men and makes some women quake at the knees. In his heyday, he must have been strikingly handsome as the picture on his desk of him being awarded a medal by Prince Charles testifies. I bet he was a lady killer too because even though he never says a single word out of place, his eyes betray him. And his eyes like breasts. In fact, his eyes like my breasts quite a lot, I'd say. He's probably got some army slang for them. Like BPT. (That's big pair of tits.)

Frosty finishes the letter, lays it on the table before him and studies me with quiet contemplation.

"Is the resignation really about the loss of commission and not your mother, Sandy?"

"No."

Frosty continues staring at me. I can see his mind theorising behind those beady eyes, pushing his flags around his map and realising there will be a big sales gap in his showroom floor. He'll be wondering what tactic he should use to try and keep me.

"But it has made the decision easier for me," I say before he can get a word in.

"I can authorise an extra thousand pounds per annum without going to HQ," says Frosty.

"Thanks," I say. "But we both know that won't even touch what I would've earnt on individual commission over the course of the year. And now my mind's made up."

"Two thousand?"

"Mr Frost," I say, sternly. "That is what you should have given me six months ago – and a whole lot more. But now nothing's going to change my mind because I need to look after my mother."

Frosty sags back in his chair. "I'm sorry, Sandy. But I had to follow directives. I told HQ this would happen but they never listen to the ground force. It's not like the army, you know. Can you imagine a military commander who doesn't listen to his men on the field? All the best sales people across the company are leaving. You're not the first."

I don't mention the deaf ears of First World War generals for fear of sending Frosty into one of his military sermons. Besides, I sort of sympathize with him; at least he said something. I know it would only have been in the form of a carefully worded memo which would have been quietly ignored. But at least he tried. The truth is these big companies don't give a damn about the little men and women behind the counters. They'll follow whatever scheme they think will keep their profits and fat bonuses up in the short term and two years later they'll reverse the decision when they realise the long term consequences.

"I don't suppose there's anything I can do that will change your mind?" says Frosty.

"An extra twenty thousand and a place in a top notch care home for my mum?" I quip.

Frosty grimaces which, by the way, is his attempt at a smile. "I'm afraid not. Only wish I could."

Frosty stares out the window for a moment. He seems almost depressed. Even though he rarely gives a proper smile he always manages to look reasonably upbeat; it's probably the stiff military back, combined with his light feet, which seems to make him bounce as he walks.

"I'm sorry to hear your mother's not so good, Sandy. Is she really that bad? She seemed fine the other day," says Frosty.

"There's been a marked deterioration lately. It's not so obvious to a bystander but, when you're with her as much as I am, it is," I reply. "She needs full-time care now. She's not safe in her own home anymore."

"I'm in the same situation. But further down the road. My mother has been in a home for the last five years."

"Really? I didn't know," I say, surprised at Frosty's unexpected revelation.

"You know how it is, Sandy," Frosty shrugs. "Best to keep everything under your hat when you're in management. That's why I left suddenly the other day.

Mother passed out and the care home thought it might be the end. Turned out it was another false alarm."

I nod, understanding now why Frosty left me in the lurch and appreciating the difficulties that are sometimes placed on managers. Before the kids, I used to be in management too but now, even with all my experience, I can't get promoted for all the graduates snapping at my heels. Besides, I think I've come to the end of the road now. I'm not sure if there's anything left to prove except, perhaps, survival.

"Where's your mother living?" I enquire.

"Sunnyside Lodge."

"That must cost a fortune," I say. "It's the best there is."

"It's why I work. The money from her bungalow and savings were gone in no time at all. She'd have been moved to some barely adequate home paid for by the state unless I agreed to pay the difference between the state contribution and the care home fee."

"That's very considerate of you," I say, knowing exactly his dilemma as I've visited some care homes in the last few days. Putting Mum in a home, especially one that doesn't meet with my expectations, does not sit well with my conscience.

"She's my mother," says Frosty, in a way that says he's a man who believes in Queen and country and duty. He may be a bit peculiar but he's an honourable man. I wouldn't be surprised if he has a picture of Her Majesty by his bed.

"I'm only able to afford it by having this job though," Frosty continues. "My army pension is good but not good enough to support my mother and Helen's lifestyle. And there's no way Helen could have coped with mother in our home. She's not the caring type. It's my biggest regret that we never had any children."

"Oh," I say, taken aback by Frosty's sudden outpourings. I didn't even know he'd never had children.

"I shouldn't be telling you all this. But now you're leaving, I don't suppose it matters. Some days, you just need to get things off your chest."

"I know what you mean," I say sympathetically, whilst wondering how I can steer the conversation back to work. Frosty's always been so reserved and now he's telling me about his mother and his marriage - I'm gobsmacked. What next? His sex life?

"To tell the truth, Sandy," continues Frosty. "Things aren't that good between Helen and me these days. We may divorce. It's not working that well between us anymore..."

Oh fuck. I think he *is* going to tell me about his sex life. I need to stall him; there are some things I do not need to know.

"And the sex...or the lack of it...is getting me down."

Oh. Dear. God. Brace yourself, Sandy Lovett.

"In fact, the other day when..."

"It sounds like working is the best thing you can possibly do," I interrupt. "Not only do you help your mother but you keep yourself occupied and have the chance to meet lots of new people. Besides, if the worst happens, you'll need the extra money if you lose half your pension."

"It's a bleak future when you put it like that," says Frosty, even more morose.

"There are worse things in life, Mr Frost. I know that sounds blasé. But you have to look on the positive side: you have a job which is fairly safe and you're still young enough to find a new partner if it doesn't work out with your wife."

"That's not what I want though. I want to stay with Helen. You're a woman, Sandy. What should I do to keep her?"

There's a momentary awkward silence as Frosty waits for my response and I contemplate throwing myself out of the window.

"Maybe Helen's bored and needs things spicing up a little?" I say tentatively, realising that throwing myself out of the window is probably not the best option. "Maybe she needs a little more affection?"

I think about the last time I met Helen at the staff summer barbecue. She's definitely bored; she's doing a calligraphy course. In my opinion, the woman is an absolute saint having put up with Frosty for thirty odd years. Making love to him must be like making love to…I'm not sure what it must be like making love to…but I bet it's over pretty damn quick. One shot of the cannon and he'll be out like a light, ready to rise and shine the next morning for a bracing fifty push-ups and a ten mile hike.

"I always give her wonderful presents," says Frosty, interrupting my thoughts.

"God give me strength!" I blurt. "It's not about presents, Mr Frost. Look, do you ever tell her she's beautiful or whisk her away for a weekend?"

"We went to France last year."

"You went to see the war graves!"

"Yes…well…"

"She's not a soldier or a military historian. She probably wanted a holiday sunbathing," I say, indignantly.

"She has everything she could possibly want," says Frosty.

"Materially, maybe. But that's not everything is it?"

"No, I don't suppose so," Frosty muses.

My cheeks begin to flame. I can't believe I came to hand in my resignation and I've ended up discussing the state of Frosty's marriage. I decide I might as well give him a wake-up call since he's brought it on himself.

"Okay, consider this, Mr Frost." I say. "Before you dump your wife of thirty years, answer this question: why has Helen followed you around the world and put up with your lengthy absences?"

Unaccustomedly, Frosty scratches his head and his nose and rubs his cheeks.

"So, what do you think?" I prompt.

"Lo…ve?" replies Frosty, almost too embarrassed to say the word.

"That's right, L.O.V.E - love. Now I tell you, Mr Frost, there are very few women whose only considerations are money and prestige. So just because you didn't have children, and Helen didn't want to look after your mother, both of which are huge responsibilities, you can't assume she's somehow callous. That's totally unfair. The question is: if you still love your wife, how are you going to save your marriage?"

"I don't know, Sandy. I'm not good at emotional stuff."

"For God's sake, no one's asking you to write poetry or declare your undying love from the rooftops. You could make a start by smiling more."

"Smiling?"

"Yes, smiling."

"I thought I smiled a lot."

"No, you don't."

"I don't?"

"No. In fact, your face looks like a smacked arse most of the time."

"Oh God," says Frosty, putting his head in his hands. "I'm not that bad, am I?"

"I'm afraid so," I say. "Sorry."

"What am I going to do?" moans Frosty. "I don't want to start all over again at my time of life and I love Helen. I really do."

I need some tranquilisers. This is worse than phoning the BT call centre. Lieutenant Colonel Frost (Rtd) is breaking down in front of me and I'm not handling it very well. In fact, I may well be exacerbating the problem.

"You need to learn how to do a proper smile first," I say with the motherly voice I use when I'm trying to sell the protective coating on the upholstery. 'Then, you can work on the displays of affection."

"How the hell do I learn to smile?"

"Look, it's easy. Watch me."

Very slowly, I begin to stretch my lips until eventually I'm wearing a beaming grin that makes me look like I've been sitting on the washing machine when it's on the extra fast spin cycle.

"Okay, so now you try," I say.

Frosty begins to smile. Unfortunately, is seems to get stuck mid-way which makes it look like a grimace caused by a red hot poker stuck up his arse. I begin to choke with laughter.

"What's the matter?" says Frosty, anxiously.

"Just swallowed a fly," I splutter. "Sorry. Let's try again. Now, imagine you've seen something you like in the distance and it's coming closer and closer towards you."

"Like what?"

"I don't know. What things do you like?"

"Cricket."

"Okay, that's not going to work," I say, wondering if Frosty is not as smart as I'd thought. "Anything else?"

"A gin and tonic."

"That's better. But that's not what I was after. Can you think of something with more visual impact?"

"A Panzer IV tank? It was a marvellous piece of machinery. It had a seventy-five millimetre dual purpose gun, you know."

"O…kay," I say, thinking out a possible scenario whilst coming to the conclusion that Helen must be on anti-depressants. "I need to help you out. Let me think…"

I contemplate the window again and whether it is high enough or if I need to go to the rooftop.

"Right," I say, visualizing the kids, Dave and Mum sobbing at my graveside. "Imagine you hear a tank rumbling towards you and it has the outline of a Panzer IV; so you start to smile. Now make it a warm, welcoming smile. Remember; it's your favourite tank."

"Alright," says Frosty. He begins to smile.

"Good, good, that's the idea," I say. "Now, imagine the tank is coming closer and closer until you can see it's definitely a Panzer IV. It's all new and shiny and it has a magnificent big gun."

"Yes, yes. I can see it!" cries Frosty, his eyes focused on his imaginary tank.

"So let that smile begin to grow," I say. "Think happy, positive thoughts. Now, as the tank comes nearer, I want you to imagine you can see a woman standing in the turret."

"Who is she?" cries Frosty with excitement.

"It's Helga, a blonde beauty with enormous full, round breasts. She's smiling at you and she wants to see you smiling back. You want to please her so gradually make your smile bigger and bigger."

"I'm trying, I'm trying!" says Frosty, stretching his mouth open to reveal his teeth.

"You're doing really well!" I say, encouragingly. "Okay, so now Helga pulls up beside you in the Panzer and says: *Guten Morgen, Lieutenant Colonel Frost I have a prezent fur you.*"

"Yes! Yes!" shouts Frosty. "I'm seeing it, I'm seeing it!"

"Then she rips off her blouse and shows you the biggest pair of boobs you've ever seen. Now, show her you're pleased with the biggest smile you ever had!"

Frosty is beaming like a hippo on heat. His mouth is so wide I reckon I could shove a whole melon in it.

"Right, hold it there! Don't move!" I shout.

I scramble in my bag for my compact as Frosty's body and face is now completely rigid as he waits for my next instruction. He follows directions surprisingly well. It must be the army background again. Maybe Helen needs to be more forceful? I find my compact and stick the mirror in front of Frosty's face.

"You're smiling!" I say.

Frosty's eyes widen as he sees himself in the mirror.

"Okay, relax," I say closing my compact. "Now, that wasn't so difficult, was it?"

"I can smile," says Frosty. "I can really smile."

"Yes, you can. Now all you need is to do it more often. Think of something that makes you feel good and how you want to share that feeling with others."

"Right," says Frosty thoughtfully. "Is that what you do, Sandy? Is that why the customers love you so much?"

"Not all the time," I say. "I guess smiling comes naturally. But when I have a difficult customer I do it. I pretend they're someone else and that I want to please them."

"Like who?"

I blush. "Well you know...Daniel Craig, George Clooney, Hugh Jackman, Robbie Williams, Ewan McGregor..."

"I think I get the idea," says Frosty.

There's an embarrassed silence.

"Sandy?"

"Yes?"

"Do you think you could give me some more tips before you leave?"

"Um...about women?" I say, awkwardly.

"About women and things in general. And sales techniques."

"You know all about sales techniques."

"In principle. But not how to apply them in practice, and anyway, your methods seem a little more lively and...interesting. The company won't replace you with a full-timer so I'll have to spend more time on the shop floor and I'm no good at this kind of communication. I'm used to barking orders." Frosty pauses. "Maybe I've done that with Helen too."

I feel sorry for Frosty as he looks so dejected again. He's a good man. He doesn't deserve to work out his retirement to provide for his mother, at the same time as trying to save himself from a cold and lonely marriage. You know, sometimes I feel there's something wrong with our society when money dictates the way we look after our elderly. But maybe money dictates everything? I don't know for sure and I've not thought about that sort of philosophical stuff since I gave birth to Andy... But I suppose it does and that makes me feel quite sad.

"Okay," I say. "One lesson a week until I leave in four weeks."

"Thank you, Sandy," says Frosty.

"You're smiling," I say.

7

I step out onto the street from the offices of The Herald. The interview went smoothly and I've had the nod from Deidre that I've got the job. I'll start mid-January, a couple of days after I finish at Hendersons. Everything is going to plan. I'm so relieved and with Christmas only three weeks away, I feel more in the Christmas spirit than I've done for years. I've been back at work full-time since Tabby went to school and, even though I know there will be hard times ahead with Mum, I feel a burden has been lifted from my shoulders. Trying to combine work and family life isn't easy but with bills to pay there's been no choice.

I turn onto the High Street and head towards Thorntons for a well-deserved packed of chocolate misshapes and a lottery ticket at the newsagents. Thorntons is busy in the run-up to Christmas which prompts me to get the kids boxes of toffees for their stockings. The assistant pops my purchases in a carrier for me and I weave my way back outside, stand in front of the window and delve inside the bag to find my tasty treat. I choose an ugly lump of dark chocolate from the bag which looks like something out of Stallone's cat litter tray but tastes a lot better. I nibble away at it whilst looking back into the shop at the queue which is now almost reaching the door and wonder how I'm going to tell Dave that I'm not keen on the idea of Mum going into a care home and maybe, just maybe, she should come and live with us.

It's then I see a short, tubby woman who looks vaguely familiar inside the shop. She has neat, tidy hair and looks smart and professional with shapely legs and heels, but she has a very pronounced stomach. It does not look good at all; it's like a joey is going to jump out at any moment. I peer through the shop window trying to recognise the familiar woman and, in a moment of dawning horror, I realise the woman is...me. It's my reflection in the plate glass window.

Oh shit.

I stare at my protruding stomach sticking out in front of the flaps of my unbuttoned coat. Is this what I really look like when I'm caught unawares? Oh shit, shit, shit. I'd no idea I'd put on that much weight. I knew I'd gained a few pounds but this much? I look at least five months pregnant, if not more. I turn to the other side and look in the window again in the hope that it's an illusion. But my stomach's still sticking out. I turn back again; the bulge is still there. It is *not* going away.

"Och, lassie, it happens to us all," says a passing rotund woman wearing a tartan beret and pushing a matching shopping trolley.

I compare our tummies. They're remarkably similar and, for once in my life, I cannot think of a retort. I am struck dumb. I'm supposed to be in my prime. I'm not supposed to look like one of the seven dwarves.

I look at my reflection again and realise I still have the chocolate poised at my lips. I'm so ashamed at my overt greediness I throw it back into the bag and fasten my coat. Only I can't. I haven't worn my best winter coat since last January and now I can't do up the middle button over my stomach. I desperately suck in a huge breath and squeeze the button through the hole. Hurrah!

I let out a huge sigh of relief. Perhaps I'm not as fat as I first thought. But as I do so the button pops off and shoots across the pavement. A man wearing a black cashmere overcoat, as gorgeous as George Clooney, picks it up and offers it back to me.

"Yours, I believe," he says with a debonair smile.

My cheeks flood with heat. I must look like a pickled beetroot, a particularly big pickled beetroot.

"Thanks," I mumble, as he drops it into the palm of my hand.

"Nothing a bit of exercise wouldn't cure," he says with a cheeky smile.

I'm glued to the pavement. My body is as hot as Mount Etna on the verge of eruption. I have never been so embarrassed in all my life. The one time I get to meet someone as hot as Gorgeous George and I look like a fucking sumo wrestler. I glance in the window one more time. Mum was absolutely right. There's no denying it. It's official:

I AM FAT.

* * * * *

That's life for you. As soon as you're on a high something comes along to knock you to the ground. I wander down the High Street towards the car park in a gloomy mood, knowing that I'll have to go on a diet immediately. If I wait till after the New Year I'll gain yet more weight through stuffing myself with mince pies and I'll end up with another half a stone to lose. The thought of gaining any more weight makes me feel ill. What happened to the slim, sexy me? What happened to my youth? And on top of all that – what's worse than having to diet over Christmas?

I shall have to exercise more and eat less. It's not as if I'm completely lazy. I do at least one dog walk a day, if not two, and I spend most days on my feet, which means to lose weight I will have to eat almost zero and take up marathon running. I don't want to be caught squatting like Paula Radcliffe though. Maybe I should pass on the marathon and aim for something more refined – like croquet?

Ahead of me, I see the lady with the tartan shopping trolley again turning into a shop; it's probably fate's way of telling me that croquet isn't a goer. I stop outside the shop, which turns out to be Age Concern, and look inside to see if I can see her again so I can torture myself with the idea of what I may look like in thirty years if I don't pull myself together. I see her browsing the romances in the second hand book section, a small pile stacked on top of her trolley. Is this what's to become of me too if I don't change my ways? Am I going to be old, fat and lonely and spend my evenings reading cheap romances?

I'm about to turn away to go home and stick my head in the oven when something catches my eye: an electric wheelchair. My mind begins to tick over. If I bought Mum a wheelchair we could get out more. It's well known that walking is the best exercise and although Mum's still able bodied, she's not so strong anymore. A wheelchair would make outings so much easier. Mum could combine some exercise with the freedom of having a chair to rest in at any time and I'd get more exercise. It would be much better than being stuck indoors playing cards and bingo all the time, and driving each other mad.

I go inside the shop and pass Tartan Lady, who's waiting in the queue to purchase her books at the counter.

"Hello again," she says in her broad Scottish accent. "There's a guid selection of romances over there."

"Thanks. Looks like you've got the best pickings though," I say, not wanting to be rude by saying I prefer thrillers. "I've come to look at that wheelchair. For my mother."

The Tartan lady hands over her books to the assistant and I wander over to the wheelchair to take a closer look. It's in pretty good condition. I'm not sure how much they're worth but I'm guessing Age Concern would have a fair and not overly inflated price. It's still £350 though and that's not money to be thrown away on a spur of the moment purchase.

"That one's got a top speed of six miles per hour."

I turn my head and see the Tartan lady is at my elbow.

"I've been looking at scooters and chairs myself," she continues. "I've read all the brochures and you cannae go wrong with that one. I'll probably need one myself soon. I've arthritis in my hips. It's not so bad today so I'm making the most of it. The arthritis doesn't help with the weight though. As you can see." The Tartan lady gives her tummy an affectionate pat.

"It's in working order," calls the assistant from the counter.

"Great," I reply, picking up the manual which has been left on the seat and flicking through. It can be used manually or on battery and as I look through the instructions it seems everything that should be here is here.

"What do you think?" I say to the Tartan lady. "I'm worried about making a rash decision and finding it's not what I need."

"Well, if you're thinking about whether your maw needs one, it probably means she does, if not now then very soon. It's a guid price and anyway you'd have no problems selling it on. There's too many of us oldies around these days."

I sit down in the chair. It's comfortable with plenty of support for the back. The controls look simple enough if Mum were to use it by herself, although I'm envisioning pushing her most of the time. I can't imagine a worse end for Mum, cooped up like a chicken in an old folks' home. One of Mum's favourite phrases she used to plague me with was, "Exercise is good for the soul, Sandy. Just you remember that!" which was why she always insisted on bracing country walks, swimming in the sea and religiously transporting me to every sports fixture in the school calendar. Have I mentioned it before? That Mum always has lots of advice? Well, she does. In fact, before I left home, she made me write a list of things to do and things not to do, which included washing my bed linen once a week, ironing my underwear and not to kiss on a first date. I ignored all of them out of principle. Peter emigrated to Australia.

"Everything seems fine," I say to Tartan Lady.

"Do you want to give me a push?" she says. "See how it steers?"

"Why not?" I grin. "Thanks."

Tartan Lady pushes her trolley to one side and plops herself down on the seat. "Quite comfy," she says. "Now let's have a wee spin round the shop. Mind that auld man over there; he's more wobbly than I am."

"Off we go!" I give a big push, expecting the chair to be heavy but it glides forwards with ease. We move in a straight line down the shop towards the front window display.

"Start turning," says Tartan Lady as we approach a rack of fashion wear near the end of the shop, "or you're going to crash. You need a wider angle!"

"I'm trying!" I say, manoeuvring the chair further out to the right before sweeping around the rail and back down the other side of the shop.

"Phew. That was close," says Tartan Lady. "For a wee moment I thought I was going to be wearing a onesie."

"The chair seems fine," I laugh. "It won't take long to get used to it. I think I'm going to take a chance and buy it."

"Guid idea," says Tartan Lady hoisting herself off the chair. "Well, I'll love you and leave you, lassie."

"Thanks for your help," I say.

"My pleasure," replies Tartan Lady, delving into her shopping trolley. "Here, take this," she says, pulling out an almost new book. "It's a particularly guid one. I think you'll enjoy it."

"Thanks," I call after her as she turns and heads off out of the shop.

I look down at the book cover which shows a man and woman in a passionate embrace and has a title of The Hot Nights of Lucinda Lovett by Morna McIntyre. I laugh out loud at the character's surname. I turn it over to read the blurb and see a black and white photo of a familiar face staring out at me. The photo must be an old one, used to suit the youthful and erotic nature of the book because, despite her age, there's no mistaking the mischievous smile; it's the Tartan Lady who obviously not only reads romantic novels but also writes them. Maybe that goes to show you should never judge a book by its cover or a person by their appearance.

I push the wheelchair to the cash desk and inspect myself in a mirror on the wall as I wait to pay. Maybe I could write romances like Morna McIntyre when I'm old? Maybe that wouldn't be so bad. It could even be fun. But the one thing I realise with absolute certainty as I study the contours of my stomach is that I don't want to be fat. Nope, the fat definitely has to go.

How I'm going to get rid of it is another matter.

8

I turn into the driveway of The Orchards, my last stop of the day. So far, all the care homes I've visited over the last few weeks, with the exception of Sunnyside Lodge, have left me a little depressed. The home where Frosty's mum lives is clearly the crème de la crème of care homes: clean, hospitable and the staff possessing a kindred spirit in the way Mum used to say Londoners endured the Blitz. It's set a benchmark and if I can't persuade Dave that Mum should live with us, which is an idea I have strong doubts about anyway as it runs the risk of driving us all insane, then I want the absolute best for her. However, I also know that the bottom line is if I sell Mum's house to fund Sunnyside Lodge, the money will be gone in no time at all. Somehow, I need to find a compromise: a home that has the ethos of Sunnyside Lodge but perhaps doesn't have all the five star luxuries. Unfortunately, The Orchards is now my last hope of finding such a home which is close enough for me to travel to on a daily basis.

I park my car on the near-empty gravel driveway and study the imposing Victorian double-fronted building, swathed with dense ivy. The front steps are extended with wheelchair ramps on both sides and the adjoining concrete pathways lead to lawns dotted with aging apple trees of a decaying orchard. The trees, their branches warped from when once they bore heavy fruit, are now frail skeletons jutting out of the unkempt grass like ancient gravestones. The flower beds are full of weeds and the bushes need pruning. I focus on the building again and examine it more thoroughly; paint is flaking off the window sills and, in between the clusters of ivy there are cracks in the walls. My hopes start to sink; The Orchards may be as dilapidated as some of its occupants.

I climb the central steps and peer through the glass door. There's two nurses deep in conversation behind a tall oak desk reminiscent of a hotel reception in an Agatha Christie movie. When I ring the bell, they immediately break off their conversation and one of the nurses comes out from behind the desk and hurries to the door. She's wearing a crisp blue dress and a starched white cap.

"Hello, I've come to see the manageress about a possible place for my mother."

"Mrs Lovett?" says the nurse. "Please do come in and have a seat. Frau Engel is expecting you."

I step inside and take off my coat, trying to hide my curiosity as to why anyone, even a native German, would be addressed as "Frau" in modern Britain.

"Mrs Lovett?"

I look up to find myself confronted by a large buxom woman also wearing a navy dress which fails to disguise possibly the largest breasts I've ever seen; the sort of breasts that could suffocate a man in the throes of passion and which in their prime you'd have seen coming around a corner before their owner.

"Mrs Lovett?"

"Um…yes," I say, feeling a wave of heat course into my cheeks as I tear my eyes away from the breasts, which I've now determined look like a pair of slowly deflating beach balls.

"I am Frau Engel. The manageress. I believe you've come to look round our home?"

"Yes," I reply, focusing on Frau Engel's face. Her heavy jaw, large eyes and hair tied rigorously back in a bun and topped with another of the starched hats, make her look distinctly formidable.

"So, let us begin with the lounge." says Frau Engel without further ado.

"Fine," I say, deciding that Frau Engel looks like a German version of Hattie Jacques in the Carry On films but with an even brusquer manner.

Frau Engel takes my coat, hands it to one of the nurses who dutifully hangs it on a nearby coat stand, whilst the other nurse furiously polishes the front desk, and frogmarches me across the hallway to a pair of double oak doors and pushes them open.

"Don't forget to polish the windows, Nurse Hobbs. There are fingerprints on the glass," says Frau Engel as a parting shot as we disappear into the next room.

I look back and see Nurse Hobbs stick out her tongue comically before heading over at a pace to the foyer windows.

"This is the lounge," says Frau Engel, moving her large frame to the side so I have a clear view.

I focus on a cluster of old ladies sitting in high backed armchairs around a television which is showing a rerun of Dad's Army. All of them are asleep, their heads lolling to one side or resting on their chests. There are two bald men: one who looks jaundiced and whose head is tipped back on the head rest of his chair snoring volubly and the other who is reading a copy of The Sun but, by the looks of it, is struggling to get past page three. In the far corner are three more ladies: one who is dropping off to sleep, her eyes randomly flicking open and closed; one who has dropped off altogether, her hand dangling down the side of her armchair clutching a half-knitted scarf, and the last who looks like she has just woken up, her eyeballs rolling around like something out of The Exorcist. Nearest to the entrance are three very elderly residents, probably in their nineties, all in wheelchairs and lined up by the side wall; I surmise that position is Death Row, which is for anyone who might possibly need a quick exit. Another television sits in front of the ancient trio but the screen is blank, its services unrequired as all three are sound asleep, omitting variable degrees of snoring, snuffling and the occasional unconscious belch. It's such a depressing scene I decide that as soon as I'm home, I'm opening a litre bottle of red.

"They always sleep after dinner," says Frau Engel by way of explanation.

"Yes," I reply, unsure what else to say but debating whether I should a) slash my wrists immediately or b) sign up for euthanasia before I get my OAP bus pass.

"What did they have for dinner?" I ask as the nearest wheelchair occupant belches loudly in his sleep.

"Roast pork, mashed potato, parsnips, carrots and gravy followed by semolina or treacle pudding."

I cringe as images of school lunchtimes flicker through my mind: the head teacher with spaghetti caught in his beard, the dinner ladies with their grease-stained hats and the lunchtime supervisors who wouldn't have been out of place in the Gestapo.

"No cabbage?" I say, trying to make polite conversation.

"They have cabbage on Tuesdays," says Frau Engel, "swede and carrots on Mondays, broccoli on Wednesdays, parsnips and carrots on Thursdays, peas and beans on Fridays and seasonal vegetables on the weekends."

"Sounds healthy," I say, nodding wisely whilst silently acknowledging that The Orchards has the air of Colditz about it.

"Enough," says Frau Engel. "I will now show you the dining room and the conservatory."

"Great," I say, walking after her. "Can I ask a question?"

"Ja, ja, ja, in a minute."

Frau Engel stops amongst the group of sleeping ladies and switches the TV from Dad's Army to Antiques Roadshow.

"I was watching that!" exclaims a haughty, aristocratic voice.

"Those silly old men are ridiculous," says Frau Engel, frowning at a slender woman leaning out of a cavernous armchair whom I hadn't noticed before.

"Frau Engel," says the woman forcefully, "Please turn the programme back on. I pay good money to be here and I will watch what I please."

The aristocratic lady is probably in her late seventies, but I can tell by the alertness in her eyes that she is still "all there". She's dressed in a chic lilac suit, with a floral silk scarf tied decorously around her neck and a matching pearl necklace and earrings. Her deep wrinkled face is made up with a heavy matte foundation, vibrant blue eyeshadow and a slash of purple lipstick. Her hair, whilst a natural white, is coiffured to perfection. She seems a peculiar resident, at odds with the other sleepy residents dressed in their woolly cardigans and voluminous skirts.

"Frau Engel," repeats the woman, "Please turn the programme back on."

"Hear, hear," shouts the old man with the newspaper, peering over the top of it with sudden interest.

"I like Dad's Army too," says the Exorcist lady who has come round from her sleep, her eyes still bulging. Instead of looking like a ghoul, she now resembles a Cavalier King Charles spaniel.

"Turn it back on," repeats the aristocratic lady.

"It's stupid. For idiots," protests Frau Engel.

"It's funny. It's for people with a sense of humour."

"Ugh. You British, you have no idea what's funny," says Frau Engel, letting out a heavy sigh and switching the channel back to Dad's Army.

"The war was bloody funny wasn't it?" shouts the old man from behind the newspaper. "That gave me a right old laugh, that did."

Frau Engel makes a guttural sound of despair and gestures to me to follow her.

"Now, now, Johnnie. No need to mention Herr Hitler again," says the aristocratic lady. "Frau Engel wasn't even born then."

"Bloody lucky for her," says Johnnie, throwing down the newspaper and wandering over to sit amongst the group of ladies who are all waking up as a result of the disturbance.

Frau Engel ushers me out of the lounge and into the adjoining dining room as a burst of laughter and clapping peals out behind us.

"I love this episode!" squeals Exorcist Lady as Frau Engel pulls the door shut with an almighty bang.

"You see what I have to put up with!" exclaims Frau Engel. "The war, always the war!"

"Well, they say old people have long memories. I suppose we'll be the same when we're pensioners," I say, trying to be conciliatory.

"Ja, ja. I know that, Mrs Lovett," says Frau Engel, raising her hands in frustration. "But always they watch Dad's Army and that even more stupid programme, 'Allo 'Allo. Sometimes I think it is deliberate!"

"I doubt it," I say, wondering if the reverse is true having witnessed the sudden, and somewhat playful, interest amongst the residents. "They're always showing repeats on the telly and those particular programmes were very popular in their heyday."

Frau Engel gives a dismissive snort.

"Actually, what I was going to ask you was whether you provide any sort of live entertainment? I'd like to think that if I'm not around to keep Mum company, there would be some activities to occupy her."

"Ja, ja" says Frau Engel, clearly relieved to be discussing something less contentious. "We regularly have pianists and singers, art and craft demonstrations and sometimes even talks on interesting subjects. But believe me, Mrs Lovett, the residents are more than capable of making their own entertainment. Cards are a big favourite, as well as Dad's Army."

"Really?"

"Oh yes. If your mutter comes here I would advise giving her a small allowance each week or she will be bankrupt before you know it. They'd gamble their entire pensions away if I didn't limit it to penny stakes."

I grin to myself. The Orchards may well be more than a little peculiar but it is beginning to appeal to me. Apart from the garden and outside maintenance, everything is absolutely spick and span. It's fairly obvious that Frau Engel keeps a tight rein on what goes on inside the building and, if the efficiency of the reception staff is anything to go by, at least I could be sure that Mum would be well looked after in a clean and safe environment.

"Now, see if you like our dining room," says Frau Engel, opening the door to the adjoining dining room and sweeping an arm around like a theatrical impresario.

Unlike the foyer and the lounge, which are full of antiquated furniture, the dining room is very modern and equipped with sleek, but comfortable-looking chairs and tables. It is also absolutely pristine. Frau Engel swells with pride, her bosom inflating to twice the size it was in the foyer. In fact, it's possible it might explode.

"What do you think?" prompts Frau Engel.

I scrutinise the dining room again. The walls are clean and painted a fresh white and the large Victorian windows are draped with bright yellow curtains. There are about a dozen round tables, covered with patterned plastic tablecloths, which are already laid out with china for afternoon tea. Each table has a vase of flowers placed in the middle and there are even named place cards. It all looks very picturesque.

"You are surprised," states Frau Engel.

"Well…yes," I admit. "It's just everything else I've seen so far looks a bit worn out…"

Frau Engel stiffens like an upright truncheon.

"But clean," I add, hastily. "Very clean."

"Ja, it's true," says Frau Engel, relaxing. "But it is very expensive to run a home like this so I spend the money on the important things. I cannot afford everything. Are you cold?"

"No," I reply, taken aback by the sudden questioning. "I'm quite warm, thank you."

"Ah, you see, Mrs Lovett, old people must be warm, they must be well fed and they must have companionship. Meals are the highlight of their day, where they interact with each other and make friendships. When they do that they eat well, stay healthy and happy. Otherwise, old age can be very long and very boring."

"I see," I nod, beginning to warm to Frau Engel's more personable and caring side which is hidden beneath her abrupt façade. The aroma of freshly baked scones wafts over from the kitchen. "It's lovely in here, Frau Engel. Truly lovely. It's like a seaside café on a sunny day. I like the idea of the place cards too."

"Ja. It is important that everyone must be friends. We are a community and this is my way of making them all get to know each other. You must understand that the community changes; some people are here for years…and others not so long. It is gut that they all have many friends. In fact, it is essential. This is my little way of helping things along. I move everyone around at each meal time so no one is lonely or bored."

"I like that," I smile. "As you probably know already, my mother has Alzheimer's. Do you think the other residents would accept her?"

"There are degrees of Alzheimer's," says Frau Engel. "In the early stages, it is not so different from the normal memory loss that occurs in old age. But everyone is fairly tolerant here as most of them have an ailment in some way or another. The only time Alzheimer's starts to become a major problem is if your mother develops an aggressive form when she's a danger to herself or the other residents. What stage do you think she is at?"

"She's getting more forgetful recently and occasionally she's delusional," I say, slightly uncomfortable discussing my mother like she's a child. I know old age and death come to us all but it still hurts to talk about mum like this and, as much as I try to be positive, sometimes I want to burst out crying.

"You are finding it hard?" says Frau Engel, as if she knows exactly what I am thinking. "You are not the only one, Mrs Lovett. I have been a nurse for many years. Watching our parents die is not easy but, eventually, you will be stronger for it. You have children?"

"Yes," I whisper, my throat hoarse as I try to hold my tears at bay.

"They will learn too. They will learn caring, compassion and responsibility. These are gut things for children to learn."

"I've been contemplating moving Mum into my own home," I say, finally spilling out what I have been thinking over and over for several months. "But I'm worried about the effects on the family."

Frau Engel takes a long, hard look at me. I feel like I'm being appraised like a naughty child before the head teacher. I stare back antagonistically and wonder if she will go for the hard sell if she feels her potential income slipping away.

"I think you can do it, Mrs Lovett," says Frau Engel after a long pause. "But it will not be easy on you or your family. You must think carefully and make your plans. Come…now I will show you the rest of the building and you can think things over. We will be here if you need us."

Again, I am taken by surprise by Frau Engel. But as she leads me around the rest of the lower floor of the building, including the staff quarters, the kitchen and administration areas, I see that in her manner and in her job, she hides nothing. Her brutal honesty may not be for all but it suits me fine. Upstairs, she shows me a variety of rooms: from swanky new bathrooms, fitted with every conceivable gadget, to old but useable ones with cracked sinks and tiles.

"So what kind of delusions does your mutter have?" says Frau Engel, closing the door on a bedroom furnished with an Edwardian dressing table, wardrobe and chest of drawers but also a modern, adjustable bed and relaxer chair.

"There's a variety," I reply. "Sometimes she's a character from history, sometimes she's a character from a film. Unfortunately, it just adds to the confusion about who she thinks I am."

"That is not gut, of course, Mrs Lovett, but your mutter is not the first. I once had a gentleman who thought he was Chuck Norris. Now that did cause problems," chuckles Frau Engel.

"I can imagine," I laugh. "Mum's pretty harmless though, but she's very exhausting at times."

"Ja, ja. I understand. So who does your mutter think she is?"

I hesitate but realise there's no point in lying. Frau Engel would realise soon enough if I placed Mum in The Orchards.

"Most of the time it's Steve McQueen," I say, grimacing.

"Steve McQueen?" replies Frau Engel, surprised. "Steve McQueen as in The Magnificent Seven?"

"No, Steve McQueen as in The Great Escape."

There's a pause as Frau Engel takes in what I am saying and then breaks out with a booming laugh that has her vast bosom gyrating so much, I'm in fear of being knocked unconscious. She pats me on the arm affectionately.

"No wonder you are here," she chortles. "Do not worry, Mrs Lovett. If you cannot cope at home, she will fit in perfectly with my ladies and gentlemen."

"I'm sorry," I say. "You must get sick to death of the residents mentioning the war."

"As you know, Mrs Lovett, old folks' chatter can be tiring at times. But we must all reap what we sow," shrugs Frau Engel. "But for me, my conscience is clear. I am of a different generation. However, I understand how some of them think, even if I don't always appreciate their humour. It is best to be philosophical."

We smile at each other. My intuition tells me that Frau Engel would be honest and open with me and that I could be the same in return. It's refreshing after all the worries I've had dealing with Mum and the times she's been passed from doctor to doctor like an unwanted gift. I guess it's not the same for everyone but I find the truth is easier to deal with than uncertainty and fear. And the truth is, Mum is slowly dying and what I need is help from someone who understands her and understands me. I need to think about my best options for Mum, for me and for the entire family. Perhaps The Orchards might be best for Mum after all?

Frau Engel shows me the rest of the premises, including three vacant airy rooms which might be suitable accommodation for Mum. The last one is the biggest and mentally I picture myself in here with her, perhaps working whilst she takes a nap or watches the telly.

"I am happy for residents to bring some of their own furniture," says Frau Engel, interrupting my thoughts. "In fact, it is gut to have things that are familiar and well loved. The Orchards is supposed to be a home, not a hospital or a hotel. The only thing I stipulate is that the bed and chair remain. When the residents are sick and need nursing, they are essential, and at times like those we do not want to be moving furniture around."

"I understand," I nod, feeling a lot happier with this arrangement than with some of the more uniform rooms I've seen elsewhere.

"You've seen nearly everything, Mrs Lovett," says Frau Engel with finality. "We will go back downstairs now and I will give you a brochure."

We descend down a wide staircase and arrive back down in the foyer, which is now empty. The door to the lounge is open and I can see the two nursing staff mingling with residents. There's lots of chatter and laughter and the television is blasting out the theme tune to Inspector Morse.

"Sssh!" exclaims Exorcist lady.

"Everyone, The Inspector is on!" says the aristocratic lady, clapping her hands together. The residents begin to seat themselves in front of the biggest of the televisions upon which John Thaw's face is now appearing in close up.

"The Inspector is also a favourite," says Frau Engel in acknowledgement. "Do you have any questions, Mrs Lovett, before I take my leave?"

"I think you've covered everything I need to know," I smile in return as she fetches my coat.

Frau Engel takes a brochure and some forms from behind the reception desk and hands them to me and we walk to the door together.

"Thank you, Frau Engel," I say. "You've been most helpful."

"It is my pleasure," says Frau Engel, opening the door for me. "Oh by the way, Mrs Lovett, in case you are worried, I do not have a cooler."

For a moment I wonder what on earth Frau Engel is talking about. And then I burst out laughing and decide I'm going to give The Orchards a chance. The decision is made. It's The Orchards.

9

Frosty has a poker up his arse again. By which I mean he is smiling at me. I don't feel like smiling back as he's craftily converted my one-to-one instruction, which I'd envisioned giving him in the privacy of his office, into staff training sessions encompassing the entire staff. However, as I remember the lecture I gave him on trying to look happy I feel obliged to be supportive so I grin back at him through gritted teeth, whilst imagining turning the poker like a corkscrew.

I take a sip of water from the glass on the podium, move to the flipchart and tear off last week's notes on product knowledge. Then I turn back and watch Frosty circulating the room, shaking hands and greeting the staff with warm, yet distant, professionalism. It's a curiously formal routine to use with people he works with every day and yet it also encourages mutual respect. Frosty would simply say it helps to "maintain order in the ranks" and he has a point; I've worked in some places where overfamiliarity breeds nothing but contempt and, in some cases, children.

This morning, Frosty is in one of his buoyant moods, bouncing up and down as if he's hopping across a minefield. I've heard on the grapevine that he's booked a holiday in Florida, so maybe things are looking up on the home front. However, I also happen to know through personal experience that staff training, presentations and conferences are the sort of scenarios he enjoys most, especially ones when someone else is doing all the work and he gets to tick all the boxes and take all the credit. Plus (and it's a big plus) as Frosty likes to court danger consorting with senior management, he has the added thrill that today Mr Baker, the area manager, and Mr Mason, the regional manager, have turned up on an unscheduled early morning visit.

I take another sip of water and fumble in my bag for some painkillers. I'm not feeling well. In fact, I am not feeling well at all. This is because a) I have a training session I don't want to give, b) Mr Baker and Mr Mason are here and c) I have a hangover. Unfortunately, it is a very bad hangover. In fact, if I didn't know better, I'd say there was a herd of stampeding wildebeest inside my head. I close my eyes momentarily and swallow the pills, whilst imagining myself throwing up over Mr Mason which, to be honest, is quite an attractive proposition. As Mum used to say during my pregnancies, and indeed anytime I looked even slightly unwell, "Vomit is better out than in!"

although I'd argue it's probably best kept in during a staff training session.

Anyway, improvising my way through a session in Frosty's office is somewhat different to delivering one to over twenty staff, especially one under the watchful eye of the big bosses when you've got a hangover. Charlie Sheen might handle it but, unluckily, I don't have a cast iron constitution or a career in acting. I swallow the acid in my mouth, open my A4 file and glance at the notes I made late last night. I've three subheadings: Greeting the Customer, Sales Techniques and Closing the Sale. Underneath each title I've made notes which, after the bottle of wine and several vodkas I consumed at Deidre's lingerie party, seemed more than enough, but now don't seem quite so thorough or amusing. I gulp down some more acid. Under the heading Greeting the Customer I've written "How to say hello. Discuss", under Sales Techniques, "Don't piss the customer off" and under Closing the Sale, "Take money, kiss arse, shut door", and if that isn't bad enough, at the bottom of the page I've written "DO NOT MENTION FROSTY'S SEX LIFE". Oh – and I underlined it three times. You know, I think I need to stay away from alcohol as at the end of this training session, I may have some explaining to do. I may also need to explain to Dave why I purchased a deluxe model vibrator called The Throbber.

"Just waiting for Mrs Morrison now," says Frosty, strutting towards me like a puffed up peacock. "And then we can get started. Don't forget to maintain eye contact with those two."

Frosty discreetly gestures towards Baker and Mason. I quickly close the flap on my file before Frosty catches a glimpse of the incriminating evidence and look towards Baker and Mason, who are drinking coffee and examining last week's sales figures in the front row. Mr Baker reminds me of an iced doughnut, with a rotund body, short legs and mop of unruly grey hair. He wouldn't look out of place in a pre-war greengrocer, especially as he usually carries a clip board and tucks a pen behind his ear. His slightly comical appearance belies his abilities though, as he has a marvellous memory for figures and can quote any company statistic at the drop of a hat. This is in stark contrast to Mr Mason, who is never without his electronic gadgets, keeps a stylus pen in his breast pocket and is always consulting his Blackberry or laptop and making calls in the middle of a conversation, so he can look important. It's not that some of his calls aren't important, it's his supercilious manner that bugs me. Mr Mason always wears a dapper suit, crisp shirt and silk tie and his eyes are like a predatory hawk, observing everything and everyone around him. These are good skills for a regional manager but, on the other hand, his observation of the female sex is probably more than absolutely necessary. In fact, rumour has it that years ago Mr Mason was dismissed from a fashion chain for paying too much attention to the young female staff, which probably explains why he is now working for a furniture retailer, where generally the sales staff tend to be more mature and less vulnerable.

I'd better clarify that last statement about maturity. You see, when people are making expensive or luxury purchases, they often prefer to be assisted by someone with a bit of experience, who knows a thing or two about the products and who can conduct a conversation without saying "um", "ah" and "I'll just find someone who knows". Naturally, being a mature parent myself, I have a lot of experience of sofas, bathroom suites and kitchen tables. This is because once you've had children you develop a huge range of household expertise and knowledge. Gone are the days when you spent a quick five minutes painting on eyeliner and lippy before work, or luxuriously sleeping in on Sunday mornings – after childbirth, you can spend a whole night examining the finer contours of your bathroom suite whilst cleaning up projectile vomiting. You may even spend numerous nights, if not years, on your sofa, whilst your child runs around in circles pretending to be a steam engine before he falls asleep on the lounge rug and you sojourn to the kitchen and crash out with your head in a bowl of cornflakes. By the way, these are generally the same mornings when you open the door to the postman and you're wearing a vomit-stained Homer Simpson night shirt, your slippers are on the wrong feet and a bogie is hanging from your nose.

"Are you alright?"

I look up and see Frosty staring at me, a concerned frown on his face. But, before I have a chance to reply and tell him I feel sick and suggest he steps in for me, he spots Mrs Morrison bustling her way through the door.

"I'm here!" says Mrs Morrison, waving with one hand and clutching three bags and an umbrella with the other. One of the bags is an enormous white stitched shoulder bag with gold plated buckles and a plaited chain. It's a favourite of hers but it clashes terribly with her purple and black check winter coat with the fur collar and the matching purple felt hat with the large black feather, which are her current favourites. Mrs Morrison, who we all usually refer to as Mrs M, is obsessed with hats. She even makes her own hats and sometimes sells them too. In fact, I have a drawer full of hats that Mrs M has given me for Christmas and birthdays and, whilst some of them are attractive, some of the others are…how can I say this without being too rude? I can't. They're fucking awful. The trouble is, Mrs M is not the sort of woman you can say "no" to, which is why I often find myself wearing a hat these days. To be honest, I think I am slowly morphing into Mrs M, so maybe it is best I've handed in my resignation. I don't want to spend my retirement looking like the Queen. Although that probably isn't being fair to HM, whose hats are a little bit more conservative than Mrs M's.

"Excellent, excellent," cries Frosty, delighted that Mrs M has caught an earlier bus to make it here so that he has a full house. "We'll make a start in a minute."

Frosty positions himself to the side of me, ready to make the introductions, whilst to everyone's amusement Mrs M spots Mr Mason's blond head several inches above everyone else's and makes a beeline for him, squashing herself into the empty seat on his left hand side which Frosty had designated for himself. Inwardly, despite my queasiness, I cackle with laughter as Frosty's shoulders stiffen with annoyance and Mr Mason squirms as Mrs M squeezes his arm and shifts sideways so their thighs are touching.

"Hold this for a moment, ducks," says Mrs M, dropping her white bag into Mr Mason's lap.

Mr Mason's lips draw tight together at the unwanted familiarity.

"Oh and this," says Mrs M, nonchalantly dropping her umbrella on top of the bag so rain droplets flick into Mr Mason's face and over his expensive suit.

"And these," continues Mrs M, dropping her purple leather gloves into his lap.

Everyone is smirking and stifling giggles, except Mr Baker who is just about managing to keep a straight face by pretending he is absorbed in the paperwork attached to his clipboard. Mr Mason has turned a deathly shade of white and Frosty, who normally has everything under control in the workplace, looks like he's about to ignite.

"Mrs Morrison, we are ready when you are," interrupts Frosty as Mrs M arranges her bags. He's trying to sound calm and upbeat but I can hear the lilt of annoyance which sometimes seeps into his voice when things aren't going exactly as he's planned.

"Almost done," says Mrs M cheerfully, so cheerfully that in fact I suspect she is deliberately ignoring the emotional undercurrents.

I'm curious about Mrs M's sudden affection for Mr Mason, which began a couple of months ago. Everyone else seems to think it's a fanciful crush but, watching the two of them up close and Mr Mason's tight-lipped awkwardness in her presence, I wonder if there's something I don't know about. Perhaps Mrs M knows some juicy scandal about Mr Mason, beyond all the usual rumours about him getting his leg over one too many times? After all, Mrs M has been with the company for years and has connections throughout Hendersons. She is, in fact, a company legend. She's even in the privileged position of having her own chair - not just any chair - but a deluxe leather model which was surreptitiously "lost" in a stocktake back in 1995.

"Thank you, ducks," says Mrs M, taking back her accessories from Mr Mason and placing them on the floor directly in front of his feet so he can't stretch out his long legs.

"All set now, Mr Frost. Ready and waiting," says Mrs M.

Frosty clears his throat and claps his hands. We all sit up to attention. Even Mr Mason and Mr Baker seem to have gained an inch or two. I suspect they must hate coming to this branch: there's Frosty the control freak,

Mrs M the gossipmonger and, of course, there's me. I'm not sure how I'd best be described.

"Good morning, everyone," says Frosty.

"Good morning, Mr Frost," bark the staff in unison. Mr Baker (ex-territorial army, Catering Support Regiment) raises his hand half-way to salute, before recalling he is in a furniture store in the Home Counties. Mr Mason looks relieved the focus is off him, and Mrs M gives me an encouraging wink. I take a last sip of my water and pray to God I don't throw up.

A burst of laughter rings out. It's all been going surprisingly well; the pills have been clearing my head and I haven't made any major faux pas. Yet. However, now it's time to open up the floor to questions, as it always is at the end of these affairs. I only hope Mrs M is not going to stitch me up, as she's been known to do with various head office speakers, which is highly possible as Mrs M knows as much, if not more than me, about sales and what's more, she has absolutely no scruples about selling. In fact, she once persuaded a customer to buy three lamps, a Parker Knoll recliner, a coffee table, a foot stool and a magazine rack at 5 pm on Christmas Eve, so we could meet the sales target for our Christmas bonus.

"Any questions?" I ask, tentatively.

There are a few technical questions from the sales staff, but mostly they want to hear my anecdotes about my rudest customer, my customer with the silliest walk, my celebrity customers and, of course, my customer with the silliest name which, unfortunately, was Mr Ivor Bottom.

He was passing through and bought a nest of tables for his wife's birthday. Her name was Fanny. Apparently. Yeah, you're right. I do tell a lot of old blarney – but for the most part it does have an element of truth.

Frosty interrupts as the laughter begins to subside.

"You haven't mentioned your smile technique, Sandy."

"My smile technique?" I feign ignorance. I cannot believe he has mentioned my little secret. Doesn't he realise I could make him look a complete idiot by recounting the episode in his office? I suppose he knows I won't; I may be leaving Hendersons but I don't want to leave it on a sour note, especially with Mason and Baker here.

"Yes, the one you demonstrated for me in my office." says Frosty.

"What demonstration is that?" says Mr Mason, with the emphasis on "demonstration" in such a way that implies I've been selling favours.

"Sandy uses an unusual sales technique to help her with her more difficult customers," says Frosty. "I think we could all benefit from using it."

"Perhaps you would enlighten us?" says Mason, delighting in my discomfort. "I'm always interested in new techniques."

The glint in Mason's eye tells me exactly what he is referring to; the man is a total lecher. I enjoy innocent flirting but I know that flirting with Mason would be a dangerous path to tread. He doesn't do innocent and, anyway, he's had it in for me since I removed his hand from my backside during a regional conference a few years ago. (I was slimmer then.) He claimed he was "brushing past" and I claimed that his hand felt less like a brush and more like a vice. He hasn't laid a finger on me since but, occasionally, he tries to put me down as a sort of punitive vengeance. I give Frosty one of my glowering stares as he nods in agreement with Mason and smiles pleadingly at me which, I suppose, is progress on a poker up the backside, although not perhaps as satisfying an image.

"Come on, ducks," says Mrs M to me, whilst patting Mr Mason on the knee and giving him an endearing look. "I'm with Wally on this one; I want to know about this new technique."

Mr Mason flinches at the physical contact and the unabashed and inappropriate use of his nickname, draws in his knees and shoulders and shifts towards Mr Baker so that the two of them are squashed up like sardines. Baker shuffles awkwardly across his seat, his bulbous body pushing Len from delivery into Sally from admin who nudges Harvey, who leans away and head butts Guy, who clasps his head, screams and dramatically lurches sideways so that he gives a large shove to Margery, who promptly falls off her end seat like an upright pencil off a table and lands with her legs in the air with her wholesome Marks and Spencer's peach coloured knickers on display underneath her twenty denier tights. The whole place descends into uproar. Frosty jumps up to the rescue, Mr Mason looks like he's about to have an embolism and I burst out in uncontrollable laughter. I look at Mrs M through my tears and she winks at me with a smug, self-satisfied smirk creeping across her powdered cheeks.

"I think we'd better end it here," says Frosty, hurriedly. "Everyone back to their stations. Doors open in five minutes. Get ready for those customers! Shoot to kill, ladies and gents. Shoot to kill!"

"Anyone would think we were going over the top," says Mrs M, idling past me towards the exit to the canteen as Mason, Baker and Frosty converge in the middle of the sales floor, the staff disband and Margery strides off to the office to file an accident report. "Coming for a cuppa?"

I look towards the main doors for the potential rush of early morning customers: there's only an elderly couple wearing matching dogtooth coats being buffeted by the wind. The man's hands are deep in his pockets and his face is buried in a paisley scarf and the woman is wearing black knitted gloves, a black beanie hat pulled down over her ears and is desperately clutching one of our flyers, which looks like it might be ripped out of her hands at any moment. It is pouring with rain and there isn't anyone else in sight, not even outside Argos, where there is usually a small clutch of folks eager to return their unwanted gifts.

"Yes, I'm coming," I reply, picking up my bag and file and trailing after Mrs M. "I think they can manage the full frontal assault without me."

10

"So how's the old girl?" says Deidre as she pulls the passenger door closed behind her and I steer away from the kerb in the direction of The Orchards where Mum has been in residence for the last week.

"Failed her MOT last week. I needed new tyres, a bulb and windscreen wipers."

"Not this old girl, the other one," snorts Deidre.

"Oh you mean my Mum," I say. "Well, you're about to find out as we're taking her tonight."

"A brave move," says Deidre. "Have you taken any Valium?"

"Not yet, but after an evening watching a Christmas nativity with Mum in tow, I may well need it."

"What's Tabby's role tonight?"

"A mammoth."

"You're joking!" screeches Deidre in painful delight.

"No, I'm not. But at least she'll be warm in her costume," I say. "Last year, she was a baboon and wore a black leotard and body paint. She was frozen by the time we got home."

"Oh dear God," says Deidre, chortling. "Who thinks up this nonsense? What's happened to cattle and sheep?"

"Some politically correct jobsworth in Westminster probably," I say, getting onto one of my favourite soapboxes, "Who thinks the nativity is a multi-cultural, global experience encompassing all religions, races and animals."

"But a mammoth?" repeats Deidre, pulling a bemused face. "They were extinct before Jesus was born."

"Apparently, it was defrosting in Iceland, saw the shining star and got a lift with a swarm of pterodactyls who were relocating to Bethlehem from Northern Europe."

"I should have known. How else would it get there?" says Deidre. "Hugh is a shepherd this year and Lily is a migrant worker."

"A shepherd and a…migrant worker?"

"Yes," replies Deidre, raising an eyebrow at me questioningly as I glance sideways at her to see if she's pulling my leg. I see she's serious.

"What are they wearing?" I ask.

"The usual tea towels, but Lily has a hoe instead of a crook."

"Tea towels? That is so unfair! I haven't had an easy costume to make since Andy was a king in 2001."

"Well at least that was a good part."

"Yeah, I suppose so. But I still haven't figured out what Elvis Presley was doing at the birth of Jesus."

"Elvis?"

"Yes. Andy wore one of Dave's large shirts, a sequinned belt and one of Mum's 1960s pendants."

"Bloody hell," says Deidre flatly. "The world has gone bananas."

We drive along in silence for a while.

"So how is she?" says Deidre. "The old girl?"

"Better than I expected," I reply. "The other oldies seem to keep her grounded and as most of them have got pretty bad memories too, they don't notice how often she repeats herself. Not yet anyway. She's not had one of her totally madcap sessions yet either. Possibly because she's playing cards so much and is occupied most of the time. She's in her element."

"That's good," says Deidre, turning up the heating. "Gosh, it's cold tonight. So, is she missing home at all?"

"Frau Engel says she's been a bit confused about where she is at times but, once she starts playing cards or watching telly with the others, she settles down. There was a slight incident the first day she arrived when she thought she was imprisoned in a stalag."

"A stalag?"

"A German prisoner of war camp."

"Good God! She's still not harping on about the war?" says Deidre.

"I'm afraid so," I grimace. "I don't know whether to laugh or cry. Sometimes it's hilarious, and at other times it does my head in. Particularly the addiction to war films. I've seen The Great Escape so many times now I can quote it verbatim."

"Steve McQueen was pretty dishy though."

"Yeah, but sometimes she thinks she *is* Steve McQueen."

"Ah well. Now there's a problem," says Deidre, who I can tell is trying very hard to keep a straight face.

"I'm hoping I don't get Alzheimer's when I'm old," I say. "I'm overdosing on fish oil to try and stave it off."

"Ugh. That oil is vile," says Deidre, pulling a disgusted face. "I'm taking it as vitamin tablets. I can't understand why they don't make those tablets smaller. Swallowing those things is worse than giving a blow job."

I erupt with laughter as we turn into The Orchards' driveway, the tyres crunching on the gravel as I pull up outside the entrance. I switch off the engine and compose myself.

"Why are you taking all those supplements anyway?" I ask as we get out and climb the steps.

"My hair's thinning."

"I hadn't noticed," I reply. "Is that why you've been wearing hats lately?"

I look at Deidre's quirky red hat, stuck jauntily on the side of her head, which matches her bright red overcoat and the red and black polka dot scarf wrapped around her neck. She looks elegant and stylish. I glance down at my faded jeans, my black polo neck covered in Mutley's hairs, and my coat that won't do up because of my bulging tummy and wish I'd made more of an effort.

I ring the bell and introduce Frau Engel to Deidre.

"I've heard a lot about you…and The Orchards," says Deidre.

"I trust it is all gut," says Frau Engel.

"Yes indeed," says Deidre, giving one of her winning smiles.

"Excellent," says Frau Engel. "Mrs Lovett, your mother is in the lounge with the other residents. I have brought her coat and accessories downstairs already, so I will fetch her for you. Please take a seat."

"By God, she's efficient," whispers Deidre in my ear as we watch Frau Engel walk briskly towards the lounge. "No wonder your mum thought she was in a prison camp."

"She's marvellous," I say. "I feel like Mum is in safe hands. She scared the pants off me at first but now I'm rather fond of her."

"She's certainly a larger-than-life character," replies Deidre as Frau Engel returns, holding Mum gently by the arm.

"Denise!" exclaims Mum as she sees me, "and Deidre!"

"How come she always remembers you?" I say grudgingly to Deidre.

"I'm just a memorable person," replies Deidre, smugly.

"Here we are," says Frau Engel, steering Mum towards me and handing me her coat and other belongings. "I will leave you with…Denise and Deidre. Now have a good time and I will see you later."

I help Mum on with her navy coat, wrap her scarf around her neck to keep out the winter chill, pop her navy felt hat on her head and place her best patent leather navy handbag in her hands.

"You look very smart. One more thing," I say, pulling out Mum's gold and sapphire brooch from my own bag and pinning it onto her lapel. "There, finished!"

"Where are we going again?" says Mum.

"We're going to see Tabby in the school play," says Deidre.

"Tabby?"

"Sandy's daughter; your granddaughter."

"Of course, of course!" says Mum, thrilled. "But where's Sandy?"

"She couldn't make it. Work commitments," I say, looking forlornly at Deidre. "So we're going instead."

"Oh what a pity. But never mind, we must do our best," says Mum.

I loop arms with Mum, Deidre opens the door and we make our way down the steps. I help Mum into the front seat of the car whilst Deidre hops nimbly into the rear seat.

"It's been ages since I've seen Tabby," says Mum. "Is she going to play Mary?"

"Not this time," I say.

"Who's she playing?"

"Um…she's playing a mammoth."

"A mammoth?" says Mum, perplexed. "Has she put on weight?"

"No."

"A mammoth?" says Mum again. "I know I'm getting old, dear. But I don't remember any mammoth in the nativity."

"I fucking don't either," mutters Deidre under her breath from her rear seat.

"What's that, Deidre?" says Mum.

"I was just saying, I don't remember any mammoth either," says Deidre raising her voice.

"Well, it's not really a nativity anymore, Mum," I explain. "It's a sort of global celebration of...of...of...niceness."

"I'm not sure if I understand, Denise," says Mum, sounding very confused.

"Don't worry," pipes up Deidre again. "Neither does anyone else."

11

The school foyer and hall is bubbling with laughter and chatter. Deidre, Mum and I are enjoying mince pies and small glasses of weak fizzy white wine whilst we wait for the proceedings to get underway. We've been joined by Deidre's daughter and her husband, Jen and Rolly, who have both cut short their working day so they could be here. Dave, on the other hand, is noticeably absent. He's explained to Tabby that he has an important business event to attend to – which is a night out with the lads. I can't complain though as he's more than done his fair share of parents' evenings and other tortuous school events, and it's also his foreman's fortieth birthday.

We are standing in a group chatting when Tina (the mum with the Botox implants) weaves her way over to us. She is looking terribly excited. I can't make my mind up whether she's had a face lift or if it's a genuine expression. Her lips seem even bigger than usual too, and are moving so fast as she gossips her way across the room, I wonder what the news is that's so exciting or if she's been wired into a plug socket.

"Hello, everyone," says Tina, breathless. "Have you heard the news?"

"Are you alright, dear?" says Mum before anyone can say a word. "You look like you've had a terrible fright."

Deidre turns away from the group, choking on her wine as she tries to suppress her laughter. Disciplined by years of customer service, I manage to stay composed, even though Jen and Rolly are openly grinning. Tina, whose face is registering all sorts of conflicting emotions, clearly doesn't know how to interpret Mum's remark.

"This is my Mum, Tina," I say, hurriedly.

Everyone's heard about my Mum, her illness and some of the crazy things she's got up to lately, which seem to be reason enough for Tina as to why Mum might have made such an odd comment. I don't like to tell Tina that, although Mum can be delusional at times, there is nothing wrong with her powers of observation.

"Oh yes. How lovely to meet you," says Tina, her composure restored and offering Mum a handshake. "Have you come to see Tabby tonight? She's adorable. You must be so proud to have such a talented granddaughter."

"Why, yes, I have come to see Tabby!" says Mum as if Tina has made some hugely difficult deduction.

I'd like to point out to Tina that nobody could deduce if Tabby was talented or not as she's hidden beneath a mass of brown imitation fur, but that wouldn't be fair as

Tina's a generous, kind hearted woman who means well. I smile at Tina in appreciation and she smiles sympathetically back, no doubt thankful her own mother isn't barking mad.

"I came over to see if you've heard the news about Tricia?" says Tina.

"No, I don't think so," I say, wondering what's so exciting we warrant a formal briefing.

"What's the gossip?" says Deidre, having regained her poise and re-joined the conversation.

"She's not standing for election, is she?" says Rolly and gives one of his hearty, booming laughs that can be heard all over the room, whilst his prosperous belly, the product of too many business and charity lunches, wobbles like a blancmange.

"Not quite," says Tina, a little deflated. "But she has put herself forward to stand for selection as an MP."

Rolly laughs even louder, whilst Jen, Deidre and I look at each other in bemusement.

"I hope she gets nominated just so I can put a bet on her losing," bellows Rolly, quaffing his wine.

"I don't know what you're laughing for, Rolly," says Jen. "I think Tricia would make a very good MP. She has all the right credentials."

"What's that? Procrastinating and fiddling expenses?" laughs Rolly again.

"Maybe you should run yourself," says Jen with a hint of sarcasm. "You might give Tricia a run for her money."

"Now, now, you two," says Deidre in her parenting mode. "Let's not get into an argument. I do think Jen has a point though. Tricia does have all the credentials and, as we all know, there's as much chance of Tricia filing a dodgy expenses claim as there is of Tony Blair making a comeback."

Everyone laughs and looks over to where Tricia is at the entrance to the hall, selling programmes for the insanely overpriced amount of two pounds. She is dressed in a navy suit, with a white blouse with a ruffle neck and nude heels. Her hair has been highlighted and cropped into a shorter bob than normal.

"Christ, she even looks like Mrs Thatcher now," says Rolly, his eyes lighting up. "Actually, I might put money on her to win!"

"If she can get past the preliminaries and the selection committee, she would have the vote of everyone at the school. Potentially, that's a lot of support. What do you think, Sandy?" says Tina.

"I don't know," I say, not wanting to commit until I've got over the horrifying image in my head of Tricia as the Prime Minster lecturing the country, not just the PTA. "She's certainly good at fleecing cash out of everyone though. Two pounds for a school programme is outrageous."

Rolly breaks out into another hearty laugh and fortuitously the bell rings for us to take our seats. The conversation comes to an abrupt halt. Mum has disappeared from my side but I find her a few metres away, examining the children's self-portraits which are stuck up on the wall.

"I wonder which one is Tabby?" says Mum.

"I don't know," I say examining all the weird faces with misshapen features. "The only thing I can say for certain is that there isn't an art teacher in the school."

Mum is singing and swaying to Little Donkey as the school choir stands to attention and belts out the lyrics. Well, to be more accurate: about five of them are belting it out, twenty are half-heartedly mumbling it whilst trying to locate their parents in the audience, two are miming it and one is staring vacantly into space, struck dumb with stage fright. However, combined with the screeching of the recorders, some totally inappropriate cymbal bashing and Mrs Timms hamming it up on the piano, the song is just about recognisable.

I look down the row to see if anyone has noticed Mum's behaviour but everyone seems occupied; Rolly has managed to acquire a bottle of the cheap plonk and is working his way through it whilst texting, Jen is eagerly looking for Hugh and Lily, and Deidre has that fixed glazed look which means she's bored rigid. I know exactly how she feels. I'm saturated with school plays and apart from the one occasion when Andy was Elvis, every role my kids have ever had has been an insignificant bit part. Ninety minutes of watching other parents preening over their kids whilst yours appears for two minutes in an indistinguishable costume is a total pisser, especially when they want to charge you £14.00 for a DVD.

As the choir sing/mouth their way through the verses, the donkey (twins Miles and Theo Gemoli from Year Four) led by Joseph (Ralph Newman, Year Five) and other members of the cast begin to parade down the central aisle, between the two sections of the audience. As with most nativities, the majority of the children look completely bewildered, except for one token exhibitionist whose mother thinks the whole thing is designed to showcase their child's huge talents. Tonight, this is Ralph, who clearly thinks he is the next Bruce Forsyth and is staring at the audience with a big cheesy grin, revealing the gaping holes in his teeth.

To avoid potential health and safety issues, Mary (Chloe Chang, Year Five) isn't riding on the back of the donkey but trailing behind it, heavily pregnant, with the aid of a pillow stuffed down her tunic and two pairs of tights rolled up inside her specially purchased 28AA bra. As Chloe walks tentatively up the central aisle, I acknowledge she's perfect for the role with her sallow skin, long dark lashes and innocent face. I'm grateful though that her only words are, "Who are you?" to the Angel Gabriel as Chloe barely talks above a whisper and the speaker system packed up during the opening hymn.

Joseph, Mary and the donkey lead the parade of subjects also going to attend the census in Bethlehem. They include some martial arts experts, some misplaced migrant workers, Santa's reindeers, a policeman and a menagerie of strange and disturbing-looking animals, including an oddly shaped koala bear, a drunken penguin and a sickly iguana. Trotting behind all these is James from Reception, whose impression of a kangaroo is given added authenticity by his bowlegged walk, caused by a large wet patch between his legs.

As the procession marches on, Jen spots Lily and begins to wave. Lily is carrying her hoe and wearing a non-standard red and white checked tea towel on her head to set her apart from the shepherds who are wearing brown checked tea towels. Hugh and the other shepherds, whose number has expanded from three to six because the class sizes are bigger this year, have appeared on a raised platform to the right of centre stage, where they are supposed to be set in a tableau pointing in wonderment at the Star of Bethlehem, which has been suspended precariously from the ceiling. Only Hugh's arm is tiring and he keeps raising it up and down like a Nazi. Jen is trying to ignore this by focusing her attention on Lily but Rolly has his phone held enthusiastically above the heads of the other parents, recording Hugh's faux pas for posterity. He'll probably dine out on Hugh's folly for the next few years.

At the end of the procession is my Tabby, in her large hairy costume that took me three weeks and three meters of fake fur at £8.99 a metre to make. Mrs M even gave me a hand to make the headwear as I was determined that, after all the years in minuscule parts, Tabby was going to get a decent costume, even if she didn't get to say a word, yet again. I have to hand it to Tabby, she's giving it her all; she's bent double, wobbling her bottom and swinging her right arm, which is acting as a trunk, from side to side. She's tickling and gently pinching the audience's arms and legs, tossing programmes, flicking off hats and causing quite a stir...and a lot of laughs. I swell with pride at her ingenuity and her attempt to make such a naff part more interesting.

"Look, there's Tabby!" says Mum.

The procession sweeps round the audience and makes its way down the side aisle towards us, with Tabby still bringing up the rear, milking the audience for all they're worth.

"She's brilliant! I wish your father was here to see it!" boasts Mum, clapping her hands together with glee.

Cameras are flashing, parents are clapping and whistling and Rolly is still filming, whilst my jaw strains from grinning knowing that, for once, Tabby is getting the applause she deserves. You see, I think Tabby's a born actress and it's perplexed me why none of her class teachers have ever recognised it. Eventually, Tabby reaches our row which is towards the back of the hall. Mum is sitting on the end seat and, as Tabby sees her, she raises her trunk and squeezes Mum's nose. Mum squeals with delight and everyone in the surrounding seats breaks out laughing. I laugh too. Seeing Mum so thrilled and proud of her granddaughter brings a lump to my throat and tears to my eyes. Knowing Mum still gets pleasure from simple things like watching children, playing cards and sipping crème de menthe, makes me feel guilty for all the times I get irritated and cross, because I know that, despite her illness, she still fulfils a role in our family. Frau Engel was right. Mum might not be performing the normal role of a younger grandparent like Deidre, but Tabby is learning a lot from Mum. Maybe that isn't knitting, or needlework, or how to bake scones or even that Grannies are good for babysitting and secret stashes of sweets. Tabby understands what compassion is and what love means. I take a gulp of my wine and hold back my tears.

As the last bars of a second rendition of Little Donkey fade away, Mary, Joseph and the donkey move to centre stage and the rest of the children file onto the tiered seats which are either side of the auditorium. Narrators, innkeepers, angels and miscellaneous shopkeepers come and go, to the accompaniment of various ear-piercing instruments and the high pitch wailing masquerading as singing, which would almost make tinnitus seem a pleasure. Finally, Baby Jesus is born and the three wise people (two boys and a girl) and the six shepherds gather round, and all the children in the tiered seats rise to attention as Mary holds the child aloft for all to see.

There is a universal gasp. The auditorium falls silent.

Baby Jesus is…black.

"I didn't know Jesus was black, dear," says Mum loudly, looking more confused than she's ever done. "When did they discover that?"

"And how the hell did he get to be black with a white father and a Chinese mother?" blurts Rolly, as the gasps from other parents turn into titters of amusement.

"That's IVF for you," quips Deidre.

I collapse with laughter, huge gulps of giggles reach down to my stomach so that I can barely breathe until, eventually, the dreaded event happens - a trickle of urine seeps into my knickers. I'm immediately restored to a serious disposition as one of my ultimate horror scenarios, on a par with nuclear war, has arisen; I must get to the loo before I wet my pants completely.

"Look after Mum, will you?" I whisper urgently to Deidre and dart out of the row and walk as quickly as I can out of the hall and up the corridor. I push past the queue of angels, nuns and worshippers, waiting to celebrate the birth of Christ. There isn't time to get to the Ladies so I have to make do with the girls' toilets where I rip down my jeans and knickers and squat on the tiny loo, which is pretty darn difficult when you're my age. I sigh with relief that I've escaped public humiliation. I blot my knickers but decide I still need to switch to my emergency pair so I kick off my jeans and rummage in my handbag. After tipping it upside down and spilling the contents, I realise I haven't replaced my knickers from my last emergency episode (three hour traffic jam on the M25) and the only ones I have are Mum's large white aerated knickers which, even with my large tummy, still look like they'd double as a swimming costume. But I've no choice. I can hear singing now and I don't want to miss the end of the show with Tabby at her best. So I slip on the knickers, roll up my own and shove them into my makeup bag, pull on my jeans and boots, gather up my clutter and hurry back to the hall.

I speed walk along the corridor as the singing comes to the end. There's some mumbling, followed by a brief silence. I swing open the hall door and look to centre stage where I expect to see a montage of angels and nuns and all things godly, waiting to burst into song which is exactly what I do see - only in the middle of them with her navy scarf wrapped over her hat is Mum.

I die a thousand deaths.

I can immediately see Mum has gone into fantasy mode and thinks she is a nun, with her hands clasped in prayer and her scarf tied beneath her chin. The children are transfixed, completely thrown by the bizarre interruption to their play, the audience is clueless and the teachers clearly don't know what to do. I am frozen in complete horror as Mum does the worst thing possible; she spreads her arms out wide like Julie Andrews in the Sound of Music, spins, and takes a deep breath as she faces the audience again. I am rooted to the spot and so is everyone else, as they watch with fascination the batty woman who has taken over the nativity, who is clearly off her rocker and whose voice begins to warble around the auditorium.

The hills are alive with the sound of music
With songs they have sung for a thousand years

I die a thousand more deaths. Deidre turns round, shrugs despairingly and mouths "sorry". A few people have begun to catch on to who the imposter is and, out of the corner of my eye, I see the head teacher making furious gestures at me to redeem the situation. So I lift up my feet, which now seem as heavy as dumbbells, and make my way through the centre aisle. I climb the stage steps as Mum continues to warble in a voice which, although reasonably tuneful, doesn't exactly match Julie Andrews for beauty. I hold Mum's hand and wait for her to finish.

I go to the hills when my heart is lonely
I know I will hear what I've heard before
My heart will be blessed with the sound of music
And I'll sing once more.

Mum ends on a long, trill note and then the auditorium falls deadly quiet. I begin to lead Mum away, the elation of my earlier joy thrown into total despair and humiliation. We are poised on the top step and, as I start to help Mum down, Tricia Marshall, who is sitting in the front row, stands up and begins to clap, her face calm and composed. Everyone follows suit; they stand up and begin to clap too. Thunderous applause echoes around the hall. I lead Mum out of the hall as she smiles and waves and curtseys, completely oblivious to the significance of what she has done. As I push open the exit doors, Deidre leaps up and follows us out and I hear Mrs Timms strike up the first notes of Away in a Manger.

"That went down well, Denise," says Mum. "I think we should come again."

"Yes, it was wonderful," I say, turning to Deidre. "I'll just be a few minutes. Can you take Mum to the car?"

Deidre leads Mum away. I slink into the girls' toilets, sit down on the loo and begin to cry.

12

I'm relaxing on Hilda, the striped sofa, in Hendersons' canteen during my afternoon tea break, sipping hot coffee and gorging on a monstrous cream cake left over from my lunchtime farewell buffet. I lick the fresh cream and jam, relishing the sweet sensations, and nibble the crisp flaky pastry. I flick off the flat sandals which I always wear during sale time, rest my stockinged feet on the sofa and recline like a debauched Roman emperor. As I indulge in the luxurious cream, I revel in the thought of being free from the monotony of nine to five and the bliss of a week off before I start at The Herald. Of course, I'll still be taking Mum for her daily outings, but it'll still be my first real day without the pressure of getting the kids to school, rushing off to work, rushing back to cook, clean, iron and look after the kids, Mum, Dave and the dog for six whole years. I repeat: six whole years. And I have plans. Big plans.

So my big plan is to take up exercise. I know to some people that isn't such a big deal but to me it's like the quest for the Holy Grail: a long, agonizing mission strewn with the bodies of knights, dragons and pious monks. Only in my case, the quest is strewn with bodies of defunct cycle machines, abdominal crunching devices with the patents still pending, and exercise instructors who haven't looked a chocolate bar in the face for thirty years. Anyway, that's my big plan - exercise - with an accompanying diet and some overpriced fat-busting pills that taste like grass cuttings Stallone's pissed on.

Exercise. Ugh. You may have guessed it's not my favourite hobby. But, nevertheless, this time around I've got to stick to some sort of routine if I'm going to have any success reducing the size of my stomach. Over Christmas, I weighed up the pros and cons of which type of exercise would best suit me and after dispensing with the obvious choices of croquet, curling and bowls I came up with – darts. Dave was a little disappointed (he snorted like a pig and shoved a cushion up my jumper) which got me thinking that maybe I ought to be more serious about losing weight. So, eventually, I decided on something revolutionary, something I'd not done before in the whole of my checkered exercise history as an adult: jogging. Okay, so maybe it's not that revolutionary, and maybe what I'm planning is more akin to brisk walking, but it'll still be the first time I've attempted rapid movement in a big way since school. On a scale of one to ten on my exercise radar, jogging is about minus thirty and brisk walking is about minus ten. Anyway, it's cheap and I'm desperate to lose weight. Yes, I know I said earlier I'd start dieting before Christmas but as they say the "flesh is weak" or, more specifically, my flesh is weak and I pigged out over the festivities with brandy puddings and chocolate-covered Brazil nuts. Besides, I had the excuse that with all the hassle of Mum going doolally at school and spending most of Christmas with us, the only way to avoid impending depression was to eat my way out of it. Strangely enough, I've eaten my way out of numerous depressions.

Anyway, tomorrow is D-Day, the first day of my new diet and my new exercise regime. I've bought black running shoes, black jogging bottoms and a black jogging top to match my nondescript black headphones and an even more nondescript black hat. Hopefully, no fucker on earth will recognise me when I'm walking round the block. I've also bought a black swimming costume and a black rubber hat. But the less said about that the better.

I pop the last mouthful of cake into my mouth, close my eyes and begin to fantasize about transforming into the size ten I was years ago, jogging in tiny pink shorts and a skimpy bra top on a hot summer's day. I'm so fit and agile again, I'm bounding over the fields, leaping over the stiles with the theme tune to Rocky blasting in my ears. Sylvester Stallone, aged about forty, (I've still got some principles) is chasing me but I can't risk capture as he doesn't have any condoms. I'm running fast, very fast, there's a slightly higher stile at the end of the field but I think I can manage it, so I speed up, sprinting faster and faster like the bionic woman until I take a flying leap over the stile. I glide in the air like Jaime Sommers until my trainer clips the highest crossbeam and I crash onto the hardened earth. I'm winded but I quickly twist my body around to see if Sly is catching me up but, to my dismay, he's completely disappeared. Bitterly disappointed (I was playing hard to get), I turn back and start to lever my body off the floor when I notice muscular, tanned legs in stylish blue and white trainers standing directly in front of me. I raise my head slowly to meet two dark brown eyes, glistening with sexuality and desire. The eyes do not belong to Sly. They belong to someone even more special, someone who makes me feel all wobbly and gooey. The eyes belong to George Clooney.

"Hi there," says George in his smooth chocolate voice, which sets my heart beating furiously. "Do you need a hand?"

"Have you got any condoms?" I reply.

"I don't think we'll need those," says George suggestively and offers his hand to me as his white teeth gleam in the sun.

I giggle and run my tongue round my lips.

"What's going on here?"

I bolt upright, wrenched out of my fantasy by a voice that doesn't sound like Gorgeous George but which sounds like...

"Mr Mason, what are you doing here?" I blurt.

"I'm the regional manager. Remember?" says Mason. "I tend to drop into my shops from time to time to check everything is going as it should."

"Ah yes," I reply, regaining my focus. "I was just relaxing - last day and all that stuff."

"Yes, you looked *very* relaxed," says Mason questioningly, as a flush of embarrassment washes over me. "Anyway, I hate to interrupt you but there's a last minute rush going on upstairs and they could do with another pair of hands. Unless you have something else more important to attend to?"

"Um…no," I say, gathering up my bag and jacket.

"I'm disappointed to see you go, Sandy," says Mason, placing his laptop bag on the coffee table. "You've always been a hard worker and I've enjoyed our repartee. It's a shame we never hit it off," Mason pauses and adds with emphasis, "Although there's still time."

Mason rakes his carnivorous eyes up and down my body. If I didn't have a stomach like a hippo I might be flattered, but at this particular moment his interest seems unwarranted. Basically I'm fat and his interest reeks of nothing more than the opportunism of an unashamed sexual predator. It dawns on me that Mason thinks he's in with a chance with me now work no longer stands between us. I stand up, hoist my handbag over my shoulder and move to pass him but he sidesteps, blocking my way.

"It's a pity I missed the Christmas party this year," says Mason, coolly. "I hear you're a bit of a goer."

A deep rage begins to well inside me. Not because Derek has blown the whistle on Dave and me, but because Mason is inferring I'm some kind of easy lay, who is going to submit to his cack-handed overtures. Dave and I might have overdone it on the booze and behaved rather foolishly that night a few years ago, but you can hardly say I'm easy when I was frolicking with a man who also happens to be my husband. Besides, I didn't know Derek had installed a new CCTV monitor as, up until that point, there was more privacy in the soft furnishings department than there was in our own bedroom. I stare Mason defiantly in the eyes whilst I search for the right words to rebuff him.

"So how about a little…extra relaxation time?" says Mason, encroaching into my space so that we are so close his breath is on my face.

I've a suspicion he's going to touch me whatever I say. "No," I spit through gritted teeth.

"Are you sure?" Mason replies and raises his hand as if to touch my breasts. Automatically, I step back, acutely aware of Mason's towering physical presence. Normally my sharp tongue gets me out of any situation but, for the first time in my life, I feel physically threatened. Mason takes another small step forward and I stumble backwards and land ungracefully on Hilda.

"Well now, what an interesting situation," says Mason with a lewd leer, eyeing up my thighs which have been partially exposed by my skirt riding up in the fall.

"I don't think Sandy finds it interesting at all," interjects a loud voice.

Relief flows through me as I see Mrs M standing inside the doorway, her hands clasped tightly around her bag and with a face like a dark, ominous cloud. My throat is now so dry with anger, I'm not sure if I could say anything that would have come out as anything more than a mousey whisper. I've never been more grateful to see a friendly face.

"Mrs Morrison," says Mason flatly in recognition and picks up his laptop case, turns around without the slightest hint of remorse and walks calmly to the door. It's only then I'm sure that all the rumours about him are true. He's so cool and collected as if he's done this many times before; it's definitely not a one-off situation driven by unrequited love or anything which seems at all justifiable. I suspect he's a womaniser who covers his tracks under a guise of professionalism, preying on women who don't have the wherewithal or the experience to resist his advances and to whom, no doubt, he makes promises of favours and promotion.

"I'll expect to see you on the shop floor in five minutes, Sandy," says Mason. "You haven't left our employment yet and your tea break is timed out."

Mason stops fleetingly as he passes Mrs M at the door and they stare at each other. Neither of them flinches but there is a small patch of red high on Mason's cheeks which reveals either his embarrassment or his anger. I sense that it's anger.

"Not on my patch," says Mrs M and with that Mr Mason gives her one last deriding glance and leaves the room.

I let out a huge sigh as the tension dissipates.

"Nasty piece of work," says Mrs M, making her way over to the sideboard where the kettle is kept and flicking it on to boil. "And I wouldn't bother going up there. It's thinned out. It's power play to get one over on you."

"Yes, you're right. I think he's best avoided altogether now," I mutter, clearing my throat and pulling myself up from my awkward position on Hilda.

Mrs M upturns another cup from the pile and starts to make tea for the two of us.

"Thank goodness you came along when you did though, Mrs M. I was beginning to get worried."

I smooth down my skirt, straighten my blouse and put on my jacket trying to disguise my shaking hands. I'm annoyed with myself too for behaving so...weakly. Is that the right word? If only I'd delivered some amazing one liner like, "I need to remove my tampon" or "Are you okay with the herpes outbreak?" Damn it, why, why, why didn't I think of something at the time, instead of behaving like a complete lemon?

"I should have punched him between the eyes," I say, as numerous heroic scenarios shoot through my imagination, all of which now involve Mr Mason doubled over, clutching his groin in agony.

"I wouldn't have blamed you. The man is a lecher," says Mrs M, spooning sugar into our cups and stirring in milk. "I've met his type before: men who look for vulnerable women."

"He tried it on with me a few years ago, not long after I'd joined the company, but I dismissed is as one of those things," I reply, trying to calm myself down and realising that imagining Mason in a vat of boiling oil probably isn't helping. "He's never given me any trouble since. Not physically anyway. Obviously, he was testing the waters back then and thought he'd give it another shot now that I'm leaving. God knows why when I look like I do."

"You're still an attractive woman, Sandy. Even with the extra weight," says Mrs M. "Don't put yourself down."

I smile and accept the tea Mrs M offers me, take a few deep breaths and sit back down on Hilda and try to relax into her comfy cushions. Mrs M picks up her cup and saucer, waddles over and plops herself beside me.

"What is it between you and Mr Mason, Mrs M?" I say, taking a sip of my sugary tea. The warm fluid soothes the dryness in my throat and my stress begins to seep away. "I know there's something. It's more than just the rumours."

"You're very observant, Sandy," replies Mrs M, good naturedly. "It's one of the reasons you're so successful at sales: you always know the right time to smooch the customers."

"I'm not as good as you, Mrs M," I say, grinning with amusement at Mrs M's colloquial expression. It amazes me how she knows so much modern slang. She even knows how to use text jargon and predictive text, which confuses the hell out of me. I suppose I prefer talking.

Mrs M reciprocates a smile and places her cup and saucer firmly on the table and sighs. "I need to tell someone as I've been bottling it all up. It's been driving me potty."

I wait patiently for Mrs M to reveal what's upsetting her, even though I'm not sure if I want to know the whole truth. Sometimes it's awkward when people unburden themselves on me, like that episode in Frosty's office and the time when Tricia Marshall told me she'd had cystitis and wet herself in Marks and Spencers; it was six months before she could look me in the eye again. But, then again, Mrs M is not just anyone; I have quite a deep affection for her. She's almost the same age as Deidre but, whereas Deidre is more like a sister to me, Mrs M feels more like a mother or perhaps a mad aunt. I study Mrs M, whilst she braces herself to tell me whatever it is that is troubling her. She's wearing her Friday outfit, which consists of luminous green beads and matching bulbous earrings and a bright orange suit with green lapels. It's marginally better than her Thursday outfit which looks like a pair of 1970s curtains. I sip my tea again and conclude that probably makes her more of a mad aunt.

Mrs M takes a deep breath and I wonder what on earth she could possibly know about Mason that makes her so angry and upset. Mason's a bit of a slime ball but surely not all that bad? Tears begin to well in Mrs M's eyes. I clasp her wrinkly hand, which reminds me of Mum's, only with fewer liver spots. Instead of Mum's simple solitaire, Mrs M wears a large amber and gold ring as big as a knuckle duster. Whatever Mrs M knows, I deduce as she sniffles, maybe it is worse than I thought; Mrs M is normally as tough as one of my burnt pizzas.

"Mrs M," I say, "Whatever it is, it looks like you need to get it off your chest. Spit it out now."

"Mr Mason is Sophie's father," gulps Mrs M.

"Sophie? Your granddaughter?"

"Yes," says Mrs M, as a big tear drops unceremoniously on her blouse.

I reflect on this news for a moment, retrieve some tissues from my bag and pass them to Mrs M, whilst her breast heaves with sobbing. Mrs M's daughter, Layla, is married with three girls and I know both her and her husband, Liam. I'd always assumed Sophie was Liam's daughter…but apparently not.

"Layla was fifteen when she got pregnant," says Mrs M, trying her best to compose herself. "She wouldn't have an abortion and pretty much dropped out of school and left with a handful of mediocre exams. She'd always wanted to go to sixth form and university, but it was impossible with a baby to look after."

I nod, absorbing the news which now doesn't seem that shocking given my recent experience.

"She would never tell me who the father was and, naturally, I assumed it was a teenage boy," continues Mrs M, letting all her angst out. "After a while, I gave up asking - believing it was probably best left with nothing to gain emotionally or financially out of a relationship that would most likely have floundered within a couple of years."

"How did you find out it was Mr Mason?" I enquire, engrossed in the story unfolding in front of me.

"Remember he came on a visit a few months ago? And Layla and Sophie had dropped in to see me?"

"Yes, yes, I do remember," I say, visualizing all that happened that day. Mr Mason had been expected for a minimum two hour visit and we'd all frantically spruced up the displays. However, within a few minutes of arriving, Mr Mason had made his excuses and left. Frosty had been most put out and gone into one of his quiet rages.

"He saw Layla. I could see at once they knew each other. It was written all over her face, especially her disgust when she saw him appraising Sophie."

"Presumably, he left because he felt that there might be a confrontation and it would all come out on the shop floor?" I say.

"I suppose so. And then later, I remembered that when she'd got pregnant, she was working in a department store on Saturdays. I got a friend at head office to delve into his background: he was the deputy manager at the time."

"Did you confirm your suspicions with Layla?"

"Oh yes. I asked her as soon as we had a quiet moment away from Sophie. He's the father alright. She didn't tell me at the time, because she didn't want to cause even more trouble, and she felt guilty about what happened."

171

"So you think he manipulated her?"

"She was only fifteen. She was still a child!" says Mrs M, tears rolling down her cheeks. "How easy it must have been to flatter her and make her a willing partner. She pretty much told me that was the case – but when she told him about the pregnancy he told her to get an abortion and refused to have anything to do with her."

"Does he know Layla had the baby? That Sophie is his child?"

"He knows Layla had the baby but whether or not he realised Sophie was his daughter when she came in here - I don't know. She looks very young for her age and he may not have tied it together."

"So he's never given a helping hand, not even financially?" I say, appalled at the idea that Mason, whose job is very well paid, might not even have made some gesture towards his own child.

"No. He left her to bring up their child without the slightest help." Mrs M sniffs again. "You have no idea how hard it was for her until Liam came along."

"I can imagine," I say, remembering my own struggles in my mid-twenties bringing up Andy even with Dave on hand. All that crying and burping, the tantrums in supermarkets and doctors' surgeries, and the inevitable sleepless nights were a complete nightmare and landed me with a twenty-year addiction to the biscuit barrel. God knows what it must have been like for Layla, with no money and no partner, even with the indomitable Mrs M at her side.

"Why on earth didn't she ask for financial support?" I enquire.

"I'm not sure: pride, guilt? Maybe later the potential effect on his family?" shrugs Mrs M.

"I suppose I can sort of see how she might have felt," I reply, trying my best to put myself in Layla's shoes but failing miserably. "But she's let him off the hook too easily. He manipulated a child, fathered another one and hasn't made any apology or contribution to their wellbeing at all. It's shameful!"

"Layla never asked him for help after he told her to get an abortion. She's too stubborn and has too much pride," says Mrs M, whose face suggests she doesn't know whether to be enormously proud of Layla's resolute determination, or whether to bang her over the head with a broomstick. "Of course, I didn't think it was so bad when I thought it was the naivety of young love - or even young lust - but now, knowing the father was Mr Mason and exactly how he behaves, I feel completely different." Mrs M dabs at her eyes. "He must have been mid-thirties at the time. He should have kept his hands off."

"And what's more, it would seem he's hasn't kept his hands off trying to take advantage of women for the last eighteen years!" I proclaim indignantly.

I recall what's just happened to me with Mr Mason. How simple it must have been for him to seduce a fifteen year old girl; a few choice words and romantic gestures and she'd have been easy prey. Mr Mason is an attractive man, even in his fifties; in his thirties he must have been even more handsome. Layla probably wouldn't have been capable of seeing anything beyond that, especially in the haze of a schoolgirl crush.

I refill our teacups and place one of the left-over cakes on a plate in front of Mrs M as she blots her smudged mascara. I put the last jam doughnut on a plate for myself, and when Mrs M closes her compact, satisfied she no longer looks like a ghoul, we sit in silence, chewing our buns and contemplating the rather problematic situation in which Mrs M has found herself. It's not one which is easy to overlook either, not when you consider Mrs M sees Mason regularly and how uncomfortable it must be knowing he once committed an offence with a minor who also happened to be her daughter.

"What are you going to do, if anything?" I ask eventually. "Contact the police?"

"I'm not sure yet," says Mrs M. "I don't want to stir up a hornets' nest. It's eighteen years ago and there would be a lot of ifs, buts and maybes hanging in the air. I know he's a predator, but unless he has a track record of seducing underage girls, who's to say it was anything but an unfortunate one-off which should be left to rest?"

"But it was illegal, Mrs M. He shouldn't be allowed to get away with it. To ignore it…well, it's almost condoning his behaviour!"

"Illegal - but not unheard of, Sandy," says Mrs M, giving me a reproachful look. "I have to think of the long term consequences for my family…and for his, if I do anything at all. He has a family too. What would be the consequences for them if he lost his job and was publically vilified?"

"I see what you mean," I say, admiring Mrs M's forgiveness and her forethought. "But he should be held accountable in some way. Only then will he acknowledge the consequences of his actions."

"True. But I'm not sure how."

"Financially is the obvious solution," I say. "He's missed out on eighteen years of child maintenance, which is totally unjust, irrespective of whether or not Layla asked for it. It's not as if he's living on the breadline, is it, with his swanky suits? His wife has a good job too. He could afford to make some sort of payment. Even if it was only a nominal one."

"What if his wife doesn't know though?" says Mrs M with a furrowed brow. "That could cause a lot of trouble."

"No more than he's caused you and Layla," I snort in disgust. "I bet his wife doesn't have any idea about his past. He'd have to either come clean, or perhaps keep it a secret if he has separate finances. Personally, I'd be ashamed if I found out Dave had fathered a child and he made no contribution to its upbringing."

"Not all women are like you, Sandy. Asking for money feels like blackmail if I'm not reporting him to the police."

"Maybe it feels like that, but it's not, is it? It's what rightfully belongs to Sophie."

"I suppose when you put it like that — it doesn't seem so bad. Sophie is going to university in the autumn," says Mrs M, thoughtfully. "Maybe he could make a contribution to her fees? I would certainly feel happier seeing him around the place, knowing he'd done something for her. I think the only other alternative is to leave before I make a huge scene - although that would affect my pension."

"You don't want to lose any of your pension, Mrs M. And you shouldn't be forced into leaving because you feel uncomfortable. I think a contribution towards her university fees is an excellent idea," I enthuse. "It's a very reasonable request and at the same time it'll force him to share some of the responsibility."

"Shall I ask Layla?"

"Mrs Lovett to the shop floor," booms Frosty over the tannoy system in his clipped military voice. "Immediately, please."

"I'd better go," I say, standing up. "But ask Layla, Mrs M. She deserves a break. University is expensive; Andy is up to his ears in debt. Mr Mason should accept some responsibility and, deep down, Layla probably knows that. Besides, he can only say no and she will have lost nothing."

"Mrs Lovett to the shop floor," repeats Frosty in a more commanding tone.

"See you in a jiffy, Mrs M."

I leave Mrs M reapplying her mascara and make my way up to the shop floor, passing Frosty's office with the door ajar. I peer around the frame and see Mason's laptop on Frosty's sideboard and, as usual, Frosty's figurines strategically rearranged on the map of the store positioned on his desk. I hesitate, knowing I should be hurrying to the showroom, but I can't resist wandering in for a last look at Frosty's war game. I push the door wider and slip inside.

For six years, I've been fascinated by Frosty's bizarre shop landscape which is manufactured out of chicken wire, paper-mache and carpet remnants. I pick up one of the small sofas, arranged in clusters around the map. It's obviously from a dolls' house although some of the other replica suites look home-made. I turn it around and inspect it; the sticky label reads; "The Majestic Suite, £2,599". I place it gently back down and pick up another, one of its armrests falls off and I see that underneath the fabric covering, it is made out of matchboxes. I place it back down, position the armrest but it falls off again. I try a third time, but it falls off yet again. I begin to panic and look around the office for something to fix it. But the whole office is so frustratingly neat, I can't even see a reel of Sellotape or a knob of Blu-Tack. I rummage desperately in my makeup bag, find a crumpled plaster and cut off a small piece and wedge it in between the two surfaces. It sticks and I let a small sigh of relief and conclude that, whilst I may have some odd personality traits, Frosty is a *whole* lot worse.

After a furtive glance back to the door, I study the placement of the figurines in Frosty's latest strategic battle plan which he must have been demonstrating to Mr Mason. I often wonder why Mason hasn't dispatched Frosty into some quiet backwater, to slip into company obscurity. I can only conclude that it's because Frosty's oddball methods produce results; our shop is the third most profitable in the company, despite not being in a major city. I bend down further and survey the new positions. Derek, who is represented by a Dalek, is the only one who appears to be in his usual position at the security post. I'm interpreting this as a form of flattery as, normally, when someone leaves the company, we have an obligatory security search in case they've decided to pocket a Queen Anne chandelier at the last moment. However, the fact that this is not happening tonight means that Frosty obviously trusts me which, ironically, is probably not wise, bearing in mind I'm standing in his office thinking about ringing social services.

Anyway, back to the figurines: I'm represented by a metal figurine of Bilbo Baggins (I know why now) and have been moved to the exit. Mrs M is a porcelain figure of Mrs Bennett from Pride and Prejudice, and has been moved into my position, Guy is a Lego Jedi Knight and has moved into Mrs M's position, Harvey is Cinderella from a McDonald's Happy Meal and has been moved into Guy's position, and Harvey's position remains vacant as they are not replacing me due to the recession. In the centre of the board are the three figurines I am most interested in: Frosty, who is represented by a tin soldier about to launch a hand grenade, Mr Baker, who is Doc from the Seven Dwarves, and Mr Mason, who is a White King from a standard chess set.

I stand rigidly in Frosty's office, transfixed by the figurines. A shiver of excitement runs up my spine. At long last, I get to do something I have always secretly desired. Something I also know is very, very wrong. I pick up the White King, pull a black biro from my bag and draw a lopsided fringe and a small square moustache where the face should be and giggle.

I turn to leave the office still giggling, when I hear a familiar electronic "pop" of a message arriving on Facebook. My curiosity gets the better of me, because there's no way Frosty would be on Facebook. The sound must be coming from Mr Mason's laptop, which he's left with the cover half-closed on the sideboard. I know I shouldn't, but I edge over to the sideboard and flick up the cover – his Facebook home screen is on show. I feel like I'm a spy from MI5 as I'm compelled to look through his friends; all the big cheeses from HQ are there, including the MD, the human resources director and the CEO. I can't believe they are all communicating with each other by Facebook. I stoop to an all-time low and read Mason's message. It's from the North West regional manager and reads: "Are you coming to the conference next week? You've got to see this new bird I've taken on at the Humberside store. She'll be there. Sending you a picture of her arse. It's a 9/10. Haven't seen a 9/10 in your region for months. Loser."

I reel backwards for a moment; I can't believe it – all those times I thought Mason was making important texts he was probably updating his Facebook status. Maybe even photographing my arse and sending it to his mates round the company. Bastard. I just know he photographed it. And I bet it didn't score 9/10.

I quickly search the Net on my phone for some dubious sites and note down the address of a particularly outrageous one. Then I update his status. "Just bought some kinky boots. Check them out!" I put a link to the website underneath and a picture appears of a male performance artist wearing black leather thigh boots and a red bra and miniskirt.

I push the lid down on the laptop and sneak out of the office.

* * * * *

"There you are, Sandy," says Frosty, slightly disgruntled as I step up onto the raised platform in the centre of the showroom upon which Frosty exhibits our premier leather seating range, Regal Dreams, and which also acts as his look-out post. "Where have you been? I've tried calling you several times."

I glance down at my walkie-talkie. It's a useful device but, unfortunately, Frosty tends to overdo his use of it and has an annoying habit of ringing me at the most inconvenient times. Like when I'm in the loo or about to bite into my sandwich. His usual instruction is something like "Mr and Mrs John Doe at four o'clock, circumnavigate and engage before exit".

"It's not working again," I say, pulling a dejected face.

Mr Mason, who is standing next to Frosty, and who is far too composed for a man with a lot of secrets, raises a sceptical eyebrow but says nothing.

"Let me see," says Frosty, holding out his hand for my walkie-talkie.

I hand it over and wait for the usual reprimand. Unfortunately, my walkie-talkie has a habit of developing problems that manage to be rectified fairly easily by everyone else. Dave says it's a curious coincidence that I seem to have the same effect on our household iron.

"The volume is turned down," says Frosty, grumpily. "I know it's your last day, Sandy, but we're still paying you for a full day's work and not to lounge around in the canteen. One needs to maintain discipline and duty at all times. I expect better of you."

"Sorry," I reply.

Frosty hands me back my walkie-talkie and I clip it back on my belt as a satisfied smirk spreads across Mason's face.

"We could have done with your help up here. We had a rush on and, instead of your fifteen minute entitlement, you took forty minutes. That is not acceptable," continues Frosty, who obviously wants to make an example of me because Mason is here, even though he knows that on numerous occasions, I've worked through my lunch hours and tea breaks.

"Sorry, it won't happen again," I say, as I can't be bothered to argue about it as it's my last day, but noticing that Mason is positively revelling in my discomfort.

"Well of course it won't," says Frosty even more annoyed. "As you're leaving today. What kind of idiot do you think I am, Sandy?"

Mr Mason is now gloating like a lion that's about to maul its victim. I look him straight in the eye and a big malicious grin spreads across his face. In that moment, I make a rather rash decision.

"As I said, I'm really sorry, Mr Frost," I reply. "I must have knocked it when I lost my balance in the canteen."

Mason instantly stiffens and a small satisfying glow lights up inside me.

"How did you lose your balance? Did you trip over something?" demands Frosty, who is paranoid about Health and Safety regulations.

"No, I caught Mrs M; she nearly fainted."

Mason is perturbed now, whereas Frosty is seriously alarmed. Not only is his number one sales person leaving, but his number two sales person might be unwell. And if Mrs M is unwell, it would cause a major upset to his strategic plans.

"What's wrong with Mrs Morrison? Is she sick?" says Frosty, anxiously.

"No, she's very upset."

"Upset?" says Frosty. "What's she upset about?"

"She just found out who Sophie's father is."

"Sophie? You mean her granddaughter? That pretty young blonde girl who was here the other week?"

The smile has been totally wiped off of Mason's face. There's a trace of shock which must be because he hadn't recognised Sophie as his own daughter, but there's a hint of venom as well. But I'm not going to dish the dirt on him as he probably expects, because it isn't my prerogative, even though it's not my prerogative to do what I'm going to next either. But I'm going to do it anyway. And I'll just have to suffer any consequences.

"Yes, that right," I reply. "Apparently Sophie's dad isn't her birth father. Sophie's mum, Layla, got pregnant when she was fifteen by a much older man who she worked for. When he found out she was pregnant he abandoned her and left Mrs M to pick up the pieces."

"I had no idea! Poor Mrs Morrison, no wonder she's upset," exclaims Frosty.

"And the real father hasn't contributed a single penny to Sophie's upbringing," I say in my most indignant voice.

"That's outrageous!" says Frosty, picking up on my disgust. "What sort of man would do that? Impregnate a minor and then abandon her? Only a man with no moral substance!"

"Yes, he's probably a very selfish and callous individual," I say, laying on the hyperbole. "I expect he's an absolute scoundrel."

"A rotten egg!" says Frosty, full of outrage.

"A mean-spirited scallywag!" I say, enjoying the rhetoric and Mason's discomfort.

"A charlatan!" adds Frosty.

"A reprobate!"

"A cad and a criminal! He should be court martialled!" cries Frosty reaching a crescendo and looking like he's about to produce some duelling pistols.

Mason is now totally aghast. He knows Frosty will definitely blow the whistle on him if he learns he is Sophie's father. His cocky self-assuredness is slipping away as he realises what is at stake: his reputation and career.

"Is Mrs M going to report this monster to the police?" says Frosty. "We wouldn't have tolerated that sort of behaviour in the army. If I had my way, this sort of scum should be shot on sight!"

God, I love Frosty sometimes. I really do. He is so deliciously predictable. I guessed he'd act like this. After all, a man who spends his retirement working to pay for a more luxurious care home for his ninety-three year old mother is not going to look too kindly on a man who shirks his responsibility for a fifteen-year-old girl and a newborn baby, is he?

"I don't know, Mr Frost," I reply. "Mrs M doesn't know what to do. She's terribly, terribly distressed. She doesn't want to dredge up the past but, at the same time, she feels the father should now make some contribution to Sophie's upkeep, especially as Sophie is going to university soon, which is a very expensive business. But, of course, if the scandal comes out about her father taking advantage of a minor, he could lose his job and that wouldn't help anyone."

"Yes, yes. I see what you mean," says Frosty, pursing his lips as he cogitates. "It's a bit of a dilemma for Mrs Morrison. I wouldn't like to be in her shoes."

"I think the scoundrel should pay up," I say. "Think of all those years when he's paid nothing. The least he could do is to contribute towards his own daughter's university fees."

"Yes, yes, I quite agree," says Frosty, nodding. "That's probably the best solution. I shall speak to Mrs M and ask her if she'd like some assistance in confronting the rogue. I didn't spend thirty years in the army without learning a thing or two about negotiations!"

Mr Mason sways on his feet like he's about to topple over with shock.

"How much do you think Mrs M should ask for, Mr Frost?" I say. "Twenty thousand pounds?"

"Hmm…let me think," says Frosty as if he's mentally calculating eighteen years of child maintenance.

"What do you think, Mr Mason?" I say, with as much virginal innocence as I can muster. "How much should Sophie's father contribute?"

Frosty and I wait in expectation. Mason looks as white and frozen as an iceberg.

"Yes, yes, give us some of your wisdom on this matter, Wallace," says Frosty. "Assuming the father is solvent, how much should this rogue contribute?"

"I…don't…know," says Mason, clearing his throat. "It's a tricky question."

"You think more than twenty thousand? Twenty-five?" I say, eagerly.

"Well...no...I'm not sure..." says Mason, his voice uncharacteristically wobbling. "Twenty five thousand or even twenty thousand is a lot of money for someone to cough up at the drop of a hat."

"True, true," says Mason as his walkie-talkie beeps. "But twenty five thousand seems a good opening figure for negotiations." Frosty whips the pager off his belt and presses the intercom. "Frost here."

Mason and I stare at each other, whilst Frosty conducts a brief conversation with Margery in accounts. Mr Mason does not look very happy with me. He does not look happy at all. In fact, he looks very, very cross. So I give him one of my dazzling smiles.

"I have to go," say Frosty, clipping the walkie-talkie back on his belt. "Margery has an immediate problem which needs resolving. I'll be back in ten minutes. Sandy, tell Mrs M I will speak to her tomorrow and, in the meantime, perhaps you'll show Mr Mason our new range of bathroom fittings."

Frosty marches off at a pace and Mason and I are left, still eyeballing each other. Eventually, Mason breaks the silence. "I don't know whether you're exceedingly stupid or exceedingly clever, Sandy."

"The same could be said of you," I say.

"Touché."

Mason sits down on the Regal Dreams settee, pulls out a cheque book and pen from his inside breast pocket and writes out a cheque. I stand in silence, waiting. He fills out an amount, signs his name, stands up and hands it to me. I look down at the cheque in my hands. It's payable to Mrs Morrison and is for twenty-five thousand pounds.

"I expect you to deal with everything, Sandy."

"I will," I say, folding the cheque in half and slipping it into my jacket pocket.

"I don't expect anyone to come knocking at my door. My wife doesn't know but I will tell her - in my own good time. When I have done that, I will let Mrs Morrison know. Only then will we talk about the future."

"That sounds reasonable."

I am about to speak again when there is a loud scream from the bathroom suite department. Mason and I look over and see a woman with her hands over her face, several children running wild and a man, gripping a pram, whose face is so distorted it's possible he might be having a heart attack. We both break out in a run, as do Guy and Harvey from their corners of the showroom, and we all weave our way furiously through the sofas, dining room tables and bedroom suites and converge on the bathroom department at the far end of the store.

The woman, who is dishevelled and clearly at the end of her tether, is red-faced and about to burst into tears, a baby in the pram is screaming at full pitch and two other children, who appear to be twins, are running around like electrified rabbits. The man, whose face is still distorted, is clearly in some kind of shock but he is obviously not dying; his eyes are fixed in frozen horror upon the Flights of Fancy bathroom collection. We all follow his stare - sitting on the Flights of Fancy premier toilet, with his pants and trousers round his ankles, is a small boy about three years old, with brown hair and big puppy eyes, who is clearly having a poo.

"Oh my God, I am so sorry," wails the woman.

"Jesus fucking Christ," curses the man, before lapsing into contorted silence again.

"Um…right," says Mason, struggling for words before he gives me a look of evil relish. "Over to you, Sandy." Then he turns on his heel and heads off with a final parting shot. "And don't forget to clear up the mess."

Harvey and Guy quickly follow Mason leaving me to sort out what is a rather awkward situation. Well, not for me as, believe it or not, this has happened before. However, I do have two embarrassed parents, a distressed baby, a pair of twins behaving like they're at the fairground and a kid who needs his bottom wiping.

I put my arm round the woman, who smells slightly of baby sick and bananas.

"Don't worry. It's happened before," I say. "We can sort it out. Does your husband need to be here?"

"Not really. It's just I can't cope with all four at the same time anymore."

"Alright, let's get rid of him and the twins and then we'll sort out Master Pooey here," I smile.

The woman smiles back at me with genuine relief.

"Right, kids," I say. "Who wants a milkshake in McDonalds?"

"Yesssssssss!" cry the twins, jumping up and down with excitement.

"Off you go now, Dad. Take these two with you. McDonalds is over the road."

Dad lets go of the pram at my command, takes hold of the twins' outstretched hands and all three of them troop off towards the exit. I can tell from the way the man's shoulders are sagging with despair, and from his v-neck pullover, checkered shirt and Barbour jacket, that about four years ago he would never have stepped across the threshold of a McDonalds. He probably works in the City and used to dine out in sushi bars and drink Martini cocktails. Today, though, he is a broken man who would happily drink cheap lager and buy shares in McDonalds. That's parenthood for you.

I unstrap the baby, a little girl dressed in a pink jumpsuit and white knitted socks, and place her in her mum's arms. The baby immediately begins to calm down.

"Any milk?"

"In the bag," says Mum, nodding towards the back of the pram.

"Sit down over there on that sofa," I say, gesturing to a nearby suite.

I fetch the bottle and pass it to her as she starts to fuss the little baby, who is nuzzling her breast, anxiously searching for a feed.

"Now, I'll sort out Master Pooey and we'll be back in a few minutes. Try and relax."

I walk over to the Flights of Fancy collection. Master Pooey is still on the loo, innocently swinging his legs.

"Are you all done?" I ask.

"Yes, but there's no loo paper," he says.

"That's because we are in a pretend bathroom, not a real one."

"Really?"

"It is a very good pretend bathroom though." I smile and pull out the wadge of the tissues experience has taught me to always carry in my pocket. "Now up you get."

I help Master Pooey off the toilet and stuff a little tissue in the back of his pants and pull them loosely up around his waist. Using the rest of the tissues, I scoop up as much of the poo as possible from the bottom of the u-bend and put down the lid. The cleaners will have to do the real scrubbing later but, for the moment, the worst of the smell will soon be gone from the showroom.

"Ugh," says Master Pooey. "That's gross."

"Yes, isn't it?" I say, grinning at the look of sheer horror on his face as he studies the guilty evidence cupped in my hand. "Now let's go and get rid of it and clean you up."

Fifty minutes later, Dad and the twins return. Dad looks far more relaxed and the colour has come back into his cheeks and the twins are back under control. They spot us and wind their way through the displays to my desk, where Master Pooey is colouring in a picture of Buzz Lightyear and sucking a lolly. Baby is now asleep in her pram and Mum and I are now chatting about pre-schools as I've already sold her a £3,500 bathroom suite paid by cheque, as well as setting up a £4,500 interest free credit arrangement for a three piece suite.

"I'm sorry about that earlier," says Dad, still looking a bit bashful. "We've just moved house and none of us are at our best."

"No worries," I say, smiling. "We're all sorted now."

"Thank you so much," says Mum, getting up and taking hold of the pram.

"Do you have everything you want?" says Dad to Mum.

"Yes," says Mum smiling.

I wave Mum and Dad and the four kids off at the door and wander back to my desk. It's almost 5.30 pm and I decide enough is enough. I'm done with Hendersons. It's time to move on. I pick up my paperwork and walk over to Frosty's look-out post, where he and Mason are studying some invoices. They both look up. I hand Mason the order forms and receipts, he looks at the total and passes them on to Frosty.

"Well done, Sandy," says Mason. "Situation salvaged."

"Excellent," says Frosty, looking at the total with glee. "That means we'll meet our weekly target."

"I'm done now," I say.

"Fair enough," says Mason, nodding. "I believe they've laid on a surprise for you in the canteen. We'll see you there in ten minutes."

I gather up the rest of my belongings, and empty my drawers, as Derek locks the main doors behind the last customers. When I'm finished, I make my way slowly down to the canteen. I'm sad now to be leaving. It wasn't so bad here and, in some ways, I had a lot of fun and I made some good friends. That counts for a lot, doesn't it?

When I reach the canteen doorway, Mrs M is at the entrance, beaming profusely. Everyone else is lined up in a row behind her, including Mason and Frosty. Even Mr Baker has turned up from nowhere. They all look strangely amused.

"We have a special present for you, Sandy," says Mrs M, grinning. "One. Two. Three!"

On Mrs M's count of three, the line of staff parts and I see my surprise gift, which was hidden behind them. It's not the male stripper I'd secretly fancied but something I would never have wanted in a thousand years. Standing by itself, dressed in a huge pink bow and decorated with rose petals, and looking as splendidly awful as only a hideous pink and yellow striped sofa can be, is my parting gift: Hilda.

As the laughter subsides, and everyone chats and tucks into the crisps and nuts Frosty has provided, I notice Mr Mason edging towards the exit. He catches my eye and we nod at each other in recognition of our agreement. When I'm sure he's gone, I walk over to the window, call Mrs M over and explain what's happened. I hand her the cheque which she stares at in amazement.

"He asks that you wait for him to tell you that he's told his wife before you see if Sophie or Layla want any further contact. He hinted there might be some sort of…reconciliation. It was only a hint though," I say.

"Well, I never," says Mrs M, smiling. "Maybe he isn't so bad after all."

"I'll reserve judgement on that," I say, watching Mason walking briskly across the car park. He's a strange man, that's for sure. I'm not sure if I trust him yet. Although I don't think he's going to renege on the cheque; he has too much to lose. Mason slips between two stationary cars as he heads over to his Mercedes, then stops for a moment and inspects the sole of his right shoe. He walks a few paces further, stops and inspects the sole of his left shoe.

"What's he doing?" says Mrs M, leaning forwards for a better view.

"I've no idea."

I smile broadly and wonder when Mr Mason will discover the poo in his briefcase.

13

I open the front door and step out into the bitter January morning, my hot breath making a long plume of condensation. This is it. This is the start of my new exercise regime and my new life. I'm wearing my black running gear and my black hat, which I've pulled down as far as possible, and I'm ready to face the world.

Only first, I wait until Mrs Andrews from number twenty-six drives by in her ancient Ford Fiesta and Mr Fredricks has tottered past on his way to the corner shop to get his daily newspaper. I glance at my watch; it's 9.35 am. This means, tomorrow, I can't face the world until at least 9.40 am, or I get up and exercise before I drop Tabby at school which does not appeal to me. In fact, exercising at any time does not appeal to me, but exercising at 7 am definitely has the least appeal; I like my soft, comfy bed and those few precious minutes snuggling up to Dave. Now that Mr Fredricks has passed, I step into the centre of the porch again and limber up. I rock up and down on my heels, stretch my arms over my head and jump up and down on the spot.

"Go for it, Mum."

I turn around and see Andy at the bottom of the stairs scoffing a bowl of overcooked porridge.

"You'll soon be running the London Marathon," says Andy, grinning.

"Oh sod off," I say and slam the door behind me. I hear Andy laughing to himself as he trudges up the stairs to play the Xbox with Max who doesn't start back to school until tomorrow. It's great to have Andy home for a while, even though he's screwed me for £500 and a Chinese takeaway.

I've decided I'm going to build up to running as I don't want to overdo it on the exercise front yet. The advice fitness gurus give is to start slowly with exercise routines and increase the vigour gradually, which is the kind of advice I like; the type that doesn't require too much exertion. So I'm going to start with brisk walking. I jump up and down several more times and finally set off down the path, which is fairly long, and build my pace into a steady rhythm until I reach the garden gate. In those few metres, the cold has begun to sink into my bones so I decide to go back and get an extra layer of clothing. I turn around and head back up the path.

"What's the matter, Mum? Has the Bogey Man got you already?"

I look up to the source of the yelling and see Andy and Max, hanging out of Max's bedroom window, laughing.

They look totally unrelated. If I didn't know Dave was their father they could have been born to different men. This is mainly because Andy is your typical student, and hasn't had his hair cut for two terms and looks like a cross between Neanderthal man and Ozzy Osbourne, whereas Max has a skin-head shave so close he resembles a psychopathic soldier from an Xbox game.

"I'm going to get a jacket; it's cold," I shout.

"Yeah, yeah, we've heard that one before," replies Andy as Max takes a picture on his phone.

Did you know children can be really, really annoying at times?

"I'm doing a "before" and "after" album for you, Mum," yells Max. "I've got a good one of you asleep on the sofa last night!"

As I said, children can be really, really annoying at times.

Max shows Andy the pictures on his phone and the two of them burst out laughing again.

I march up the pathway, open the door and grab my jacket hanging over the stair bannister, put it on and run back down the path. I hear Andy and Max laughing hysterically and I know (because I'm their mother and mothers have eyes in the backs of their heads) that they are taking photographs of my bottom.

By the way, did I say that children can be really, really, really annoying at times? In fact, most of the time.

I close the garden gate behind me and look back at Andy and Max still giggling.

"You!" I point my finger at Max. "Get that bedroom tidy or I'm cancelling your Xbox subscription!" I point my finger at Andy. "And you get that hair cut before I get back or your bank is CLOSING!"

The boys' laughter immediately stops and the window slams shut, just as Dave pulls up next to me in one of his vans. He leans across from the driver's seat and the electric window slides down. "Can you pick me up a pack of Stella? I don't want to stop on my way home tonight."

"I'm going for a run!" I protest.

"Later then?"

"Yes, yes, okay," I say, grudgingly.

"It's great you've taken up jogging, love," says Dave, smiling. "Your arse will soon be half its size."

And with that Dave closes the window and drives off, whilst I'm left, mouth agape, staring at the back of his van. Men are so bloody frustrating aren't they? Sometimes I wish I'd been born a lesbian.

I walk briskly down the pavement towards the nearby fields, trying to keep my mind occupied so my body doesn't recognise the early signs of fatigue; I don't want to suffer the humiliation of having to catch a bus back before I get to the end of the road. Dave's inept compliment sets me wondering about the difference between men and women and how they often handle situations in different ways. I start to wonder if I'd be better off in a relationship with a lesbian. Would I have less housework? Would I have to do less cooking? Would I need to produce a route map for my genitals like I do for Dave? It crosses my mind that maybe I am a lesbian if I'm thinking about lesbians. I sort of fancy Angelina Jolie – or maybe that's jealousy? I don't know. Anyway, Angelina and I are not suited as she likes kids so much it's sort of abnormal. And she has big lips; I have small lips. If we kissed I'd probably get sucked inside her and absorbed into some kind of weird rubbery collagen.

I think Jennifer Aniston is more my style anyway. She seems so sweet and she hasn't had children so if we got it together we wouldn't have any hassle from her kids, only mine, and that would probably be enough. The only trouble is, what if Jennifer felt left out and decided to adopt some kids from the Third World like Angelina and Madonna? Then I'd get stuck with the babysitting whilst she went out on the town. That would piss me off. I mean, I've done all that childcare business; I don't want to do it again. Besides, there's the hair. I spend about point four of a nanosecond on my hair in the morning and Jennifer probably spends hours, perhaps weeks, getting her hair styled. We might fall out over the inordinate time she spends with her hairdresser, or I might get jealous of a can of hairspray. That wouldn't be a good foundation for any relationship. And what if my hair thinned like Deidre's? I think Jennifer would probably leave me for someone with better hair.

So, Jennifer is out as I need a woman with less hair, and Angelina is out as I need a woman with smaller lips. I suppose that means that I prefer men as generally they have less hair (on their heads anyway) and thinner lips.

I stop thinking for a moment and notice I've made it into the field and I haven't passed out yet. This is good news. My attempt to distract myself is obviously working because I reckon I've covered – about half a mile. And I am not dead, even though I can feel my heart pumping in my ears which is slightly worrying because at school they told me my heart was in my chest. Still, as I said before, we studied mainly sprouting beans and reproductive organs in biology. What am I to know?

I look across to the other side of the field. I calculate that if I go across this field and the next one, work my way around the back of the housing estate beyond that and walk back in a loop, it will be about three and a half miles in total. By that time I will be either dead or I will have lost at least a pound or two. I set off again at a slightly faster pace. I've forgotten to bring any water but I find some chewing gum in my jacket pocket and use that to keep my mouth moist.

So where was I? So men are less hairy on their heads. That's a good thing as I'm not into hairy heads or bodies. At school, there was a girl with the most amazing long hair. It was very beautiful and shiny but she had a habit of swinging it side to side like a hypnotist, and occasionally it would flick into my face in the dinner queue. School dinners weren't appetising at the best of times but after a mouthful of hair they were even less so. Anyway, luckily, Dave has a full head of hair, which is good for a forty-nine year old. It's not that I don't like baldies, because if they've got a nice shaped head they can be very attractive. It's that in-between stage, when they're still clinging to the hope that no one's noticed their hair loss that bothers me; when they're manufacturing comb-overs and spiking what's left with hair gel.

What I've always been curious to know though is, when blokes go bald on top, do they go bald down below? God, what a thought. Those turkey necks look vile at the best of times but a bald one? I'm not sure I could cope. It was bad enough when Dave shaved his for his vasectomy. I've never seen such a fuss and bother. Anyone would have thought he was sculpturing the next Picasso. And to top it all, he chickened out at the last moment. I wonder if hair loss is the same for women? I'll have to ask Deidre. Maybe hair loss down below won't be such a bad thing then. I could tolerate the loss of a bit on top if I didn't have to use a lawnmower on my fanny.

I can't believe it! By distracting myself I've already passed the back of the housing estate and now I'm on my return journey. Jaggi's corner shop is about fifty metres away, and after that, it's less than half a mile home. I'm desperate for a drink of water though and there's enough loose change in my jacket pocket for a bottle at Jaggi's. I'm going to risk being seen as my body is now craving water like it normally craves chocolate. Thinking about my bodily needs was totally stupid because, as I approach Jaggi's, I'm so utterly exhausted I begin to wander all over the place like a drunk. I stumble up the step to Jaggi's and lurch inside as the bell rings to announce my arrival. I'm completely shattered and my chest is heaving like a trampoline.

"Water," I gasp.

Jaggi looks up from sorting a pile of magazines behind the counter. "Holy shit, Mrs Lovett. What happened to you?" says Jaggi in his stilted Pakistani accent.

"Jogging," I splutter, not wanting to admit I've only been walking briskly.

"Ladies of your age should not be jogging, Mrs Lovett," says Jaggi, knowledgably. "Mrs Jaggi always says, once the babies come, you will have a fat arse forever."

Mrs Jaggi appears at the mention of her name from behind the bread shelf to the side of me. Mrs Jaggi is smaller than me at about five foot and has a larger bottom; I like her a lot. Sometimes we chat in the school playground, as despite our different heritages, we have a lot in common: we have too many kids, work long hours in retail and we both have big bottoms. Mrs Jaggi looks at me with concern.

"Mrs Lovett! What is wrong? Are you ill?"

"Jogging," I gasp again and rummage in my pocket for the loose change to pay for the bottled water that Jaggi has put on the counter for me.

"No, no, no, no," says Mrs Jaggi, shaking her head from side to side. "What have I said before, Mrs Lovett? Once a big arse, always a big arse. Jogging will not make any difference."

"See," says Jaggi, shrugging.

"New Year's resolution," I say, by way of explanation to Mrs Jaggi as my pulse begins to slow. Unable to find all the change for the water, I pull out the collection of gunk in my pocket.

Mrs Jaggi raises her eyes to the heavens. I'm not sure if that's because I'm jogging or because of the contents of my pockets.

"Seventy pence, please," says Jaggi.

I find seventy pence in amongst the dirty tissues and sweet wrappers, as well as a crumpled five pound note. On the spur of the moment, I decide to get Dave's Stella.

"Thanks," I say, putting the fiver and loose change on the counter. "And four Stella please."

"Are you sure that's wise, Mrs Lovett? It's a bit early to be drinking," says Jaggi.

"They're for Dave," I say.

"Ah yes," says Jaggi, grinning at his own joke. "How is Mr Lovett?"

"He's fine. But business is a bit slack."

"Ah yes. This recession is not good. Mrs Jaggi would like a new car but I say not until we are out of the recession. We must save our money."

I give Mrs Jaggi a sympathetic smile; she drives a 1972 Ford Cortina. I suspect Mr Jaggi has conveniently been in a recession for at least twenty years. I pick up the water and the cans of Stella Jaggi has transferred into a blue carrier bag for me and head back to the door. "Thanks," I say. "Gotta go."

Jaggi comes out from behind his desk and follows me to the door, as does Mrs Jaggi. I begin to panic when I realise that they're going to watch me jog. I categorically don't want to attempt running. However, it would be even more embarrassing to admit I was only walking than to actually jog round the corner.

"Bye!" I say with exaggerated cheerfulness at the door, hoping they don't follow. But Jaggi holds the door open and trails out after me, closely followed by Mrs Jaggi.

"See you at school," says Mrs Jaggi.

"See you!" I say with finality.

I walk a few paces away but sense Mr and Mrs Jaggi's eyes on the back of my head. I'm definitely going to have to run if I'm going to salvage any pride. I stop, wind the plastic handle of Jaggi's carrier around my wrist, and stare straight ahead at the red post box on the corner. If I can make it to the post box, they will probably have lost interest and be gone by then. Yes, that should do.

I break out into a very slow jog. Not that I could go any faster but I don't have to overdo it trying to impress, I just need to survive. I run about ten paces and already I feel like the Grim Reaper is approaching. My heart is beginning to pump furiously and my breathing sounds like a perverted phone caller. I focus on the post box and try to remember the instructions the midwife told me when I was in labour.

"Focus…Breath…Focus…Breath…Focus…Breath."

I keep jogging, regretting the four Stella which now feels like a whole crate, rhythmically bashing into my legs.

Why, why, why, did I buy Dave's beer at Jaggi's? What was I thinking of? My right arm feels like it's going to drop off and my legs feel as heavy as two pillars of concrete. The fact I'm alive can only be an act of God. Maybe he's got something else in store for me, because my body is telling me that I should probably be dead by now.

"Focus…Breath…Focus…Breath…Focus…Breath."

The post box is looming closer and closer; I'm only a few metres away. My adrenaline begins to kick in and I speed up as the finish line approaches. I will be victorious - Mr and Mrs Jaggi will be gone and I will have won my first fight against the flab. I take three big strides and reach the post box and elation courses through me. I come to an abrupt halt and grin to myself, punching the air. I did it. I won. I take a satisfied look behind me which quickly turns to horror.

Mr and Mrs Jaggi are still on the doorstep, watching.

Fuck. Fuck. Fuck. Fuck. FUCK.

"Are you alright?" calls Mr Jaggi.

"Yes," I call breathlessly. "Just posting a letter!"

I scrabble in my pockets for something to post. Please God, let there be something. There is. In one of the breast pockets is a folded up newsletter from school. I have never been so grateful to see a letter from school in my whole life. I push it into the letterbox, wave at Mr and Mrs Jaggi again, take another deep breath and set off running again.

In a few paces I'm finally round the corner and out of sight. I'm utterly exhausted. In fact, I think I'm going to have a stroke. I drop down on the pavement, pull the water out of the blue plastic bag, unscrew the lid and begin to drink. Water has never tasted so good. I rest for a few minutes until my breathing has returned to normal. I'm thinking about setting off again, when I see a blue Ford C-max approaching. It begins to slow down as it nears me and I see it's my C-max and Max is leaning out the window, waving a Microsoft points package to attract my attention and Andy is at the wheel, driving. I also see that Andy's hair has been cut the same as Max's and now they both look like a pair of psychopaths. I scramble to my feet, dropping my water bottle, which splits on the pavement, forming a pool of water around my trainers.

"What the hell have you done to your hair?" I shout furiously, as they pull up beside me and wind down the window.

"You said to get it cut," says Andy, grinning.

"Not like that!"

"How was I to know?" says Andy, who clearly does know by the smug look on his face.

"Race you," says Max.

"What?" I say, my eyes still fixed upon Andy's ridiculous haircut.

"Last one back cooks dinner and tidies the house. We'll give you a head start though, Mum."

"What?" I say again, beginning to grasp what Max is saying. "But I always cook the dinner and tidy the house! That's completely unfair!"

"Do you want to race or not?" grins Andy, leaning further over towards the passenger window. "I haven't got all day. I've got an essay to write."

"You cheeky little bastard," I say as my competitive streak bursts into fire. I decide to take the boys on. What's more, the rubbish truck's coming up the road and that may hold Andy up for a minute or two. I pick up the broken water bottle, fling it through the car window to distract Andy, and take off like an Olympic athlete, legging it as fast as possible down the road towards home.

"Cheat!" calls Max.

Andy tries to pull away after me but stalls the car, giving me an extra second or two. I pound down the road, listening to Andy trying to start the engine again, grating the gears. I know in order to win I must focus again so I imagine I'm Usain Bolt. Yohan Blake is a few steps behind me and Justin Gaitlin is coming up on the inside. They are trying to get my medal but I'm not going to let them. No fucking way. The medal is going to be mine, all mine. I imagine I've big, powerful muscles like Usain and I'm thrusting forwards, cutting through the air like a knife. I'm approaching the rubbish truck and now I'm running like a mad woman and the collectors are watching me in total astonishment. I hear Andy revving the engine and he finally takes off in pursuit.

"Don't...let...that...car...through!" I cry as I draw level with the rubbish truck. "Sons...race...must...win..." I call out between breaths like a demented idiot.

"Stop that car!" calls one of the men after a momentary hesitation. I hear the rubbish truck rev up and slew across the road as I race past. I thank God that I always remember to give the rubbish men a big tip at Christmas. And that I always separate my recycling. I keep on running, even though I can feel my legs turning to jelly beneath me. But the gate is only a few footsteps away. I fling it open and stagger up the path and splatter into the door like a massive paintball and slip down onto the floor into a pathetic heap of sweaty flesh. Slowly, I turn around and prop myself up against the door as Andy and Max pull up outside.

I pull out one of Dave's Stellas from the blue bag, rip off the tag and take a giant mouthful as Andy and Max jump out.

"Well done, Mum," says Andy, grinning.

"Awesome, Mum," says Max.

"I'll have steak and salad and don't forget to clean the bathroom," I say, smugly.

14

Today, Mum is bonkers. She thinks she is Steve McQueen again and I am "The Scrounger". I've just bartered half the contents of my handbag including some Nivea hand cream, a pen, half a packet of chewing gum, some nail clippers and some black mascara in exchange for Mum's packet of tissues and an old pair of her bed socks. I'm deeply suspicious Mum is thinking about making her third breakout this month. Last week, Frau Engel found Mum trying to cut her way through the laurel hedge at the bottom of the garden with some poultry scissors and the week before she found her attempting to prise up the floorboards in the linen cupboard with a shoehorn.

"Would you like another biscuit?" I ask Mum.

"Have the Red Cross parcels come in?" says Mum, her eyes lighting up with excitement.

"Yes," I say pushing the plate of shortbread biscuits from one side of the table to the other and pocketing the nail clippers with the other hand. God knows what damage Mum could do with a pair of nail clippers, but the thought of Frau Engel telephoning to tell me that Mum is trying to clip her way to freedom through the curtains would be too much to bear.

Mum picks up one of the shortbread biscuits and begins to nibble.

"Delicious," says Mum and leans over the table furtively, so that no one else can hear. Not that any of the other residents are interested in our conversation, of course, as it's not long after lunch and all but Mrs Levinson-Rice and Mr Patterson are asleep.

"What's in it? Anything we could use?" whispers Mum.

I look cautiously from side to side, playing along with Mum's delusion. Mrs Levinson-Rice is absorbed in a book from The Orchards' library and is making all sorts of expressions: her eyebrows rising up in surprise, her lips twitching with amusement and, occasionally, even pulling her lips back over her teeth in disgust. In contrast, Mr Patterson's eyes are set in his usual unblinking trance on page three of The Sun. I lean forward so Mum and I are almost touching heads.

"Tea," I say.

"Oh," squeals Mum. "Breakfast or Earl Grey?"

"Earl Grey."

"Ooohh," says Mum, clearly delighted. "Anything else?"

I reach down by my side and pull my handbag secretively onto my lap and remove something I know

Mum will covet. I cover it with a hanky and slide it slowly across the table.

"What is it?" whispers Mum, barely able to contain her excitement.

I slide the hanky slowly off the object.

"Cadbury's Fruit and Nut!" squeals Mum again, her eyes practically popping out of her head.

"You can have it in exchange for that black mascara," I say, as I need my mascara back. It's the one that gives the least smudges and I'm worried about Mum blackening her face with it and trying to steal out of The Orchards after dark.

"Deal," says Mum, pushing the mascara over and slipping the Fruit and Nut into her cardigan pocket.

Mrs Levinson-Rice snorts loudly and Mum and I glance over to where she's sitting in one of the larger armchairs, dressed in one of her majestic twinsets. She gives a second snort and pulls her lips back over her teeth once more in another disgusted grimace.

"Ugh. How revolting. They actually have sex!" says Mrs Levinson-Rice, her upper crust voice rising above the snoring that is reverberating around the room. "It's too hideous to even think about!"

Mr Patterson looks up from page three at the mention of the word "sex" but Mrs Levinson-Rice is so absorbed in her book she doesn't notice, turns the page and carries on reading. Mr Patterson, knocked out of his page three trance, turns to the back page of The Sun and begins reading the sports headlines.

Mum and I turn back to face each other again.

"I wonder what she's reading?" says Mum.

"Maybe it's Jackie Collins?" I reply.

"No, it can't be. Everyone has sex in a Jackie Collins novel," says Mum knowledgably.

Mum nibbles her shortbread biscuit and her eyes flicker as if she's experiencing a surge of random memories. The mention of Jackie Collins has somehow moved her into another realm, her thoughts clutching at the fragments of another life. Maybe it's memories of the Seventies and the days when her life was full of sex and vigour and passion. Maybe it's Tom Jones, gyrating his hips. Maybe it's Denise again.

"I read The Stud, you know," says Mum out of the blue. "And The Bitch and The World is Full of Married Men. And nearly all of Jackie's other books."

"Really?" I say, covering my pen up with my hand and rolling it towards me and off the table into my lap.

"And very good they were too," says Mum. "My husband approved."

I giggle, thankful that, despite her madness, Mum still brings laughter and joy into my world even though I'm somewhat put out that I never saw a copy of Jackie Collins on the bookshelves at home. I wouldn't have minded reading them. I've been trying to get back into the swing of reading lately. In fact, the other day I read The Hot Nights of Lucinda Lovett by Morna McIntyre and it was rather good and rather saucy. Anyway, I'm digressing again – our bookshelves at home were always stacked with Jane Austen and Georgette Heyer.

"I never knew you'd read Jackie Collins," I say.

It's funny how you learn stuff about your parents all the time, isn't it? We think we know them and then you learn something that makes you see a whole new side of them.

"Oh yes. I had to hide them though as Denise was always reading the dirty bits," says Mum.

I laugh and for a moment I'm pleased I'm not Denise, even if I'm still The Scrounger. But then it becomes apparent in the space of a few seconds that Mum is rapidly retreating into her own reclusive thoughts and a wave of tiredness is sweeping over her. My laughter dies out. It's as if truth and reality are the painful alternatives to the madcap world of Mum's dementia, draining her of life and laughter. I suppose sleep is an easy alternative to the pain of loss. I know somehow, call it instinct or intuition, that Mum is thinking about Denise again. I think Mum accepted Dad's death more easily; it was part of that wider picture they call the Circle of Life, I guess. But a child's death? That's different. People don't expect their children to die before them do they? Sometimes, I wonder what my life would have been like with Denise still here; an older sister to share my life and the responsibilities of our ageing parents. Peter is great, of course. He's very supportive over the phone and will happily talk for several hours but, at the end of the day, he's across the other side of the world.

The responsibility has been mine. All mine. Thank goodness I have Dave.

"You look tired, Mum," I say. "It must be that big dinner. Why don't you have a nap in the conservatory? Maybe afterwards, we could have a stroll around the grounds?"

Mum doesn't reply. She's gone into her solitary world. So I take her hand and lead her into the conservatory, settle her into an armchair and tuck a fleece blanket over her knees and legs for a bit of extra warmth and comfort. I pull up another armchair and sit next to her and together we look out over the ramshackle grounds of The Orchards.

"The bulbs are breaking through already," I say after a while. "That's definitely earlier than last year. I wonder if that's global warming or an anomaly? I don't suppose we'll find out until it's too late. Tabby says that her generation will pay for the selfishness of ours. Last week, she made me buy a hideous ceramic composting bin for the kitchen. It's green, of course, with a handle the shape of a potato. Have you noticed everything to do with recycling is either green or orange? Why can't they be different colours? Green bags, green pots, green bins. On my birthday, Tabby bought me a green jumper with Save the Rainforests on it, and Max bought me a green hat made from recycled wool. I looked like a garden gnome."

Mum snores.

I glance sideways and confirm Mum has drifted off to sleep. Hopefully, it wasn't my conversation, just the steak and kidney pie.

I sit silently for a few minutes longer before I return to the lounge and collect my handbag and laptop. I put my bartered belongings back into my handbag and replace Mum's bed socks and tissues in her knitting bag. Not that Mum does much knitting anymore but she's had that bag for so many years now she won't be parted from it for long. The fabric isn't so bold and colourful as it once was, and the embroidered yellow and red roses have a number of threads missing, but Mum still loves it. These days she stuffs it with all sorts of bits and bobs. It's a bit like her mind at the moment, mixed up with no discernible order.

Back in the conservatory, Mum is sleeping peacefully, her breathing rhythmic and quiet as she's slipped into deeper sleep. I place my laptop on a table and pull up a chair and set to work. Deidre has contracted me for four hours a day and I can't thank her enough for allowing me the flexibility of a job that gives me so much time with Mum. Deidre has it all worked out; I spend four hours in the office on Mondays and Fridays and on Tuesdays, Wednesdays and Thursdays I essentially "work from home". On those days, Deidre forwards me the vast proportion of the email enquiries so that I can chase them up around my time with Mum. Any other time I've got available, I'm either renewing advertisement subscriptions or doing what Deidre has really employed me for, which is soliciting business. I put on my Bluetooth, switch on my email and a flood of email enquiries arrive and I'm all set to go.

Even with my long career in retail, my first few calls were nerve racking. Cold calling is different to retail outlets, where you know that for the main part if someone comes into your shop they're interested in buying, even if they can't afford what you've got right at that very moment. But I've found that applying the same principles as I've used for twenty five years - be friendly, be efficient and be patient - works a treat. I work on the basis that everyone wants their business to be successful so, apart from the rare exception, advertising is a must. All I need to do is unlock the key that makes the client want to buy space. I've been working on my patter too. Deidre says I'm a natural and that I was born to sell. Maybe I was, but I think part of it is, I like talking to people and finding out all about them.

I like to do things my own way though so, as well as Deidre's spread sheets, I keep my own manual records of whom I've contacted, shorthand notes of the conversations and whether I've sent them further information by email or post. Most importantly, I use my own personal scoring system where I rate how likely they are to purchase advertising space, which I use to decide how soon I should chase them up. My methods seem to be working because, nearly three months on, and I have a steady stream of clients coming back to me as well as those biting at the first hurdle.

I'm busy typing when my mobile vibrates. I glance at the screen; it's Tricia Marshall. I make a small groan as, nine times out of ten, that means she wants something from me. Occasionally, there's an invite to her house at Christmas or Easter for mince pies or hot cross buns, or some other social function designed to secure my support throughout the rest of the year but, usually, when Tricia wants me it's to press gang me into something. However, I've learnt from experience that avoiding her doesn't help as she'll soon have me cornered at school where it's even harder to say no when everyone else is looking on and they've already been commandeered. I pick up the phone and accept the call.

"Hi. Sandy?"

"Yes?" I reply, trying not to sound too abrupt but knowing I don't want to be lumbered with any good deeds at the moment. Everything is going well: Mum is settled, Dave and the kids are very happy with my new hours, I'm happy too and I've been losing weight at a very good rate until recently. I don't want anything to upset the applecart.

"How are you?"

Dear God. Tricia saw me in the playground this morning, and has seen me every day since mid-January, and I haven't had a spray tan, turned up in Mum's wheelchair or brought Pierce Brosnan along with me, so I think it would be fair to say that nothing too dramatic has happened in my life.

"Good. Thanks. And you?"

"Yes, fine."

I can hear a hint of excitement in Tricia's voice though. She's obviously building up to asking me something hideous, like being the human target at the spring school fair for the "Flan the Parent" stall, or to join the Morris Dancing Society or, failing that, she'll want me to sell five hundred raffle tickets by a week on Thursday.

"I was wondering if you'd like a coffee sometime? Perhaps in Costa?"

"A coffee?" I say, barely able to keep the surprise out of my voice. I have never been asked out for coffee before by Tricia. She must be up to no good. Whatever it is she wants, I decide I'm going to say no. I am not going to be persuaded. Nope, definitely not. My curiosity is piqued though; it's such a normal overture. I mean, a coffee instead of being speared against the gym wall? Who am I to refuse? Maybe I'll accept the offer just to find out what she's got planned.

"Yes, you know that brown liquid," says Tricia, amused. "I can do today after school if that's any good?"

Today? Blimey, whatever she wants to ask me is beyond her usual remit if she's this keen. I'm not sure if I should go and allow myself to be cornered…but Costa with Tricia in school social terms is like dinner with the PM. I will be the talk of the playground, my social status will zoom to an all-time high and a place on the PTA will be assured. Hmm…okay…I don't want a place on the PTA, and I don't want to be known as an arse-licker, but I ought to hear out what Tricia's got to say, bearing in mind how kind and supportive she was to Mum at the Christmas concert.

"I'd have to bring Tabby with me if it's today, Tricia."

"Oh, that's fine. I'll have Oliver with me. How about 4 pm in Costa?"

The conversation finishes as Frau Engel and Mrs Honor appear in the lounge with a tea trolley, the cups and saucers rattling as they make their way down the central aisle, distributing a mid-afternoon cup of tea. The residents begin to rouse and Mr Patterson puts down his paper and turns up the volume on the television; life is returning to The Orchards. Mum begins to stir too but I reckon I've got time for one more call before she wakes up completely.

"Roland Carter, please."

"Who's calling?"

"Sandra Lovett."

The line goes quiet for a minute and then Rolly comes on the line.

"Sandy!" laughs Rolly so loud I pull my ear away from the phone for a moment. "I've been expecting your call. Did Deidre put you up to this?"

"Absolutely not," I say with mock seriousness. "But you do know that you need some quality advertising, don't you?"

"I do?" laughs Rolly, heartily.

"Yes, imagine it now, Rolly. You're Joe Bloggs sitting at the breakfast table, eating your toast and marmalade, reading The Herald and checking the obituaries. Your gran's died and you've inherited three hundred thousand pounds which means you can divorce your miserable wife, move out, buy a new house, marry the girl from the chip shop you've been secretly dating and have another child, which means you'll need a bigger house and a better job. Then the ex-wife will come after you for more alimony, so you'll agree to meet her to discuss payments and new wife will think you've betrayed her and will want to divorce you. So you'll move out, divorce her, thrash out new payments to her and the ex-wife and end up buying a small one bedroomed apartment in Bognor because you can't afford anything else. But throughout all this angst, all this trauma and heartbreak, you'll know you'll be safe in the hands of your solicitor because, on that day you checked your gran's obituary, you saw in the top right hand corner of the announcements page, beautifully printed in majestic script accompanied by a small scroll and a quill…."

I take a deep breath…

"Roland Carter and Partners, Solicitors of Distinction."

"And how much will this advert cost me, Sandy?" guffaws Rolly. "Because I'm not sure I need it. I have far too much work as it is."

"Ah," I say, "You may have far too much work, Rolly. But what about your partners? Haven't you noticed on your way to your modest lunch at Monsieur Pascal's Rotisserie, that new young conveyancer, shuffling his papers, stacking envelopes and flitting to and from the filing cabinet, trying to look busy? And what about that time you caught him picking his nose and shining his shoes as you went for your mid-afternoon break at Madame Bovary's Petite Patisserie? Are you *absolutely* sure he's got enough work?"

Rolly is now laughing so hard I can't help laughing too. I love Rolly's booming laugh. It's got to be one of the best sounds in the world.

"Alright, alright. You win," splutters Rolly. "You can have the bloody adverts!"

"I tell you what," I say. "I like to play fair, so I'll send you an email with all the rates and two sample adverts I've drafted. If you like what you see, you can go ahead and if not we'll forget it. I wouldn't ever want to be accused of doing a hard sell."

"I'd love to hear the hard sell, Sandy, if that's the soft one," exclaims Rolly.

A few seconds later, I send Rolly an email with the costings and two attachments. The first attachment is an advert, featuring a rumbustious pot-bellied gentleman with a scroll and quill who reminds me of Mr Pickwick, and the second is the advert as it will appear in the paper. A minute or two later, an email pings back with a reply. I open it up and read:

You're hired, Sandy Lovett. Four weeks' trial. Only on the condition you use the second advert though! Send me the invoice.

Rolly.

I grin. You see, you've just got to find the right key if you want to sell which, I admit, is pretty darn easy with Rolly.

"You look happy, Sandy," says Mum.

I look up at the sound of Mum's voice and the mention of my name and see from the look in Mum's eyes that Mum is Mum and I am Sandy. I close my laptop immediately; the times Mum is lucid are increasingly precious.

Mum and I stroll through the grounds of The Orchards, arms looped through each other's.

"I'm enjoying it at The Orchards," says Mum. "I didn't think I would. But now I'm here, having lots of company is wonderful. The house wasn't the same after your father died."

"A house is only bricks and mortar at the end of the day," I say, sympathetically. "It's people who make homes."

"What's happening to Primrose Cottage though, Sandy?" says Mum, a flash of concern flickering across her face.

I decide Mum can take a little bit of truth today – not that it matters as, in a few minutes, she may well have forgotten everything we've said. But sometimes it's good, even for a moment or two, to know whether I've done the right thing. I suppose I want to do right by her. Does that make sense?

"Dave's men have given it a lick of paint and we've modernised the bathroom and kitchen a little," I say. "And now we've got a lovely young couple with two small children renting it. The rental fee covers the cost of The Orchards so you'll be able to stay here as long as you want, but Primrose Cottage will still be there if you want to go back."

The rental fee doesn't cover all Mum's fees, of course, but I'm not going to tell her that. There's no need. At the moment, her savings are covering the difference but in about a year or two, Dave and I and Peter and Lucy will have to cover the surplus or sell Primrose Cottage – or I'll have to come up with an alternative arrangement.

"That's good news," says Mum. "I'm glad there's a young family in it. It's a house suited for growing children. You all used to spend ages playing in the garden."

"I remember," I say, recalling the safe haven of our large garden and shrubbery. "We were very lucky."

"I know," says Mum, smugly. "Your father and I deliberately chose a house with a big garden so you had plenty of space to play – not like these poor children today, stuck in those tiny square boxes. I don't know why these silly governments don't make sure children have safe places to play and plenty of sport in school. Then they wouldn't get into half so much trouble."

"I don't suppose so," I say diplomatically, trying not to antagonise Mum as she's clearly on the edge of a full blown Brown Owl/Everything Was Better in the Good Old Days rant. "But there doesn't seem any easy way of getting anything done these days with all the rules and regulations. Life is a lot more complicated."

"There's always a way if you want it," says Mum, argumentatively. "These politicians need to lead from the front. Not behave like a bunch of namby-pamby girls on a school outing. It would never have happened during the war; Churchill would have sent them packing."

"Hmm," I murmur non-commitally, not wanting to spend Mum's few lucid moments talking about politics, even though I think she's probably right. I used to get all worked up about stuff like that but now just getting through the day is more important.

"Well, don't you have an opinion?" says Mum.

"Of course I do," I say. "But it's such a lovely day. I'd rather enjoy the sun than argue about politics."

"Good Lord, Sandy, have you turned into a mouse? I remember the times I could barely restrain you from burning your bra outside No. 10. You'll have to get your act together, my girl. I don't want a daughter who's more interested in soap operas than saving the world."

"Mum, I am not Jesus Christ or Gandhi. I'm a mother of three with a part-time job in sales. Can we agree that I do something less grand than saving the world? How about I agree to save the whales?"

"Humph," snorts Mum, derisively.

We follow the path and reach the end of the garden and turn back to view the picturesque sight of The Orchards set against the clear blue horizon. It still looks rather grand in spite of the much needed repairs. I tilt my face to the sky and enjoy the first rays of spring sunshine. It's a beautiful day. A day to enjoy the sight of shoots bursting forth from the ground, the uncurling leaves of the trees and the scent of new life and new beginnings. I'm glad I still have the occasional moment like this with Mum. There's something to be said for enjoying the simple things in life with those you love.

"Your new job must suit you," says Mum, having forgotten her last train of thought. "You look far more relaxed. It's obviously doing you the world of good. You look slimmer too. Dave must be pleased."

"You bet," I reply. "But I've got about another stone and a half to go."

I know Dave will be ecstatic when I reach my target weight. In fact, he's already planning a big celebration.

"But it's getting more difficult to lose the weight now," I add. "I haven't lost anything for two weeks."

"You'll have to work harder," says Mum, resuming her bossy role again. "Remember how good you were at cross-country running at school. You could run off the last of that flab."

"That was thirty years ago, Mum. And I was never placed higher than third."

"That's because of your chest. If you'd had a completely flat chest like Madeline Gibson and Lyn Tattler you would have beaten them all!"

I look down at my chest; it's not ideal for running and never will be, but at least it's not on a par with Frau Engel's chest. If she ran, she'd knock herself out. At least I could do short runs if I was strapped up like an Egyptian mummy.

"Right, off you go."

"Off where?" I say, confused and wondering if Mum has slipped into madness again.

"To the gate and back."

"To the gate and back?"

"Good God, Sandy. Are you going to repeat everything I say? What's got into you? You used to be as sharp as a knife. Now run to the gate and back. I'll time you."

"Are you serious?"

"Of course I am."

Mum pulls up the sleeve of her coat to expose the simple men's watch she wears with its large digital display.

"But...but..."

"No buts, Sandy," says Mum, in her Brown Owl voice again. "Do you want Dave to go off with a woman with a smaller butt?"

"No...but..."

"Right then. After three. One...two...three."

I sprint off towards the gate, wondering why on earth I'm happy when Mum is lucid. Now we're definitely back in mother and daughter roles and I feel a complete twit, running to the gate in my boots and duffel coat. I touch the gates and sprint back. I admit it's a lot easier than my first attempt outside Jaggi's but I'm definitely happier with brisk walking. It's more stately and dignified at my age. I draw level with Mum who looks at me sternly.

"One minute and seventeen seconds. That's atrocious. If you ran any slower you'd be going back in time. Now go faster a second time. Put some effort in!"

"Mum!"

"Off you go."

I run to the gate again, turn around and run back to Mum.

"Better. You knocked ten seconds off. Tomorrow, we'll go to the park and run. We'll take my wheelchair so I can keep up with you."

"But Mum…"

"No buts, Sandy. I'm doing this for your own good. You can't go into middle age with a backside the size of a walrus's."

"I thought you said I was looking slimmer?"

"Did I say your backside was slimmer?"

"No…but…"

"So it's the park tomorrow," says Mum, firmly. "Now let's go and get a cup of tea; it's nearly time for cards."

Mum is settled in her seat. Mr Patterson, Mrs Lowry (that's the Exorcist lady) and three of the other residents are also sitting around the table, stacking up piles of coins. Mum is shuffling the cards like she's at Vegas so I know it's going to be a very serious game indeed; there's at least a two quid in pennies at stake.

"Shall I deal you in, Sandy?" says Mum.

"Not today, Mum. It's nearly time to pick up Tabby and then we're off to see Tricia Marshall."

"Is that the lady who sounds like Margaret Thatcher?"

"That's the one," I laugh. You see, when Mum's lucid she's always on the ball.

"She'll go far that one. Mark my words," says Mum.

"Deal me in, June," calls Mrs Levinson-Rice from her chair across the aisle and slamming her book down on the coffee table. "I can't take any more of this sycophantic nonsense!"

"Bye, Mum. Bye, everyone," I say. "See you tomorrow."

A chorus of goodbyes resound and Mum gives me a little wave before becoming absorbed in the cards again. I collect my belongings and make my way out, noticing Mrs Levinson-Rice's book on the table.

It's Tony Blair's autobiography.

15

"There they are!" cries Tabby, spotting Tricia and Oliver in the corner of Costa. Tricia hears Tabby's enthusiastic squeal, looks over in our direction and waves. I indicate that I'm getting drinks and line up at the counter, whilst Tabby weaves her way to the back of the coffee shop to sit with Tricia and Oliver.

"A medium skinny cappuccino and a hot chocolate with marshmallows," I say as I reach the front of the queue.

"Any cakes?"

I eye up the chocolate muffins, granola bars and the almond and raspberry slices which I've been drooling over for the last five minutes. Saliva gathers in my mouth at the thought of biting into a moist chocolate muffin and letting it melt slowly in my mouth. I'm hit with the awful realisation that I could probably eat one of each of the cakes and still have room for more. I also know that if I do start eating cakes, the assistants may well be dragging me out of the shop by my ankles at closing time.

"No thanks," I say.

"Are you sure?" says the barista, a young woman in her early twenties who can probably consume pastries by the dozen without the slightest effect on her waistline. "The almond pastries are delicious."

I hesitate, my tongue practically hanging out of my mouth, before taking a deep breath and uttering the words I've come to hate. "I'm on a diet."

"Oh, never mind," says the girl, in a pleasant, conciliatory tone. "Perhaps you can have one when you reach your goal."

"Maybe," I say, handing over a ten pound note.

"My neighbour lost three stone a couple of years ago."

"That's fantastic!" I say, feeling suitably smug for having denied myself a pastry.

"Then she put four stone back on."

"Oh."

"And got diabetes."

"Oh," I say again, my elation now reduced to depression.

"And then my mum found her face down in the flowerbed in her front garden."

"Oh my God!" I exclaim, unable to stop myself from being sucked into the girl's morbid story. "Was she dead?"

"No. She tripped over on her way to sign up with Weight Watchers."

I accept my change and debate whether there's a subliminal message in the girl's sorry tale, or whether I should stuff myself with cakes now and save the future heartache. It's been two and a half months since I touched a cake or a chocolate bar and, as much as I'd love to get my gnashers into one, I haven't come this far to give up just yet.

I place my cappuccino and Tabby's hot chocolate on a tray, offer my thanks to the girl, and head over towards Tricia who has settled Tabby and Oliver on the adjoining table, where they are happily comparing game scores on their Nintendos.

"Thanks for coming," says Tricia.

I smile appreciatively and take off my coat and hook it over the back of my chair.

"Wow! You've lost so much weight, Sandy," says Tricia.

"Thanks," I say, grinning. Apart from Dave and Deidre, Tricia is the first person to comment on my weight loss. I suppose the fact I've been covered up all winter, in long voluminous coats and big chunky boots to accommodate my new burgeoning toenail, no one has noticed. "I've been dieting but the real difference has been the exercise."

"How's your mum?" enquires Tricia.

"Still mad I'm afraid," I say with a sheepish smile. "But it's more manageable now she's in full time care and she's made friends. Loneliness seemed to be exacerbating her delusions."

"Yes, I see a lot of loneliness amongst the elderly when I'm doing my voluntary work. I suppose I'll have to face all those hurdles with my parents sometime. At the moment though they're enjoying the good life in Australia."

I drop a sachet of sweetener into my coffee, whilst Tricia looks thoughtful, no doubt contemplating what lies ahead for her when her parents need some help. I also notice I'm not the only one who has lost weight. Tricia, who has always been very trim, is even skinnier than normal. In fact, she's too skinny. Yes, I know women often say those things and people think they're jealous of a slim woman, but Tricia does genuinely look too thin; her collar bone is too prominent and her beige cashmere jumper is positively baggy around the boobs.

"By the way, thanks again for what you did at the school play, Tricia. I appreciate it."

"You know your mum was really quite good, especially when you consider her age," says Tricia, focusing on our conversation again.

I smile graciously as Tricia takes another sip of her black Americano. I know she's being far too generous in her praise but, nevertheless, it's sweet of her to try and make me feel less awkward about the whole affair.

"So are you busy planning the Spring Fair and working on all those other committees you sit on?" I say, changing the direction of the conversation. "Because I hope you don't mind me saying, but you've lost some weight too and, to be honest, you're as skinny as a rake now. I'd happily donate some of my flab for implants for you."

"That's what I like about you, Sandy," laughs Tricia. "You always say what you feel."

"It's called having a big gob."

"I wouldn't have put it quite like that," laughs Tricia. "Impetuous maybe."

"Let's not go off subject," I say, curious to know how Tricia has lost so much weight that she now looks positively unhealthy. "What have you been doing that's made you lose so much weight?"

"I've no idea. It's been falling off me. I think it's all the adrenaline!" says Tricia, her eyes lighting up with the same excitement I heard in her voice during our phone conversation. "It's the reason I wanted to see you; I wanted you to be one of the first to know!"

I scoop up a teaspoon of the froth on the top of my cappuccino and suck it up, revelling in the creamy essence of coffee. I decide I'll make it easier for Tricia who is obviously so excited about some utterly wild moneymaking scheme for the school's Spring Fair, she's making herself ill. Tricia's a strange creature at times; she's the sort of woman who creates a division of opinion but, somehow, you can't help siding with her because she has so much confidence in what she believes. I like her in the same way I like dark chocolate: in small doses.

"Tricia, I'm happy to do whatever it is you dreamed up for me at the Spring Fair," I say, spooning up some more froth.

"Really? That's fantastic!" says Tricia. "I've got some great ideas!"

"I don't have to do any running, do I?"

"No," says Tricia with a curious expression.

"Excellent," I say, not relishing the thought of having to endure a mums' running race or something equally hideous.

"But there's something else I wanted to tell you," says Tricia, like an overexcited teenager.

"There is?" I say, somewhat dazzled by Tricia's bubbly enthusiasm.

"Yes…I'm going to stand for Parliament!" says Tricia, barely able to keep her bottom on her seat. Not that she has much of a bottom, of course.

"Are you serious?" I say, putting down my cup.

"Yes!"

"I thought…"

"I know, I know…everyone thought I wouldn't make it through the selection process but I have and, as of this morning, I'm the official party candidate!"

"Bloody hell," I say so loud that Tabby and Oliver look up from their Nintendos. Tabby frowns at my indiscretion.

"Mum," says Tabby, sternly.

"Sorry."

"Mum's always screwing up in public," says Tabby to Oliver.

"I know," says Oliver, before the two of them reabsorb themselves in their shooting games.

"I can hardly believe it," exclaims Tricia. "In twelve to eighteen months, I could be sitting in the House of Commons!"

"Well…well done," I say, momentarily at a loss for words. "That's amazing. And you deserve the role, Tricia. You really do."

"Thanks," says Tricia, grinning inanely.

"We'll be a very lucky community if you're representing us in Parliament," I say, thinking about the numerous voluntary roles Tricia performs and how she approaches everything she does with the utmost dedication. Tricia really is a deserving candidate. Not like some of those self-seeking MPs, who have let the side down. It's no wonder she's lost weight; she's probably been running herself ragged.

"I'm positive all the hard work you've done will secure lots of votes," I say, as Tricia's ebullient mood rubs off on me so that I find myself grinning inanely too. "You can absolutely count on my vote."

"Thanks," says Tricia, still grinning like a court jester. "Now, I have something to ask you; will you join my campaign team?"

My coffee fires out of my nose and I start snorting like a pig, which attracts the attention of people on the surrounding tables. I turn a bright shade of red, knowing I probably look and sound like Miss Piggy.

"See," says Tabby to Oliver who looks up and shrugs his shoulders like he's seen it all before, ignoring the fact that I am practically convulsing on the table next to him.

Tricia gets up and calmly pats me on the back until, eventually, I've recuperated enough to speak. "Sorry about that. Coffee went down the wrong way."

"So I see," says Tricia, amused at my antics. "Now, what do you think? Will you join me? I need someone persuasive like you."

"Persuasive?"

"Sandy, you have the gift of the gab and could talk the hind legs off a donkey. I don't have those skills. I need people like you and Deidre to help me at social gatherings, on the phone and on the doorsteps."

Tricia leans forward over the table, a look of serious intent gracing her delicate features. "I know I don't have the charisma but I do have the ideas and the willpower. I want to help change society. I want to be in Westminster and make a difference."

"That sounds persuasive to me," I say in awe of Tricia's determination. "I'm convinced already. A bit of practice and you'll soon sound like Martin Luther King!"

"That's you talking, Sandy, not the electorate. I'm not good at public speaking and I know it," says Tricia.

"You need to be less stilted, that's all. Be more natural," I say encouragingly as a wave of gloom spreads over Tricia's pale face. "Talk to people from the heart and not from a prepared speech. Remember how you won over everyone at the committee meeting when you forgot about procedures? It worked a treat."

"I think that was more what you said," says Tricia.

"No way, I only primed them. If you hadn't shown emotion, and said what you felt, there would have been a backlash within a very short space of time."

"But I have a habit of annoying people," says Tricia, looking even more gloomy.

"Maybe you need a more moderate approach?" I say, knowing how Tricia's dictatorial manner often rubs people up the wrong way, even if they agree with her. "Sometimes, you need to back down for a while and give people space. Then later, you can come at it from a different angle. Let people come round to your way of thinking. It's the same with sales – if you're too pushy, it turns people off. People need time to make their own decisions, otherwise they leave or what they've bought comes back later as a refund."

"I suppose I'm impatient to get things done," says Tricia. "I don't mean to be bullish."

"I know," I say, graciously.

"I'm being sent on a communication course. The selection committee thought it would be a good idea."

"There you go," I enthuse. "They can obviously see you've got lots of potential. You just need to work on a few things."

"It's not going to be easy but I want to do the best I possibly can," says Tricia with renewed passion. "But will you help me, Sandy? I need help from people I trust. There are some terribly unscrupulous types in politics, even at local level."

"I'm not sure if I'm the trustworthy type," I say, knowing how I almost nearly ousted Tricia at the committee meeting. I feel a bit of a fraud now that Tricia is taking me into her confidence.

"Of course you are! How long have we known each other?"

I recall the first time I met Tricia was when Oliver and Tabby were in nursery together. Tricia pulled up in her spanking clean, shiny Land Rover, wearing spotless jodhpurs and gleaming riding boots. I was wearing my slippers (on the wrong feet), old jeans and stained tee-shirt. I was so impressed at the vision of cleanliness, I tripped over the kerb on the pavement and split my head open.

"Roughly eight years," I reply.

"Well, I think we've learnt a lot about each other even if we've not lived in each other's pockets."

I stare into my coffee cup. "I guess so," I say, remembering the time when Tricia told me she'd got cystitis. She's not the type of person to reveal personal information. Maybe it was a convoluted offer of closer friendship? I suppose I was so wrapped up in surviving with the three kids I didn't see it at the time.

"So will you help me? It's not going to be easy. It's a marginal seat," says Tricia, regaining some of her enthusiasm. "I know it's a lot to ask when you're winding down a bit, but even if you can only spare a few hours a week, I'd really appreciate it."

I hesitate, not sure I want to commit to anything. I want to support Tricia and I do believe in her. But my life is only just getting back on track. It's been changing for the better and I don't want to get on board with something and blow it all apart too soon.

"Let me talk to Dave," I say. "I need to run it by him."

"Thanks," says Tricia. "Take your time and think it over. You don't have to make a rush decision."

* * * * *

I pull the car into the driveway. The garage door is open and Dave's feet are sticking out from underneath his old Saab. My excitement about Tricia's news recedes. Dave only ever works on the Saab during the holidays or on the weekends, unless something is wrong and he needs time out to think.

"Why don't you go and ask Max what he fancies for tea?" I say to Tabby.

"Okay," says Tabby, collecting her school bag off the back seat and running into the house.

Dave is bashing vigorously at some unfortunate piece of metal and cursing. I get down on my knees and look under the car. He turns and looks at me, revealing a face almost entirely covered in black, dirty oil.

"Blimey, it's Al Johnson," I say.

A big smile spreads across Dave's face. "That's my girl," he says affectionately and propels himself out from underneath the car on his creeper.

"So what's up?" I say, helping Dave to his feet and unzipping his boiler suit to slip my arms inside and give him the cuddle he probably needs.

"We've lost the Sheraton contract. They've gone bust. It was five months' work for nine men."

"Hmm…not good," I say, knowing at once that our brief respite is about to come to an end. The Sheraton contract was a big one which we could ill afford to lose.

"Yep," says Dave. "As Tom Hanks would say: *Houston, we have a problem.*"

16

I put down my mobile phone and bang my head repeatedly on my desk at The Herald.

"Problem?" says Deidre.

"Andy," I say, lifting my head up to answer. "He's lent two hundred and fifty pounds to another student who promised to pay him back before the end of term but, needless to say, the boy's packed up after his last exam without so much as a word to anyone and left Andy out of pocket. Now Andy hasn't got enough money for himself. I can't believe he's been so gullible!"

"He needs to wise up," commiserates Deidre. "Get Dave to take him on a trip to Amsterdam."

"Deidre!"

"Just a suggestion," says Deidre with a wicked grin.

"I've told him hundreds of times he needs to be careful with his spending," I say. "Only two weeks ago I told him there's absolutely no spare cash to keep bailing him out and the business cash flow is rapidly drying up. And now look what he's done!"

"He probably didn't realise it was that bad," says Deidre.

"He's been thoroughly irresponsible whilst he's been at university. God knows how many times I've told him to get his act together."

"Are you going to give him the money?"

"No, not this time. He's got to learn. I've told him to ask for an extension to his overdraft. Besides, it's not long now before he finishes. Then he can come home and do some hard graft with Dave."

I sigh, knowing that unless some big job comes up in the near future the months ahead are going to become increasingly difficult. Soon there won't be enough work for all of Dave's workforce, without lumbering Andy onto them as well.

"I'm not sure how much longer we can carry on before we have to lay off someone," I confess to Deidre. "At the moment, Dave's managing to get the men hopping from one small job to another but that won't last forever."

"Any luck with that advert you placed?" says Deidre, angling her backside on the corner of my desk.

"Some. But the designs and planning applications have to be processed first and they're mainly small jobs anyway like garage conversions and extensions; the work people do when they can't afford to move home. We need something bigger. Dave's already cut his salary so we can delay laying off the two apprentices for as long as possible."

"You've got a good one there," smiles Deidre. "Not many men would do that."

"He's like Andy. He's too soft sometimes," I say, knowing that whilst Deidre is right about my kind-hearted Dave, it doesn't exactly help our family budget.

"You wouldn't love him so much if he was any other way but I'll have him if you don't want him. I like a younger man," says Deidre, with the humorous glint in her eye which makes her a honeypot to men of all ages.

"He's still taken," I grin. "But with this recession, I don't know how much further we can economize before we do have to lay off someone. I'm not sure Dave will even be able to do it – I may have to do it myself if things don't pick up in a month or two. I don't think he's laid off anyone before, unless they didn't come up to scratch or were on the fiddle. Those lads are like family to him."

"That's rare these days," says Deidre. "It's worth making a few sacrifices for. If you do have to let someone go, at least they'll know you did your very best to avoid it."

"I suppose so," I say, knowing that if we do have to make some difficult decisions it will not be easy. Dave's firm is more than a business to him; it's his life, his passion. He loves being with his mates and building stuff. It gives him a great sense of achievement and self-worth. There's nothing that pleases him more than when we drive past one of the houses he's built and he fills me in on all the tiny details: how they found two cat skeletons when they dug the foundations, or how Jim, his foreman, bruised his leg when he fell off the third rung of the ladder, or how there was a tree root so big it took all morning to dig it out. But that's Dave for you. He loves detail as much as he loves his work. One of his biggest disappointments in life was discovering Andy and Max had no interest in his meticulously constructed train set. He still says that one day they will appreciate it, but I'm not sure. How can a train set compete with the thrill of an Xbox?

"If you're interested," says Deidre, sliding off the desk and pulling up a chair. "I can get you some more work."

"I'm really grateful that you got me this job," I say, knowing how Deidre often manages to find a way to help people even when it's to her own detriment. "But I can't see any more hours here. If things get worse, I'm sure Frosty would take me back on the weekends, although I don't fancy that – it's a step backwards if you know what I mean."

"I wasn't thinking of more hours at The Herald," says Deidre, leaning forward conspiratorially. "I was thinking of you helping me in my other line of business. You'd only need to do a few hours a week if you want, but it pays well. Far better than Hendersons."

"I didn't think you did anything else," I say, surprised that Deidre can manage yet more work on top of what she already does.

"Oh yes. This job doesn't pay enough to fund my extravagant lifestyle," laughs Deidre. "It costs a lot to keep an old girl like me looking this chic."

I suppose I never thought about it that much but Deidre always looks smart, and I don't mean cheap smart but expensive smart. Even when she wears jeans, they are always top quality designer ones, rather than bog standard ones straight off the supermarket shelves like mine. I've never wondered how she's afforded it. I just assumed she'd been left a wealthy widow when her husband died years ago.

"Well, what is it? Don't tell me you're the regional controller for Ann Summers?" I joke, thinking about Deidre's frequent and infamous lingerie parties, which reminds me about my last purchase from Deidre which is still hidden in the back of the wardrobe. (Alongside the brand new size ten jeans, two skirts and the bikini I bought in the January sales, which I still can't get my butt into, but about which I also haven't told Dave.)

"No," smirks Deidre. "But I think you can work it out with a little imagination."

I tap my desk with my pen and wonder what Deidre can possibly be doing that fits in with all the other stuff she already does. Bar work perhaps? I give Deidre a puzzled look. She smiles and pats a finger on her Bluetooth headset and it dawns on me.

"You're kidding!"

"Sssh," whispers Deidre.

"You are a madam?" I whisper, incredulously. "You sell sex? On the telephone?"

Deidre tilts her head to one side and gives a salacious smile.

"But you let me practically grovel on my knees when that rumour went around at school!" I whisper in horror.

"A necessary evil," says Deidre. "I can't have my secret coming out in the public domain."

"How long have you been doing it?"

"About twenty years."

"Twenty years!"

"Sssh!"

"Sorry," I say, trying hard to keep my voice muted.

"Things were tight after Trev died," says Deidre without a trace of self-pity. "The house was paid off but, with four children to clothe and feed, it wasn't easy. I did what I had to do to make sure they had the best possible chances to succeed."

I nod appreciatively, knowing how expensive kids can be, and realise that Deidre probably supplemented all of her four children's student finances and none of them chose an easy option. Jen's a solicitor, but there's also Steve who's a vet, Shaun who's a GP and, finally, there's the youngest, Si, who still costs Deidre a fortune as he's a struggling actor and is always requiring "loans". It's not that he's irresponsible like Andy; he genuinely has no cash. Deidre believes he'll hit the big time one day and pay her back and, frankly, I think I'd do the same as Si looks like a God. How he hasn't been cast as some superhero or romantic lead yet, I don't know. It can only be a matter of time before some producer, or maybe even some rich cougar, snaps him up.

"So what do you reckon? A couple of evenings a week and a few hours elsewhere would probably be enough to keep on those apprentices until things improve."

"Maybe…" I say, thinking over how Dave might possibly react. "I'm not sure Dave would appreciate me… talking dirty… to other men though."

"He might love it," chuckles Deidre.

"I don't know…he can be a bit jealous at times," I say, knowing that whilst Dave is very easy-going about most things, selling sex, even if it is only over the phone, might be asking too much of his forgiving nature.

"But if it meant that financially things were a little easier, he might be okay with it for a short while. Unless you ask, you'll never know. Although you could just not tell him," says Deidre with a grin.

"Possibly," I muse. "I don't like the idea of keeping it a secret…but what would be the point of making him worry unnecessarily when I could simply say I'm doing a few more hours at The Herald? He has enough to worry about at the moment."

"What he doesn't know about won't hurt him," agrees Deidre. "And he'll feel less stressed, knowing those young lads can stay on and you're not out of pocket."

"I'm not sure if I could do it though," I say, a quiver of nervousness shooting through me as I think about the possibility of saying intimate things to complete strangers. "Whispering sweet nothings in Dave's ear is presumably a lot different to getting fruity over the airwaves?"

"It's as easy as pie," says Deidre, nonchalantly. "You don't need to be complicated with men. Just keep it simple. Maybe toss in a bit of spanking for the hard of hearing. I once cleaned out the oven whilst giving a man from Dundee an erection which he said was as big as the Eiffel Tower."

"Aren't they all a bit…odd though?" I say, not knowing whether to be appalled or to be consumed by the giggles at Deidre's descriptions.

"There are some nutters, of course, but anyone who oversteps the boundaries we cut off," says Deidre, in a pragmatic way which suggests she's more likely to be flummoxed choosing between ten and fifteen denier tights. "Most are normal guys who are a bit lonesome or whatever. People are doing it all the time these days. It's nothing to get screwed up about."

"You're not going to sell me this as a public service are you?" I say.

"Absolutely," says Deidre with a grin. "Anyway, didn't you know telephone sex, sexting and cybersex are all the rage now? Honestly, where have you been living the last ten years, Sandy?"

"Underneath the laundry pile mostly."

"Believe me, you could do it easily with a bit of guidance and a few tips. You'd be a natural. I'd market you as Sexy Sally or Sweet Virginia Rose or Felicity…"

"Sweet Virginia Rose?" I interrupt. "No one would ever believe that about me!"

"Ah, but it's all make-believe in the listener's imagination. No one will know who you are. Besides, you have a lovely innocent voice. The regulars will love it."

"I have an innocent voice? I always thought it was quite deep."

"How we hear ourselves is different to how others hear us. By the time you've unzipped your man's trousers, it'll be almost all over. One tug of his ding-a-ling and… voila!"

"May…be," I muse, contemplating the reality of Deidre's suggestion. The thing is I'm not sure if I'm as tough as Deidre. She's a cockney working class girl, made good through hard work and resilience, and she's seen the rough edge of life. She's pretty thick skinned and tells it how it is. When it comes to sheer ballsy courage, I don't think I can match her at all.

"I guarantee that once you've done a few calls, you'll switch onto autopilot," says Deidre, seeing my indecision. "It's easier than some other dead beat jobs."

"Really?" I say, unable to hide my disbelief.

"Oh yes, and I should know as I've done almost everything in my time," says Deidre. "Trust me. It beats the hell out of bar work or selling fish and chips at the local chippy. I tried both after Trev died. I can't eat fish and chips to this day; I smelt of haddock for a year afterwards."

Deidre screws up her face in total disgust, presumably remembering the repugnant smell of greasy chips and fried fish, whilst I'm flooded with images of myself sweating in the local chippy; I've blisters on my feet, scald marks on my arms and I'm breaking up a fight between two yobs chucking saveloys at each other, whilst a third is vomiting on the pavement outside. As I imagine myself knocked unconscious by an overcooked sausage and spread-eagled in a pool of curry sauce, telephone sex seems a lot more appealing… and definitely less dangerous…

"Sandy?"

I wonder if anyone has ever died from injuries sustained from a burnt sausage?

"Sandy?"

Sandra Lovett. Born March 22nd 1967. Died tragically from sausage burns.

"SANDY!"

I jolt out of my daydream.

"So what do you think? Are you game?" says Deidre.

"Maybe…maybe…I could do it for a short while until things turned around?" I say.

"Why don't you come and meet some of the girls and have a chat about it? See how they've coped? A few of us are meeting tonight for a regular get-together. It'll be fun."

"Okay, I will," I say, pleased to have the opportunity to sound out some other opinions before I commit.

"It's just an excuse for a gossip really," says Deidre. "Although sometimes we discuss whatever's the latest trend."

"What…like staff training?"

"Sort of. Only there's wine…and plenty of nuts," says Deidre with a wink.

"Deidre," I protest, "Sometimes you're disgusting!"

"I know," grins Deidre, sliding off the table. "They don't call me Madame la Pompadour for nothing."

* * * * *

"Come in, come in!" says Deidre, opening the door with one hand and holding a large glass of red wine in the other. "The girls are all here and keen to meet you!"

Butterflies stir in my stomach and I wonder about the other women who the silver-tongued Deidre's coerced into this job. What happens if they live up to my worst, if somewhat predictable, expectations?

"What are you going to have to drink, Sandy?" says Deidre, her heels clicking on the wooden floor as she sashays down the hallway in tight black satin evening trousers and a glamorous lacy blouse looking a picture of sexy elegance.

"A glass of the red will be fine," I say as Deidre throws open her lounge door.

"Miss Virginia Rose is here!" cries Deidre with unadulterated glee.

I step from behind Deidre to meet my potential new colleagues and see five ladies, happily ensconced on the red leather sofas I sold Deidre two years ago, each holding a large glass of wine and smiling enthusiastically.

"Welcome to the club!" says Deidre, turning around to face me and raising her glass of wine as a toast. The other ladies join in the toast with a chorus of good wishes.

"I don't believe it," I say, recognising the woman nearest to me. "Mrs M!"

"Hello, ducks," says Mrs M, eyes sparkling with fun. "I knew Deidre would talk you round sometime. Thank goodness our club is no longer a secret. I've got so many stories to tell you."

But before I can quiz Mrs M about her obvious delight in her more amusing sexual encounters, my eyes fall on another face which leaves me even more aghast.

"Tina!"

"Hi Sandy," says Tina with a shyness I'm not used to seeing her wearing. "Martin got made redundant a year ago," she continues as if by way of explanation for her presence.

"You kept that quiet," I say, wondering if Martin, Tina's husband, is now working or whether Tina is the major breadwinner.

"I knew we'd meet again sooner or later, aye I did!" a voice pipes up from the far corner of the room.

I look over and see a plump lady, who seems vaguely familiar, reclining amongst an array of cushions with a pot of peanuts on her lap.

"You've lost a lot of weight, Sandy Lovett. Aye, you're a bonny wee lassie now."

"Morna McIntyre!"

"Aye, that's me," says Morna, looking pleased that I've remembered her from our brief meeting in the charity shop last December.

"I enjoyed your book," I say.

"Aye. It comes as no surprise. It's one of my best," says Morna. "I borrowed your surname. I couldnae think of one; it was Deidre's idea."

"And I thought it was a coincidence!" I say, making myself comfortable on the sofa next to Mrs M.

"Morna also writes explicit erotica," says Deidre, passing me a large glass of wine.

"Under a pen name," says Morna. "And I've had no shortage of ideas since I joined Deidre's club. It's been a blessing in disguise."

"Why's that, Morna?" laughs Deidre.

"Och, I'm putting it down to a filthy Scouser who calls me. I've nae heard such fantastical stuff in all my life. Still, my books are selling like hotcakes so I'll not be complaining."

"I thought you said the clients were fairly predictable?" I say to Deidre, slightly alarmed by Morna's admission.

"Oh, generally they are," interrupts Mrs M. "But, occasionally, there's an unusual one and you'll have to make the decision whether you want to go with it or not. It's no worse than an objectionable customer at Hendersons and at least you can cut them off, rather than feign politeness."

"I've never had any weird ones," giggles a pretty young woman with a pixie face and black hair, held back by an Alice band, and who looks no more than twenty. "Well, not yet."

"Sandy, this is Kate. She's studying law," says Deidre.

"I'm paying my way," explains Kate. "I don't want to leave with a big debt."

"If only my eldest would do the same," I groan.

"If Andy's interested, I can always branch out," says Deidre. "In fact, I may well ring him myself being as he's such a lovely young man now he's had his hair cut."

"That was over three months ago, Deidre. He's probably reverted to caveman style," I reply, knowing Andy's ZZ Top look is bound to have made a comeback.

"Oh, I've got a call coming in," says Deidre, gesturing to the Bluetooth clipped discreetly over her ear. "I'll leave you ladies for a few minutes. Mrs M, will you finish the introductions?"

As Deidre leaves the room, Mrs M introduces me to Josie, a lady of a similar age to myself but who's frightfully posh and who apparently goes down a storm with clients under her pseudonym of The Duchess of Porn. Josie is about to elaborate on her tricks of the trade when Deidre waltzes back through the door.

"It just so happens I do have some friends here, Professor." Deidre pulls an amused face. "But I'm not sure if you can handle us all at the same time…you think you can? You are a very naughty, naughty boy, Professor. I think I shall have to discipline you soon."

There's a long pause whilst Deidre listens to the Professor talk. Unfortunately or fortunately (I'm not sure which), none of us can hear but as Deidre is contorting her face into all sorts of shocked, confused and revolted expressions, we all have a very good idea what the Professor is saying.

"Oh my, you are one hot Professor!" says Deidre. "You are so hot, I think I'm going to cool you down with some ice cream. In fact, I'm going to smear it all over you, and my girlfriends and I are going to lick it all off. We are going to lick it off…everywhere!"

Deidre listens again and pulls her face into such a horrific expression she looks like she's seen the ghost of Liberace. After a brief pause, she nods to indicate that the Professor is ready and waiting.

"Okay, baby," says Deidre in a smooth, sensual voice. "I'm going to run my tongue luxuriously up your legs, licking off the rich vanilla ice cream which melts on my tongue and runs smoothly down my throat like a river of semen…"

I convulse with silent laughter. Deidre whips off her Bluetooth and passes it to Mrs M, takes a big slurp of her wine and gives me one of her extra-special winning grins.

"I'm nibbling your pert round arse like I would nibble a crumbly chocolate flake…." says Mrs M.

I slide off the sofa onto the floor, clutching my stomach as Mrs M elaborates what she is doing with a chocolate flake. I'm hoping I don't wet myself like I did at the school play but, unfortunately, there is absolutely nothing I can do about it; I cannot stop laughing.

"I'm wrapping my legs round you as I suck the raspberry jam off your nipples," says Tina.

Deidre, now sitting on the sofa, lifts her legs in the air and waves them around.

"Stop it, stop it," I groan. "I'm going to die!"

"Oh, honey, you turn me on so much," says Josie. "I think I'm going to sit on your face and dribble some more ice cream over you."

"Oh God, I'm literally dying," I whisper as I lie, aching with laughter, on Deidre's shag pile carpet.

"Not yet, you don't," says Morna with a grin.

"Are your almonds tasty, Professor?" says Kate. "I do so love the sweet crunchy texture of nuts and grinding them between my teeth. But you should hear what my sister likes to do…"

Kate yanks off the Bluetooth, kneels down and slips it over my head, despite the fact that I'm hardly capable of breathing, let alone talking. I hear heavy puffing and some weird groaning I'd rather not know about. Out of the corner of my eyes, I see Deidre making furious gestures to me to hurry up and say something.

"Hello," I whisper, clearing my throat.

"You must be Virginia," says a croaky old voice that sounds like the man on the other end genuinely is an ancient professor from the spires of Oxford.

"Yes," I whisper.

"Madame la Pompadour said you'd be shy at first. You sound so sweet and innocent. But you can be bold with me, Miss Virginia. Now…what would you like to do to me?"

I pause and see Deidre still gesturing furiously and the other ladies all grinning at my discomfort. I close my eyes and attempt to block everything out.

"Why, Professor," I say, trying to sound my sexiest. "There's nothing left for me to do but cover your lollipop with sprinkles and slowly lick each one up with the tip of my tongue, suck it between my lips and gently roll it around in my mouth until there's an explosion of colour fizzing on my tongue."

"Oh, Virginia!" cries the Professor. "You are delightful!"

I give the thumbs up and Deidre, Mrs M, Tina, Josie, Morna and Kate raise their glasses and cheer me.

My initiation is over; I am part of The Beaver Club.

17

I swig back the last dregs of a bottle of wine that has been in the fridge for a few days. It's cold and refreshing. However, I know I'm going to need more than a few mouthfuls of wine if I'm to make it through Deidre's one-to-one coaching and my first sex chat session. I wander over to the wine rack and pull out a bottle each of red, white and rosé and arrange them in a horizontal line. As an afterthought, I add a bottle of gin.

I study the bottles with the intensity of someone who is already half-cut, which I probably am as my lips feel like rubber. Finally, I know what it must feel like to be Angelina Jolie; it must be hell trying to suck up spaghetti. Anyway, choosing the wine (and there must be some) to accompany my first exploration into sex chatting since my initiation into The Beaver Club has become inexplicably difficult. I pick up the wines in turn and examine the labels; the quality red might boost my flagging confidence but, on the other hand, the sparkling rosé might add some much needed sparkle and sauciness to my conversation. The cheap white, however, is more befitting to my new role. I put down the white and pick up the gin - maybe I should just go for the hard stuff? I could do with it. Just thinking about what lies ahead, never mind actually doing it, is enough to make me want to resort to spirits. But then again, if I drink too much spirits, I could pass out before I've actually even spoken a word. I pick up the red again. Perhaps it should be this one? I deserve the red for sacrificing my self-worth for Luke and Kev. But then again, I probably equally deserve the cheap white for not telling Dave. Maybe I should split the difference and go for the mid-price rosé? I decide to go for my old wooden spoon trick. I tap the bottles in turn.

"Eeny, meeny, Spanish red

Gets my fella into bed.

Eeny, meeny Aussie white

Makes me want to scream and fight."

I discard the red and centre up the remaining three bottles.

"Eeny meeny, luscious pink

Gets me over the kitchen sink.

Eeny meeny cold sloe gin

Makes me want to dance and sing."

I discard the rosé which leaves the cheap white and the gin. I start tapping the bottles again with my spoon. The last stroke lands on the gin which means I'm left with the cheap white. It's probably fate telling me that's what I deserve, although that may not being fair to myself as really I'm doing the sex chat for Dave, Luke and Kev. In a way, it's also for Andy, Max and Tabby because they'll benefit from it too. Perhaps, it's even going to be for all the frustrated men in bedsits who need my services. I'll probably be keeping them off the streets and saving unsuspecting sheep from a lifetime of misery. Maybe Her Majesty will give me an OBE or a knighthood for services to the dissatisfied. Oh, wait a minute - I can't have a knighthood without having a sex change, so that means I'd have to be a Dame. I'd be a Dame like Dame Judi Dench. We could go to the Oscars together. Me and Judy. How special would that be? Judi would wear something by Versace and I'd wear something from…Marks and Spencer. I owe it to Marks because of Mum stealing those pants. I'd probably end up on the front page of The Daily Mail. "Dame Sandy wears stunning M & S frock complete with shoes from Clarks." I might even oust Kim Cardiganshire, or whatever she's called, from the gossip columns.

I'm probably more than tipsy.

What the hell, I might as well go all the way. I unscrew the lid of the white, pour out a big glass and take a mouthful and wash it around my mouth; it's not too bad, but certainly not the best. It needs some more oomph; I open the gin and pour a large measure into the wine and plop in an olive.

"That's better," I say and take another mouthful.

"What are you doing, love?

I look up and see Dave leaning against the kitchen door, grinning.

"Umm…just experimenting with cocktails for your birthday party," I say. "I thought it would be nice to do something different."

"So that's what you and Deidre are up to this evening. I'm not sure it's safe to let you two get together."

"Oh, we'll be fine," I say as the doorbell rings. "That'll be her now."

"I'll let her in on my way out," says Dave. "Be a good girl. I don't want any trouble when I get home."

"I'm never any trouble."

"Yeah, right," says Dave with another grin and saunters off.

"All set?" says Deidre, appearing in the kitchen as the front door slams.

"I'm slightly tipsy, so I reckon that's a good start," I say.

"You're a natural. Don't worry," says Deidre. "And after your expert training this evening with moi, Madame La Pompadour, you'll be prepared for any client."

"Even the Pope?" I giggle.

"Pah, the Pope would be a doddle," says Deidre." It's those power-hungry bureaucrats you've got to worry about."

I hand Deidre one of my cocktails to which I've now added several cherries, a decorative umbrella, a slice each of lemon and lime, an olive and a curly straw.

"What's this?" says Deidre, pulling an amused face.

"Dave thinks we're experimenting with cocktails for his birthday party. So I thought I might as well go with it."

"I thought it was a Philip Treacy hat or at least one of Mrs M's."

I sit down opposite Deidre and begin to tuck nervously into some peanuts and slurp my wine, as she opens her file and takes out some sheets of paper.

"Right, this is some basic information for you. This first sheet is a list of useful vocabulary."

Deidre pushes the sheet over to me and I study it for a moment.

"Penis euphemisms?"

"Men have more names for penises than they have for cars. You have to be able to pick and choose what will work best. You'll soon work out who likes what very quickly. Some men like it just plain crude and dirty and some, like the Professor, prefer a range of more subtle euphemisms."

"Love gun, master-blaster, passion pistol?" I say, taking another gulp of my cocktail and looking at Deidre. "Seriously? Men really like their penises described like that? I must be more conservative than I thought."

"Absolutely, it really gets them going," says Deidre, switching to a sultry voice. "Come here, you gorgeous man-hunk. I want to suck your master-blaster."

"Ok…ay," I say, as I imagine what Dave would say if I said I wanted to go down on his master-blaster. "I'm not sure if that would work with Dave. He'd probably think I wanted to rewire his stereo."

"Dave is Dave," grins Deidre, "But I bet there's at least one on that list that would get him up and ready for action," says Deidre, knocking back her drink.

I look down at the list again. "Pinocchio?"

"Penises enlarge," says Deidre with a nonchalant shrug.

"Nimrod?"

"A favourite with Ministry of Defence employees."

"Tonsil toothbrush?"

"Dental surgeons."

"Sabre?"

"Star Wars fans."

"Mr Potato Head?"

"Some are just perverts," says Deidre, topping up our glasses with gin.

Deidre and I go through the rest of her list and some shorter lists for euphemisms for parts of the female anatomy. By the time I've been shocked, perturbed and doubled over with laughter we are half-way through the gin and onto the rosé. I am grateful I'm sitting down because standing up is beginning to feel like it might be a problem.

"So now we get to the adjectives," says Deidre.

"Adjectives?"

"Yes, ad…jec…tives," repeats Deidre slowly, so it sinks into my brain. "Describing words."

"Oh…adjectives!"

"How much did you have to drink before I got here?" says Deidre.

"Not much…I think," I say. "What do I need to know about adjectives?"

"They're useful," says Deidre. "For spicing up the conversation and getting things moving along. I've made a list of ones that should help you. Keep it by your side the first few weeks so, if you get stuck, you can take a glimpse and get a few ideas."

"Fruity, horny, tangy, sweet, salty, moist…moist?"

"It's a good word," says Deidre. "You and I might be appalled at the idea of moist knickers but men love it."

"Juicy?"

"You've got to say it right," says Deidre, leaning over the table towards me. "Juuuu…ceee."

"Juuuuuu……ceeeeeeee," I say, copying Deidre with exaggerated lip movements.

"That's much better," says Deidre leaning back in her chair, sipping her cocktail. "You're getting the hang of this. Just try and make everything sound sexy."

"Okay," I say, referring to the list. "I'll try."

"Shoot," says Deidre, knocking back the last of her cocktail and refilling it with yet more rosé and gin.

"Deee….lici….oooous."

"Fantastic," says Deidre. "You've got a real talent for this. When Tina started she was so stilted I thought she'd never sound natural. You've got to sound like you're enjoying it, even if you aren't."

"*Suck*….ulent."

"Perfect emphasis," says Deidre, laughing "You're almost as good as me!"

"Squir....mmm," I say, enjoying myself and trying to get my lips and teeth around some random words, "pusssssshhhh, plunnnnnge, saussssssage."

"Put it all together now!" encourages Deidre.

"Oh baby, your master-blaster is so *suck*...ulent and deee...lici...ooous. It makes me so hot and juuuu....ceeee. I just want you to plunnnnnge your sausssage into me."

Deidre screams with laughter. "You got it girl!"

When Dave returns home from the pub, I'm lying on my bed semi-comatosed from drink and having completed my first sex-chat session with the Professor who, fortunately, made it really easy for me.

"It looks like you've sorted out those cocktails," says Dave when he sees me spread-eagled on the bed still in my jeans and tee-shirt.

"Oh definitely," I slur, propping myself up on my elbow. "I wanted to crash out but I thought I'd wait up for you."

"Oh, what for?" says Dave.

"I wanted to see your master-blaster," I say, drunkenly waving him towards me.

"My master-blaster? I didn't know you knew such terms," says Dave, willingly unzipping his jeans and walking across to the bed.

"Have I told you what I've got in the back of the wardrobe?" I say.

"No," says Dave, grinning. "But I think I'm going to like it."

18

It is simply the biggest turkey I have ever thought about stuffing. I heave it out of the fridge and unceremoniously dump it onto the kitchen table.

"How long will that take to cook?" says Tabby.

"I reckon about seven or eight hours." I say, peeling off the cling film and pulling out the giblets from the neck cavity.

"Ugh. That's gross," says Tabby, screwing up her face at the sight of the bloody innards.

"I thought you might like to help me stuff it," I say. "A bit of mother and daughter bonding?"

"No thanks," says Tabby, slipping off the bar stool. "I think I'll go to bed now."

"Okay, we've got a busy day tomorrow anyway so maybe that's just as well," I say, trying not to grin at Tabby's disdain for the fleshy carcass.

"What about you, Max?" I say. "Fancy a bit of mother and son bonding?"

Max looks up from his iPhone and pulls out one earplug.

"Want to stuff a turkey?" I say.

"How much?"

"I'm not paying you to stuff it. Honestly, it's your father's fiftieth birthday tomorrow and neither of you have made the slightest effort to help around the house."

"Can I have quiche tomorrow?" says Tabby on her way out the door.

"Me too," says Max, sauntering over from the breakfast bar and giving the turkey the once over. "I wonder if it had a name?"

"Of course it didn't, Max. It's from a turkey farm where they have hundreds of turkeys. The farmer can't name each individual one."

"You don't know that. He could have been called Harold or Tom or even Justin."

I throw a spatula at Max's back as he idles out the door. "Don't be ridiculous! No one in their right minds would call a turkey Justin."

"I bet you would," says Max, closing the door behind him.

"No, I wouldn't!" I shout after Max.

"Yes you would!" shouts Max in return.

I focus on the turkey, a forlorn and headless creature. A pang of pity runs through me. A few days ago, it was probably gobbling its way around a farmyard, blissfully unaware that it would soon be served up with spuds and gravy. Poor creature, it would've been nice if it had owned a name at some point in its life.

"Alright…Justin. I'm sorry to have to say this," I say, tapping a spoon on the table and bracing myself for the job in hand. "Prepare to be stuffed. But first, you've a temporary respite."

I go to my secret kitchen drawer (the one which used to contain my stash of chocolate but now contains a selection of dried fruit and nuts), pull out my Bluetooth from underneath the pumpkin seeds and let Deidre know I am going to be around for about two hours. The very earliest Dave will be back from the pub is 11 pm and, as it's now 8.30 pm, I reckon I can be available for two hours, which will still give me thirty minutes breathing space.

My first call of the evening is from Len from Leicester. He's a new client. I quickly deduce that what he wants to talk about is his recent divorce, so I let him do most of the talking and make lots of sympathetic noises which, fortunately, are greatly assisted by my peeling and dicing three onions. By the time Len has built up enough courage to move from his divorce to getting his pants down, I am practically weeping down the phone. (They're particularly strong onions.) This seems to turn him on, and within a minute or two, Len is full of the joys of life, promising to phone again soon as I'm such an understanding woman.

I stir up the sausage meat, eggs and the onions into a big sticky mix, ready to stuff the turkey and wander over to the fridge to get some lard when another call comes in.

"Hello. This is Virginia," I say, wandering back to the kitchen table and taking a sip of my red wine, which is my habitual requirement for producing a roast dinner. It also helps to loosen up my inhibitions over the phone.

"Hello, Virginia."

It's not a voice I recognise. But it's mature and has an attractive quality to it, even though there's a slight nervous quaver; it's another new client.

"You have a lovely voice," I say, a phrase which I've discovered is a good ice breaker - even if it's a ninety-year-old with a lisp.

"Thank you."

"What would you like me to call you?" I ask, which is a question Deidre says is a relatively safe option and potentially less embarrassing for the client if he hasn't thought about potential scenarios.

"Joh….Justin."

"Justin?"

"What's wrong with the name Justin?" queries the caller.

"Oh nothing, nothing at all, Justin. As it happens, I'm very, very fond of Justin. All the Justins I've ever met have been surprisingly…delicious. And you sound just the same. In fact, you sound scrumptious…you make me want to eat you." I giggle and take another gulp of the wine.

"I'm naked," says the caller, who's clearly now distracted from my little faux pas and sounding more than just a little excited.

"I know," I say looking down at Justin the Turkey's featherless carcass.

"How…how… do you know?"

"Let's just say, Justin, I have a very good imagination," I giggle again.

"You sound hot."

"Oh, I am hot. But I think you're going to be hotter than me in a minute, Justin. I like my Justins to be positively roasting."

The caller chuckles, his confidence growing. "I like you, Virginia. Tell me what you look like."

"I'm five foot seven in my stockings," I lie. "I'm a brunette and…" I look down at my breasts and add on a couple of cup sizes for good measure, "I'm a 38DD."

"That's nice, very nice," says the caller. "Now, what are you going to do for me, Virginia?"

"Would you like a massage?" I say, unwrapping the lard and plopping it on top of Justin the Turkey.

"Oh, yes please," groans the caller.

"I'll just put some lubrication on my hands," I say squeezing my fingers through the lard. "Mmm…that's so sensual. I'm going to start by rubbing it gently over your smooth, hard chest. You feel slightly cold, Justin…it must be your nakedness…but I'm soon going to have you warmed up. Why don't you lie down and spread your legs so I can massage you everywhere."

"Oh yes, Virginia, yes!"

I begin to massage the lard into Justin the Turkey's legs. "Oh my, what lovely firm thighs you have," I say. "So strong and muscular. Like an athlete's. I bet you do a lot of exercise."

"I do," groans the man. "I'm a farmer."

"Ohhhhh," I say, barely able to control my laughter.

By the time I've greased Justin the Turkey and Justin the Farmer all over and added some condiments, Justin the Farmer is ready to blow.

"I can't wait much longer!" says Justin.

"Alright, baby," I say moulding a large handful of the stuffing into my hand and switching to my dominatrix voice. "Are you ready to be stuffed?"

"Oh yes!" cries Justin.

By the time I've shoved five handfuls of the stuffing into Justin the Turkey's cavity Justin the Farmer is replete and singing my praises. I can't help grinning as Justin thanks me ebulliently and signs off. I reach out for the string to tie up the turkey's legs and hear a movement. I turn around and see Dave standing in the doorway with a face as dark as thunder. I don't think I've ever seen him look so furious. I sense the blood draining out of my face and my body turning cold with fear. We look at each other for a moment.

"I came home early to make love to my beautiful wife, but I see you've found satisfaction elsewhere," says Dave, with a calm exterior which I know belies a deep and burgeoning anger; Dave does not lose his temper easily.

"I'm doing it for the money to help keep the business afloat. I'm not doing it for pleasure," I protest feebly.

"It didn't look that way to me."

Dave turns away and slams the door behind him. His feet thud up the stairs. The bedroom door opens and shuts with a stupendous crash.

I fill up my glass of red wine and gulp it down all in one go. It's Dave's fiftieth tomorrow and I've completely screwed up and I have no idea if he's going to forgive me.

19

"For God's sake, Dave, why on earth would I be doing sex chat for pleasure when I have you?"

Dave turns away and puts a third spoonful of sugar in his coffee. He doesn't even take sugar.

"I was doing it for us and so that we didn't have to let Luke and Kev go."

"I wouldn't have fired them anyway," Dave says, sullenly.

"Well I would have," I say. "Look, I know you're very fond of all the lads but you can't keep people on by cutting your own salary indefinitely. Where would that leave us? I don't want to see the boys in the dole queue with no hope of a job, any more than you do, but at least this way we get to keep our standard of living and try and keep the boys on – even if it's only in the short term."

"You could go back to work full-time."

I make a protracted groan. "If that's what you want, I'll do it. But I think our lives have been much improved by my working only part-time. I see Mum during the day, pick Tabby up from school, you have a meal ready for you when you get home and I'm a lot more relaxed and have time to look after myself. I've lost nearly three stone and I feel better than I've done for years."

"You look great," says Dave reluctantly.

"So why would I want to change that by going back to work at Hendersons or somewhere else and getting swamped by everything again?"

Dave shrugs and says nothing. I know he is sulking. Big time. This is all to do with the threat to his sexuality and nothing to do with logic.

"You should have told me," states Dave.

"I knew you'd get all worked up about it. So it seemed better to keep it a secret."

"This is Deidre's fault. I bet she persuaded you. She's more devious that I thought."

"That's rubbish," I say. "I'm not having you blame Deidre. She offered me a way out and I took it. Nothing more, nothing less."

"She's a bad influence on you."

"Dave, stop it! I won't hear you say another word against Deidre. She brought up four kids singlehandedly through their teenage years, with no husband and no money, and did every job under the sun to give them the best chance in life. That's something to be admired."

"So I should admire her now for operating a sex service?"

"Oh grow up," I say, finally beginning to lose my temper. I've spent forty eight hours grovelling and apologising and Dave is resolutely refusing to come even half-way towards understanding.

"You're the one who needs to grow up," says Dave. "You can't do these things and expect them to have no consequences."

"Fine," I say. "Let's both think about the consequences. You think about the consequences on your ego and I'll think about the consequences of going back to work full-time. In the meantime, I'm going out."

"Where are you going?"

I pick up my bag. "I'm going to deliver Tricia's leaflets and then I'm taking Mum to the park."

I turn away and back again. I don't want to involve anyone else in our marital dispute but, after blubbing my heart out to Tina last night, she suggested Dave should ring Martin. I think maybe now's the time to take up her offer as we're simply not getting anywhere by ourselves.

"Dave?"

"Yes?" says Dave with a trace of optimism.

"Why don't you give Martin Simpson a call?"

"Martin?"

"Tina's husband."

"Oh, Martin. Why would I want to ring Martin?"

"Tina's been doing sex chat for over a year - since Martin got made redundant. He tried for sixth months to get a job with no luck and now he's re-training as a teacher. The training salary isn't enough to live on so

Tina's supplementing it until he qualifies. Martin knows and says he's happy to talk it through with you."

Dave looks genuinely surprised for a moment before returning to his sullen disposition.

"Think about it anyway," I say.

* * * * *

I run as fast as I can. Yes, that's right. I'm running of my own free will. Mum is on the other side of the park in her wheelchair, stopwatch in hand, and I'm running like I've never run before. My lungs are aching and my thighs are beginning to get that heavy feeling that signifies I'm pushing myself beyond my normal limits. My feet pound hard on the concrete pavement, the rhythm of their sound and the movement of my arms driving me forward. I know I must not stop until I'm utterly and totally exhausted. I need to rid myself of all the pent up hurt and frustration of the last few days. I try to move my legs faster to overtake a lady jogging sedately in front of me, but nothing happens, but then this morning's argument with Dave comes to the forefront of my mind and a surge of energy, driven by anger, propels me forward. I stride past the woman jogger and into the home straight towards Mum.

I keep on running as I dissect this morning's argument with Dave. It's been a long time, if ever, since we've kept up an argument for so long. Usually, one of us will admit to being in the wrong and we patch it up within an hour or two. But the bottom line is Dave is not accepting my arguments because his male pride is wounded. I understand that and I know I'm culpable - but I don't know what else to do to heal the rift. Maybe time will be the healer, or maybe Dave will ring Martin who might be able to reason with him. Tina said Martin was the same at first but soon came around to the idea when he realised they would have to sell their house if they didn't take action.

I'm within ten metres of Mum now and begin to slow down. The tiredness kicks in and my footsteps hit the pavement harder, their impact juddering up through my hips.

"Don't slow down!" says Mum. "This is your fastest time. Keep going!"

Not wanting to incur Mum's wrath, I try to surge forward again but find I can't speed up at all. I can just about keep up momentum long enough to reach Mum's wheelchair.

"Pity you slowed down at the end," says Mum. "But that's still your best time."

"Well done," says an elderly man sitting on a nearby bench, feeding pigeons. "No wonder you've lost so much weight. Fantastic effort."

Inwardly, I cringe. Mum has obviously been discussing my weight problems with the pensioner. Outwardly, I'm too exhausted to say anything but I nod in appreciation, put my hand on my knees and pant away until my breathing begins to slow. Mum passes me my water bottle and I take a long, greedy drink.

"I think you should do one more lap," says Mum.

"Mum, I'm exhausted," I moan. "I ran my absolute fastest."

"How much more weight have you got to lose?"

"About half a stone."

"Well, you won't do it wimping out. The last bit is always the hardest. I suggest you walk round and then, if you've any energy, you do some intermittent jogging."

"She's right, love," says the man. "A little bit more effort could make all the difference."

I glance from Mum to the stranger and deduce that the pair of them have ganged up against me. Mum's look of steely determination is the one she wears when someone is close to beating her at cards and she's not going to let it happen. I might as well concede defeat now and start walking before she starts discussing my sex life in public. Not that Mum knows about my sex life, but let's just say Mum is not averse to using underhand tactics.

"Alright, alright," I say. "I'm going."

"Take the last of these leaflets with you," says Mum, handing me the near empty carrier of Tricia's leaflets. "You can hand them out as you go round."

"Yes, Mum," I say. After all my arguing with Dave, I don't have the energy to do the same with Mum. No doubt everyone in the park will object to me thrusting Tricia's propaganda in their face whilst they idle away an afternoon in the sun, but, frankly, it'll be easier to accept a few rejections than spend ten minutes debating the ins and outs of it with Mum.

"What's her name again?" says Mum.

"Tricia Marshall."

"Ah yes. That's it," says Mum, turning towards her new friend. "Tricia is Sandy's friend who is standing for Parliament at the next election. That woman will go far. Mark my words."

Tricia is Mum's latest project. Everywhere we go, Mum is spouting praise for Tricia. I think everyone at The Orchards has agreed to vote for Tricia so Mum will stop interrupting Inspector Morse with Tricia's political agenda. Bizarrely, even though Mum has only met Tricia on a few brief occasions, she seems to be one of the few, like Deidre, that Mum seems to have fixed firmly in her memory. I'm not sure though if it's really Tricia, or whether the resemblance to Margaret Thatcher is stimulating memories which are somehow filtering through into her perceptions of Tricia. Alzheimer's plays lots of dirty tricks.

I take a last gulp of water, hand my bottle to Mum and set off at a brisk pace, leaving Mum chatting with her new kindred spirit. It was a bit embarrassing knowing Mum had been talking about me behind my back but, on the other hand, it's good to know she's preoccupied. It's when she's by herself, and gets lost in her thoughts, that she's at her most vulnerable. Luckily, today seems like one of Mum's fairly lucid days although the reality is, as Frau Engel told me bluntly this morning, there has been a pronounced deterioration in Mum's condition lately. I knew it, of course, as Mum is far more willing to spend time in her wheelchair than she was six months ago, but when someone tells you the truth there's no denying it or hiding it under the carpet. The fact is, after a good six or seven months of relative stability, Mum has got considerably worse.

I walk around the first curve of the park and Mum comes into view. She's ferreting in her handbag and the old gentleman is still sitting on the bench. I relax and dip into my plastic carrier with the last of Tricia's leaflets and look for unsuspecting victims.

Tricia's campaign is going extraordinarily well. The sitting MP is retiring so he's already backing Tricia to win, even though it'll be a while before the next election is announced. I've delivered thousands of leaflets already and Tricia's presence in the town seems to be growing stronger by the day. Everywhere I go, everyone is talking about "Our Tricia" making it into the corridors of power. There's an excitement at the school gate, at the swimming lessons and at the clubs and societies Tricia has supported for years. I'm beginning to believe that maybe, just maybe, Tricia can do it. Despite her abrasiveness, people seem to sense that Tricia can be trusted. It's not just about party politics anymore. It's about Tricia.

As I contemplate Tricia's future, I spy a young mum having a picnic with two pre-school children; another potential victim of my new-found conversion to Tricia's campaign.

"Hello. Could I give you one of these?" I say, proffering one of the leaflets. "My friend, Tricia Marshall, is going to be standing for MP. She's one of the good guys."

The young woman smiles at my casual approach, reaches out and takes the leaflet. "I think I've heard of her."

"She's chair of the PTA at St Matthews and governor of Kingswood School but you could've come across her in pretty much every institution in the town. To be honest, she makes me feel wholly inadequate."

The woman laughs and then reprimands one of her children for pulling up some grass. I stay, sensing she wants to talk. It can be a long and lonely business looking after small children.

"I don't know how some women juggle so many things," she says, when her children settle back to munching crisps and biscuits. "I seem to have enough to do looking after these two without doing anything else. I need to go back to work but the childcare is so expensive it doesn't make any sense." She pauses. "I was thinking of sending my children to St Matthews. Is it any good?"

"My daughter's in Year Four and my two elder children went there," I say, sitting down on the grass. "It's a good school. I've never had any issues bar none of my children starring in the school play."

The woman laughs again.

"Besides, there's always been Tricia to sort out any real problems," I say. "She keeps everyone in check."

"But I suppose she'd leave if she gets elected?" says the woman, thoughtfully.

"You're right," I say, thinking about the consequences for a lot of the local organisations that rely on Tricia. "I guess she'd have to eventually. But she'd be leaving it in a very good place. She'll probably make the PTA and governors swear affidavits of allegiance for the next five years."

"It sounds like it has a good community spirit," laughs the woman. "I should probably go and have a look round sometime."

"They get oversubscribed so I would get your children down on the waiting list as soon as you can if you decide it's the right place."

"I never thought about that."

"Parenthood is one long journey of discovery isn't it? I'd better go," I say, snatching a look at Mum. "My mother's keeping a watchful eye on me."

I say goodbye and set off walking again, enjoying the sunshine and clear skies and pushing my argument with Dave to the back of my mind. The other people I approach with Tricia's leaflet seem receptive, the good weather dispersing the usual British reserve. It's not until a few minutes have passed that I remember to check on Mum and notice that both she and the old gentleman have disappeared. My carefree disposition turns into one of impending doom. I've been incredibly foolish to take my eyes off Mum, even for a minute. How stupid, stupid, stupid am I? I scan the park but can't see her anywhere. I begin to panic. Mum could get into all sorts of trouble unless I find her soon. I scan the horizon again and see a vaguely familiar figure walking up the path towards me. I shield my eyes from the sun and recognise the figure as Dave. He recognises me too but I force myself to turn away and continue my search. This is neither the time nor the place for another argument - I have to find Mum. I continue searching and spot her emerging from behind some bushes at maximum speed in her wheelchair and heading away from me towards the lake.

"Oh shit," I cry, if the lake isn't enough to worry about, there's also a series of ten or fifteen steps before it. Even if Mum steers away from the steps, she could still go over the embankment. Either could result in a potentially fatal fall. I turn back towards Dave, not knowing what to do, but then decide I can't wait for him to catch me up. I have to go after Mum. If she's gone into one of her delusional modes, anything could happen.

I throw down the leaflets, leave the path and run directly across the grass towards Mum. I regret having exhausted myself earlier. My legs still feel tired and heavy. I grit my teeth and try to break through the pain barrier as I see Mum speeding further away.

"Sandy! Sandy!" I hear Dave shouting behind me. "Stop!"

I ignore Dave and keep on running, jumping over a man sleeping with a newspaper over his face and skimming around a young couple kissing.

"Sandy, Sandy! For God's sake stop! Don't run away from me. We need to talk!" Dave is almost level with me and tugs on the back of my tee-shirt. "Sandy, please stop!"

I carry on running. Dave draws level with me. I glance sideways at him and see the anguish on his face because he thinks I'm running away from him. I want to stop and tell him I love him, but I can't. I have to get to Mum.

"It's Mum," I say, squeezing the words out between breaths. "She's heading towards the steps."

Dave looks towards where I'm running and realises what's happening. He curses and begins to surge forwards, his long muscular legs gathering speed and momentum. Within two or three strides he is already a metre ahead of me. We run through a crowd of youths playing football.

"Look at those fucking weirdos giving it some!" yells a lad with a baseball cap.

"Pair of nutters," says another with a tattoo on his arm so big I can hardly see the skin underneath. "Anyone got a defibrillator?"

I give the finger to the lad with the tattoo and make a rash decision. "Anyone who catches the woman in the wheelchair before she crashes gets...a hundred pounds!"

The lads follow my gaze; Mum's not far from the steps now and there's no sign she's slowing down.

To my surprise, the lad with the tattoo throws down the football and takes off at breakneck speed. Within a few seconds, he's overtaken me and in a few more, he's close upon Dave's heels. To my even bigger surprise, the other lads all pass me by and are all running manically towards

Mum too. I'm astounded. I didn't think any of them would take any notice but now they're all running like their lives depend on it. I don't know whether their motivation is concern for an old lady or the money but I don't care. I'm just grateful. The lad with the tattoo overtakes Dave, who is fitter than most fifty year olds but who cannot match the speed of a young man, and he begins to rapidly close in on Mum, his legs striding purposefully across the grass. My energy begins to drain away. There's nothing more I can do. My legs begin to buckle beneath me. I run a few more steps and then just as I start to fall, I see Mum waving her stick in the air and hear her shouting:

"Up yours, Adolf!"

I fall onto the hard sunburnt grass, exhausted. Mum has clearly gone into one of her delusions and by the sounds of it she thinks she's Steve McQueen again and her wheelchair is his motorcycle in The Great Escape. I groan and look up in time to see the lad with the tattoo catching hold of the wheelchair just before Mum tumbles down the steps.

I roll on my back and look up to the heavens. "Dear God," I say. "What have I done to deserve this?"

I lie on my back, breathless, unable to move and trusting that Dave is dealing with the fallout. A face peers over me, blocking out the sunlight. "Are you okay?"

It's the young mother with her two children, now strapped into a double buggy. "I've collected your leaflets for you."

"Oh, thanks," I say, propping myself on my elbows.

"Is that your Mum?"

"I'm afraid so. She's got Alzheimer's," I say. "I shouldn't have taken my eyes off her."

"I suppose it's like having a child again."

"In a sense it's worse," I reply. "Because you know it's never going to get any better. And, one day, you know they're going to die and leave you."

This time it's the young woman's turn to smile sympathetically. Her toddlers begin to fidget, eager to move on. I get to my feet and take the bag off her. "Thanks ever so much," I say.

"I'm going to vote for your friend. I like her sentiments about making better provision for the young and the elderly and rooting out all the corruption."

We both look in Mum's direction and watch Dave pushing her towards me, with the group of lads joking and laughing beside him. Mum is still waving her stick and ranting.

"I suppose we have similar problems," says the woman. "Just in a different way."

"I guess so," I say.

The young woman heads off across the grass towards the main exit.

"That was a close call," says Dave as he steers Mum to a halt.

"Bloody Hun," says Mum, pursing her lips and laying her cane resolutely across her lap.

"I'd better get you home," I say to Mum. "I think we've had enough excitement for today."

"What about my money?" says the lad with the tattoo.

"Money?" says Dave.

"Um…yes," I say, sheepishly. "I said anyone who catches Mum gets a hundred pounds."

Dave gives me a look that says he can't believe I've said such a stupid thing when we're in the middle of a financial crisis. Then he breaks into a smile and pulls out his wallet from his back pocket.

"Aren't you a local builder?" says the boy in the baseball cap as Dave counts out the cash. "Got any jobs? None of us have had a job for over a year. Everyone thinks we're layabouts but we all want to work."

"Yeah, I'm a builder," replies Dave. "But I've got no jobs going at the moment. Times are hard for everyone. We're just keeping afloat. But I promise you, when things pick up, if you lads keep in touch, there'll be work for you. Strong young men, who want to work, are what every builder needs."

Dave hands over a business card, as well as the money, to the lad with the tattoo. The lads all nod in appreciation and wander off, clapping their friend on the back for his success in getting some cash.

Dave and I push Mum across the park towards the exit. Mum seems to have gone into a trance-like state, lost deep in her thoughts. My mind is all over the place too. The shock of Mum's latest escapade and my argument with Dave has left me tired and confused. I don't even have the energy to speak. After a while, Dave takes his hands off Mum's wheelchair and puts them on my shoulders. I look into his soft, brown eyes.

"Look, I'm sorry, love," says Dave. "I understand why you did that sex chat stuff but that doesn't stop me from being hurt. But I've talked to Martin and he's made me see it from another angle. I still don't want you to carry on with it, but maybe you should, just for a short while, whilst I think of something else. Maybe I can find another way to keep Luke and Kev. Perhaps hire out some equipment to raise some cash."

"I wasn't enjoying it," I say. "Not like you think anyway."

"Yeah, alright," Dave grins. "But you were having fun."

"I'd had two glasses of wine and I was stuffing a turkey, whilst giving a farmer called Justin a good time. Of course I was having fun. I could only do it by making light of it. I couldn't do it seriously."

"That's a pity," says Dave.

"A pity?"

"I was expecting some sort of compensation for putting me through this trauma," says Dave with a twinkle in his eye.

"Oh, were you?" I say, smiling.

"Yes," says Dave. "And you won't be needing a turkey."

20

I disentangle myself from Dave's arms, roll over and rummage for my mobile phone on my bedside table.

"Hello, Mrs Lovett?"

I bolt upright in the dark as I recognise Frau Engel's voice.

"Yes?"

"I am afraid all is not gut, Mrs Lovett. Your mother will not last until morning."

"I'll be there straight away."

I switch on the bedside light, leap out of bed and pull on my jeans.

"What's the matter, love?" says Dave, opening a weary eye.

"It's Mum. She's dying."

"I'll come," says Dave, swinging his legs out of bed.

"You can't. We can't leave the kids on their own at this time of night," I say, glancing at the alarm clock. It's 12.15 am and I probably don't have much time left with

288

my mother. I grab yesterday's discarded tee-shirt and stretch it over my head.

"I'll get someone to babysit and then I'll come over."

"Ask Deidre or Maggie," I say, pushing my feet into my summer sandals and grabbing a cardigan.

"Alright, love. I'll be there as soon as I can."

I pick up my bag and car keys from the hallway and run to my car. It's a cool summer's night in late August and it's a week since Mum took to her bed with a heavy cold. Despite the doctor's reassurances that Mum was taking longer to recover because of her age, I suspected there was something else, but maybe nothing quite so…final. Mum hadn't been herself since the incident in the park two weeks ago, her usual gregarious madness replaced by incoherent mutterings and long periods of unnerving silence. I'd begun to wonder if it was the beginning of a long, slow decline. A demise that would make interacting with Mum, in whatever form of delusion she'd invented, seem far better than the agony of watching her drift silently and slowly away from me.

Frau Engel opens the door and ushers me inside. We climb the stairs in silence so as not to disturb the other residents. She opens the door to Mum's room and we step inside. There's a low light in the far corner casting out a soft glow. Mum lies motionless under the covers, her mouth open, hands resting by her side on top of her favourite eiderdown.

"Your mother was awake earlier this evening and seemed a little better. But now her pulse has changed. I am sorry, Mrs Lovett, I do not think she will wake now. She may be able to hear you though. They say that is the last sense to go. I am sorry."

"Are you sure?" I say, holding back my tears.

"I have seen many pass to the other side, Mrs Lovett. There is no going back now."

I nod, unable to speak.

"I will bring you a cup of tea."

Frau Engel, despite her bulky frame, slips quietly from the room.

I move to Mum's bedside. Her face looks softer and less lined, as if the stress of living is seeping away from her in death. I stroke her hair, her face and kiss her forehead. There is no movement, no sign that she feels or hears my presence.

I pull up a chair and sit by her side, taking her hand in mine. For a moment I imagine a fleeting squeeze but I cannot be certain, although, somehow, I'm sure she senses my presence.

I close my eyes and, in the darkness, remember all that we have shared.

A faint clink of china disturbs the flow of memories. Frau Engel enters the room, followed closely by Dave. She places a tea tray on the dressing table, pours two cups of tea, leaves one on the dresser for Dave and places mine on the bedside table. She checks Mum's pulse, moistens her lips and leaves again.

Dave stands behind me and rests his hands on my shoulders for a while. Then he moves to the armchair by the dresser, sips his tea, and as the night wears on, he drifts into a light slumber.

Mum's breath begins to slow as the first rays of dawn begin to filter through a gap in the curtains. I get up and pull back the velvet fabric and a golden light glows on the horizon. I open the window and the first melodies of a songbird drift across the garden.

I go back to the bed, lean over my mother and kiss her one more time. "I love you," I whisper.

I sit at Mum's side, take her hand in mine again and place her palm against my cheek. Mum takes another long, slow breath and as night passes into day, my mother leaves me.

21

I lie on my bed and look at the patterns on the ceiling, which form bouffant clouds and winds with curved cheeks and swirling breath. It's been a month since we buried Mum and I haven't had the will to do much other than the usual routines except deliver more of Tricia's leaflets. It's been hard trying to keep the motivation, but Mum's voice is in my head, nagging me that I can't let myself and Tricia down by sitting on my backside and getting fat again. I know Mum's right.

People don't stop being with you because they die, do they? I think Mum will always be with me gently (and not so gently) chiding me, trying to make me a better person. Maybe that's because she expected me to somehow be the sum of two people after Denise died. Denise had big ambitions, like Tricia, whereas I stumbled from one thing to another, riding on the crest of life rather than confronting it. Maybe Tricia's aspirations were another reason Mum admired her so much. I don't know for sure.

That's the thing about death; it makes you think about the events and people that shape you and make you who you are. I suppose the reflection is a kind of healing; even if you don't necessarily come up with any answers.

"A penny for your thoughts," says Dave, padding across the carpet in his bare feet and sitting down on the edge of the bed.

"I was thinking it's about time we plastered over that artex."

"And there was I thinking it was going to be something profound," teases Dave.

"I'm no good at profound. Profound is for people like Tricia, with the big ideas and concepts. I'm more into woodchip and Dulux," I say, turning on my side to admire Dave's naked torso.

"I guess that's why you married a builder rather than a big executive cheese."

"The trouble with the big executive cheeses is they tend to end up with big executive stomachs," I grin. "Did you see Rolly's stomach at Mum's funeral? I thought an alien was going to burst out."

"And you've still got a husband with a six pack," laughs Dave, patting his abs. "Who's a lucky girl then?"

I smile and stick my foot under the towel wrapped around Dave's midriff.

"Hey ho, is it my lucky day?" says Dave with a lecherous grin.

I run my toes up Dave's thigh. "You know, I really have been thinking."

"Oh yes, about what?"

"I was thinking that now I've got more time on my hands and we've Mum's inheritance…maybe it's not too late to have another baby."

Dave's mouth falls open, his face frozen in abject terror.

"Don't you think it would be nice to hear the patter of tiny feet again, darling? If we had a girl, I'd like to call her June after Mum. If it's a boy, I'd call him Leonard after Dad."

"Are you serious?"

"What's wrong with my parents' names? Leonard is particularly nice."

"Surely, you're not serious?" says Dave, looking like he's about to have open heart surgery.

I give Dave one of my earnest expressions. "No."

Dave exhales like an exploding hot air balloon. "You wicked witch," he says, pinning me down on the bed. "Now I'm going to have to punish you for being such a despicable tease."

Dave lies on top of me and covers my face and neck with kisses. After a month of being entirely wrapped up in my own thoughts, I'd forgotten how good the firm intimate warmth of Dave's body is against mine. My lips part beneath his and we kiss like we're teenagers. I break off for a moment to whisper in Dave's ear. "In case we have an accident can we agree on Leonard now?"

"If you must," groans Dave. "The poor kid would be persecuted from dawn to dusk but you can call it anything you want so long as I get to ravage you."

"Deal," I giggle.

We start to kiss again. I rip off Dave's towel and he pulls off my tee-shirt and unclasps my bra.

"My favourite pair of beauties," says Dave, beaming as he gives my breasts an affectionate squeeze. "God, I've missed them."

"Muuum! Muuuum!" shouts Andy up the stairs.

"Oh God, please, please, not now," groans Dave in despair and his lips hover above my nipples.

"Mum!"

"Please God," moans Dave. "Please let me have sex just this once without an interruption."

"What is it?" I shout back, stroking Dave's bottom.

"Tina's here!" shouts Andy.

"Oh. I wasn't expecting Tina," I say to Dave. "I suppose I'd better go down and see what she wants."

"Shit, shit, shit," says Dave, rolling off me. "If it's anything to do with Tricia and the PTA, I'm going to throttle the pair of them!"

"I'll be down in a minute," I yell and toss Dave his towel to cover up his deflating assets.

I open the door to the kitchen. Tina is sitting at the breakfast bar with her back to me and Andy is making coffee. Tina hears me and turns around. Her face is blotchy and streaked with tears.

"What's happened?" I say, looking from Tina to Andy for an answer.

Tina tries to speak but is so distressed she is unable to utter a word.

"Have you argued with Martin?" I say, wondering if Martin's changed his stance on the sex chat.

Tina shakes her head from side to side.

"It's Trisha, Mum," says Andy.

"Oh my God, she's not quit the campaign after all our effort?"

"No," says Andy, who has obviously heard whatever the news is from Tina who's now sobbing uncontrollably into a tissue. "No, Mum. I'm afraid Tricia's got terminal cancer."

I look at the solemn expression on Andy's face as Tina continues sobbing and know that this isn't some stupid joke. Andy pushes me a mug of tea across the breakfast bar. I wrap my arms around Tina who rests her head on my shoulder and cries for a long time.

"It's not fair," says Tina, when her sobs begin to subside. "She had so many plans. She did so much for everyone. How could this happen to her?"

"Is it definitely terminal?" I say. "Is there no hope?"

"It's very aggressive. She told me so herself this morning. The consultant says she has only a few weeks - a month or two at most." Tina starts to sob again.

"I thought her weight loss was due to overwork," I say, thinking back to our meeting in the café earlier in the year and regretting I hadn't raised the issue of her continued weight loss since then.

"We all did," chokes Tina.

After an hour of comforting, Tina leaves in a slightly more composed fashion than when she arrived. I go into the hallway, push my feet into my trainers and begin to tie up the laces.

"You alright, love?" says Dave, opening the door from the lounge. "Andy told me the news."

"I'm going to go for a run."

"Good idea," says Dave with an encouraging smile. "Andy and I will get tea ready tonight."

I run down the road and into the open fields. I haven't run as fast as this since Dave and I argued. If ever. You see, I knew at some point Mum was going to die. But Tricia? Tricia's death is unjust, like Denise's. At moments like these life - or death - seems so bloody cruel.

I keep on running until I can run no more.

22

"Andy is doing a great job," says Dave. "He's doing some real graft in the office. And this plan of his to develop the land around Mum's bungalow should keep us on track till some big jobs come in. There's two of them in the offing now. I only need to pull one off and we'll be sound for the next year."

I unravel myself from Dave's arms and roll over and look at him. He looks more relaxed than he has done for months.

"I know," I smile, tracing my fingers down Dave's nose. "He's doing well. I'm surprised how the lads have taken to him, bearing in mind he's so young."

"He's a charmer. Just like his old dad," grins Dave.

"I can't believe we didn't think of developing the land around Mum's bungalow before now," I say.

"Well, it wouldn't have been right while she was alive and you needed some time to put your thoughts together. Andy's plans are great though. I've gone over and over them and I can't see any flaws. We should be able to keep all the lads in work and net a tidy profit."

I lie back onto the pillows and look up at the new ceiling.

"What are you thinking about?" says Dave after a while.

"Nothing."

"No woman ever has nothing on her mind. You might as well come out with it."

I turn back onto my side to look at Dave. "I was thinking how lucky we are when Tricia is losing everything."

"You can't dwell on it, love," says Dave, running his fingers through my hair. "It's awful. But you have to move forward."

"I know," I say, still thinking how painful things must be for Tricia and her family.

"So what are you going to do now that you have all this spare time? Do you want to quit the paper and go back to work full-time?" says Dave.

"I don't know."

"You don't want to carry on sex chatting do you?" says Dave with mock anxiety.

"No," I laugh. "I've haven't been able to do it since Mum died. I haven't been in the right frame of mind. Anyway, our circumstances aren't quite so bad now. I guess I don't really know what I want to do."

"Well, there's no hurry is there?" says Dave, moving his hand from my hair to my thigh. "Besides, I like us having more time together now Andy is doing a lot of the paperwork."

"I can't just be a sex object, you know," I say, smiling. "I have to do something constructive as well."

"Pity," grins Dave. "I rather like the sex object idea."

"I thought you did," I say, sliding out of bed. "But you've had your allowance for today. And I've got to go over to Tricia's."

"Are you sure that's wise? You don't want to upset yourself again. You've had a lot on your plate this year."

"Tricia's mum rang," I explain. "Tricia asked to see me. I can't say no. What sort of person would say no to a dying woman? Besides, I don't think she has much longer left."

"You're right. You have to go. But it's not going to be easy."

"I know. I'm dreading it. Not because I don't want to see her. It's just…so sad. I don't know if I'll be able to stop myself from crying."

Dave hops out of bed, pulls on his jeans, hugs me and looks me in the eyes. "You'll be fine, love. Just do the best you can. That's all you can do."

"I guess so," I say, uncertainly.

"Look, why don't we take the kids for a meal tonight? It will give you something to look forward to."

"Alright," I smile. "But no wearing that Texan hat that Jim brought you back from his holidays. I can only take so much stress in one day."

"You got it, babe," says Dave with a cheerful salute.

* * * * *

Tricia's mum opens the door. She looks ten years older than when she arrived from Australia a month ago.

"Hello Sandy. Thanks for coming."

"That's okay, Mrs Reynolds. How is she?"

"Not good."

A tear forms in the corner of Mrs Reynolds' eye before she quickly wipes it away. "We must be strong, my dear," she says, taking my hand. "For Tricia."

I nod and follow Mrs Reynolds into Tricia's pretty, feminine bedroom. Tricia is sitting up in bed, boosted by pillows and looking out towards the garden. She looks strangely peaceful covered in her pink quilt and surrounded by pristine white furniture and delicate flowered wallpaper. Yet I know from the syringe driver pumping morphine into her body that she is probably not as comfortable as she seems.

"Sandy's here," says Mrs Reynolds.

Tricia turns towards us yet somehow doesn't appear to see me. "Hello Sandy."

Tricia's voice is frail and thin, so completely different from the strong, ferocious woman of a year ago. I walk to the side of the bed and take a seat where I imagine Mrs Reynolds has been keeping her daily vigil. Mrs Reynolds lowers herself gently onto the mattress on the other side of the bed. Tricia turns towards me and offers her hand. I take it and we sit in silence for a few moments.

"I can't see properly anymore," says Tricia, breaking the silence. She turns her head to the window. "Everything's a blur. All I can see in the garden is green."

I look out to Tricia's garden, at the sea of shrubs and grass, the dense fir trees reaching for the sky. I imagine it through her eyes. And I imagine not being able to see my children's faces.

"Green is good," I say. "Now pink would be awful."

Tricia manages a smile. "That's what I like about you, Sandy. You always look on the bright side of things."

"I try," I say.

"Have you ever thought about the future, Sandy?"

"Sometimes. But not really more than what I'm going to cook for tomorrow's dinner. And that's hard enough."

Tricia manages another smile. "I mean – have you ever thought what you're going to do with the rest of your life?"

"Occasionally," I say, not wanting to admit that, since Mum died and Tricia's illness, I've not thought about much else. Some things are better left unsaid.

"I had mine all mapped out from when I was a girl. I didn't plan on dying this young."

"I know," I say, squeezing Tricia's hand as I'm not sure what to say.

"Maybe you should go into politics, Sandy. I think you'd be great. You could make a difference."

"I don't think politics is for me, Tricia," I say light-heartedly. "I don't think I even have a political opinion anymore."

"Oh, but you do. You have an opinion on everything."

"I used to, but not anymore. I've changed."

"Not that much. It's all still there, Sandy. Waiting. Besides, you can talk anyone, except perhaps Deidre, into a corner."

"Now Deirdre is the one who should be in politics," I say with mock seriousness. "If it wasn't for the fact she runs a sex chat line. Imagine what a scandal that would be!"

"I thought that was a rumour?"

"Oh God, no. It's all true!" I say.

"Well I never," says Tricia, smiling. "Naughty Deidre."

Mrs Reynolds' face lights up for a moment at Tricia's simple pleasure in a saucy scandal.

"But don't try and distract me with gossip, Sandy," continues Tricia. "Promise me you'll think about going into politics. You know, they'll have to select another candidate to replace me."

Mrs Reynolds looks at me with eyes that beg me to say whatever Tricia wants to hear if it makes her happy.

"Well…alright. But I promise only to think about it. I can't promise anything more."

The doorbell rings. Mrs Reynolds smiles thankfully at me and leaves the room.

"That's all I ask," says Tricia, "that you think about it. That you imagine the possibilities; think about the contribution you could make."

"It's Deidre," says Mrs Reynolds entering the room with Deidre at her side.

"Hello love," says Deidre, bustling in and going straight up to Tricia and plonking a kiss on her cheek. "How are you today?"

"I've been trying to persuade Sandy to go into politics."

"She's certainly cunning enough," laughs Deidre.

"What a nerve," I say. "And this from the woman who's been running an undercover sex service for twenty years!"

"Deidre," says Tricia. "I had no idea."

For the next thirty minutes, Deidre entertains Tricia with stories and gossip about her secret life. I realise through the conversation that Deidre has been here every day for several weeks, helping out Mrs Reynolds who has relaxed enough in Deidre's presence to the extent that she's dozed off in a chair in the corner. The poor woman must be so tired. Eventually, Tricia begins to tire too, her head lolling back on the pillow.

"Time for a rest now," says Deidre and gives me a nod to indicate that we should leave.

I get up and kiss Tricia's cheek. "Bye now," I say. "Take care."

"Don't forget your promise," says Tricia.

"I won't," I say as Tricia closes her eyes.

A week later, as I'm putting the lights on the Christmas tree, the phone rings; it's Deidre to tell me that Tricia has died peacefully in her sleep. When our call is finished I put the star on the tree and turn on the lights.

Somehow, they don't shine so brightly.

23

"Maybe you should think about politics," says Deidre, knocking back a large mouthful of Bacardi and Coke, her Mother Superior costume looking more ironic as every minute passes. "Weren't you president of the student union?"

"Deidre, you know as well as I do, I'm not cut out for it," I say, cramming a vol-au-vent which Tabby has stuffed with couscous and peanut butter into my mouth and washing it down with a mouthful of red wine. "It was youthful ideals. Besides, it's not as if I went to Oxford or Cambridge."

"What do you think, Mum?" interrupts Tabby, who is keen to know how her contribution to our New Year's Eve party is being received by the most important tester - me.

"Delicious, darling," I say, not wanting to say the unusual combination is probably the reason there's almost a whole plateful left on the sideboard. I pick up the plate and offer one to Deidre, who has no choice but to accept, whilst Tabby looks on with the studious expression of a master chef.

Deidre takes a bite. "Wonderful," she says to Tabby who breaks out in a huge smile.

"Why don't you offer one to your father?" I say, passing the plate to Tabby and looking across the room. Dave is holding court with some of the lads who are dressed in an assortment of weird and wonderful costumes, including all five of The Village People. Dave has thrown his hood back on his Chewbacca costume, which he is wearing to compliment my Princess Leia. He looks a bit hot and sweaty in all that fur and takes another swig of his cold beer. I begin to regret we didn't stick with the Flash Gordon costume. I catch his eye and smile sweetly as Tabby makes her way across the room, carrying her plate like a royal platter.

"On the other hand, you could stay at home and teach your kids how to cook," says Deidre, popping the rest of her vol-au-vent in her mouth and then taking another gulp of her drink and gargling away the taste. "Now seriously, why don't you think about party politics?"

"I have," I say, thinking back to my conversation with Tricia. I owed it to her to consider it. "But as much as I admired Tricia for her work and ambitions, she had the perfect background for it. I don't. I can't live someone else's dreams."

"What's a perfect background though?" challenges Deidre. "All those buffoons in Parliament with their so-called "perfect" backgrounds haven't exactly made a good job of it, have they?"

"But who's to say I, or anyone else, could do any better?"

"Well, unless people from other walks of life come forward we'll never know," says Deidre. "Government needs people with experience of life on the streets, big business and the armed forces. Not just those born into it or backgrounds in marketing and PR. They're all so bloody predictable."

"So you think my secretarial credentials from Luton Poly will suffice?" I giggle, topping up my glass from the bottle of wine on the table.

"At least you'd be able to type your own letters."

"Anyway, I've worked for the notorious Madame la Pompadour. I don't think that would look good on my curriculum vitae."

"It's a first class credential," chuckles Deidre, as her surplus of Bacardi kicks in. "And what's more, I hear Madame la Pompadour is an excellent employer with extremely high standards."

"Imagine if it all became public knowledge," I say. "I wouldn't win a place on the local WI Board let alone election to Parliament!"

"Oh rubbish," snorts Deidre. "That's nothing compared to what those toffs get up to at Oxford and Cambridge. Next to them, you'd look like the Virgin Mary."

"Hardly," I laugh. "I can imagine it now; *MP caught on tape selling sex to university professors and farmers.*"

Deidre and I collapse into giggles. We've both had far too much to drink. It's been a difficult year, ending on a sad note with Tricia's death and New Year's Eve is just the time to relax and look forward to the future.

"What are you two giggling about?" says Tina, ambling over with Mrs M and Morna. Morna is dressed as Bonnie Prince Charlie and Mrs M as Agnetha from Abba, which is really quite frightening when you know Mrs M was sixty-four last week.

"I was trying to persuade Sandy to go in for party politics," says Deidre.

"And I was explaining one of the many reasons I can't. Like my work with Madame La Pompadour," I giggle.

"I think that line of work should help you in politics," says Mrs M. "And you could pick up some good trade in the House of Lords."

Deidre, Morna and I collapse with laughter.

"Och, I could get a guid story or two out of that," says Morna.

"I think you should do it," interrupts Tina, with a deadpan face that brings Mrs M, Morna, Deidre and me back to attention. The fact she is dressed as Napoleon probably helps.

"I can't, Tina," I explain. "I don't have the skills or the qualifications. Besides, there's more to it than that. There's my family to consider. There's no way Dave would agree to it in a million years."

"She's right, ducks," says Mrs M, putting her arm around Tina. "Family are all important. Dave and the kids would have to agree. Politics, even at local level, can be very time consuming."

"Let's ask Dave," says Deidre drunkenly waving at him. "Come over here, gorgeous!"

Dave looks up and sees Deidre waving suggestively at him, breaks off from his mates and saunters over with his pint in his hand. "What is it, ladies?" he grins. "Are my services required?"

"We have a question for you," says Deidre. "Would you mind if Sandy went into politics?"

"And maybe even became an MP?" says Tina.

"I think that's a little premature," says Dave. "But if that's what she wants to do then, of course, she'd have my backing. I think she'd be a wonderful politician. She certainly knows how to twist me around her little finger."

My mouth falls open in surprise. Deidre looks flabbergasted as, even in her drunken state, she clearly didn't imagine Dave would give his permission. I certainly didn't think he'd agree to it. Not ever. He must be well on the way to getting totally, utterly smashed.

"I'd never win," I say.

"Let's ask the voters," says Dave, putting down his pint and clapping his hands. "Can I have your attention, everyone?!"

The dancing and chatter in the room grinds to a halt as Max who, as DJ for the night, is wearing half a dozen gold necklaces around his neck, lowers the volume down on the music. Frosty and Helen, who are dressed as The Queen and Prince Philip give a final twirl in the conservatory as Dave grabs me round the waist and squeezes my bottom.

"Right, everyone," booms Dave. "I need a show of hands. I want to know who would vote for my lovely wife to become an MP and show those poncey knobs in Westminster a thing or two!" Dave looks over to his mates. "What d'you reckon, lads?"

A huge roar erupts as about twenty drunken men raise their pints and shout their approval. The rest of the room, consisting of partners, friends, neighbours and almost everyone we know, who are all also completely sozzled, cheer and raise their hands.

"Hear, hear," cries Frosty in his clipped tones over the din.

"That's settled then," says Tina.

"They're all paralytic and completely prejudiced," I say.

"You're more likely to get an honest opinion when someone's drunk," says Tina, smugly.

"Mum, are you going to stand as an MP?" says Tabby, reappearing at my side, looking sweet and innocent for once in her Snow White dress and still carrying her tray of vol-au-vents.

"I'm only thinking about it, darling. It's nothing to worry about."

"I think you should. You'd be much better at that than you are at cooking."

I look forlornly at Dave who, instead of jumping to my defence, nods in drunken agreement.

"Okay, people," says Max over his microphone as Saturday Night Fever bursts through the speakers. "The show's over. Mum's going to stand for election. You're all going to vote for her. So let's parrrrrrrrrty!"

I turn around and look at Deidre, who gives a big cheesy grin and toasts me with her glass.

"Bugger," I mouth.

24

I gaze at the photograph of the Prime Minister smiling out at me from the pages of the party newsletter. God, he looks smug. I notice it's almost identical to the photograph of him on the wall opposite to where I'm seated in the local party offices. However, to be fair, the PM doesn't look half as smug as Trewin Thackeray, one of the prospective candidates as Tricia's replacement, who is currently greasing up to the local party chairman's secretary.

"I must say, Ethel," says Thackeray, "you're looking particularly charming today. That scarf works perfectly with that delightful suit. Now how long did you say it would be before I could see Mr Frobisher?"

I flick over the page of my newsletter and try to disguise my dislike at Trewin Thackeray's efforts to ingratiate himself with the secretary. Unfortunately, Ethel appears to be completely smitten by Thackeray's good looks, dapper suit and slick black hair.

"I'm sure Mrs Lovett won't mind you going in ahead of her," says Ethel, twisting her necklace like a gauche ingénue.

I let out a sigh; loud enough to demonstrate my discontent but not enough to be overly rude. Ethel shoots me a pleading glance.

"No, of course not," I say, reluctantly. "So long as you don't intend to be too long, Mr Thackeray. My appointment was over half-an-hour ago."

A flicker of annoyance crosses Thackeray's face, before it vanishes beneath a veneer of sophisticated charm.

"You must be Sandra Lovett, my potential new adversary," says Thackeray, walking over to greet me.

Thackeray's domineering presence makes me uncomfortable. I place my newsletter back on the pile on the coffee table and stand up to accept his handshake. I already know that he's going to be the person to beat in the contest to replace Tricia. A shiver of disgust runs through me as he raises it to his mouth, his moist lips lingering a moment too long.

"You're not what I was expecting," says Thackeray.

"Which was…?" I say, holding his gaze.

"Oh, just someone older and less…appealing. I'm delighted to meet you, Mrs Lovett. I trust we will become firm friends, whatever the outcome of the selection process. We must all stick together in these troubled times."

"Indeed," I say, wondering with whom Thackeray has been discussing me and who has obviously described me in a less than flattering light.

"Between you and me," says Thackeray, edging closer as if we are old buddies with secrets to share. "I suspect the contest will be mainly between us. The other candidates are particularly ancient and the party needs young, dynamic people."

Thackeray's description of himself as "dynamic" is in exact contrast to his appearance. The embroidered handkerchief in his breast pocket, and gold albert tucked into his pinstriped waistcoat, make him look like a cross between Disraeli and a gentleman cad. He does, however, have a sort of magnetism about him, which is probably why Ethel is still swooning over him like a schoolgirl.

"What do you think, Mrs Lovett?" continues Thackeray, pressing me for an opinion. "Do you think the party needs fresh blood?"

"I would say it needs fresh ideas," I reply.

"You hear that," says Thackeray spinning around towards Ethel. "Mrs Lovett reckons the party needs fresh blood."

"That's not very nice," says Ethel, curtly.

"That's not what I said," I say, annoyed at Thackeray's deviousness. "I said it needed fresh ideas. You're the one who said it needed fresh blood."

Thackeray looks at Ethel and raises a singular eyebrow but says nothing; the implication being that I'm lying and he doesn't want to cause a scene. I realise that his friendly overtures have all been for Ethel's sake and he's going to be a manipulative and cunning adversary. I begin to doubt whether I have Tricia's tenacity.

The door to the chairman's office opens and Mr Frobisher appears.

"Sorry to keep you waiting, Mrs Lovett," says Frobisher. "I just had to deal with an unexpected problem that came up in the course of a conference call just now. You know how it is."

"Actually, Mr Thackeray is next," says Ethel before I've even finished giving a sympathetic smile.

Thackeray gives me a dashing smile, puts his arm round Mr Frobisher's shoulder like they are best buddies, and ushers him back in to the office. The door closes firmly behind them. I begin to rue the fact that I'd let myself be steamrollered into applying for the candidature. I console myself in the knowledge that, so long as I give it my best shot, everyone, including me, will be satisfied.

"I'm going to get some paper for the photocopier," says Ethel, giving me a hard stare.

I nod in acknowledgement deciding it's best just to ignore Ethel's antagonistic nature and pick up the newsletter again and pretend to read it. When the door finally closes behind her, I throw it down, annoyed at Ethel's and Thackeray's behaviour, and stroll over to the water fountain to alleviate my boredom. As I sip my water and contemplate why I'm here, I become aware of some indistinguishable murmurings. I look around for the source and realise it's coming from the region of Ethel's desk. I move closer but still can't make out the exact source until it dawns on me that Ethel and Frobisher must somehow have left their intercoms on, perhaps during their recent conference call, and the dull noise is actually the voices of the two men inside the office. I know I shouldn't, but the temptation to hear the odious Thackeray sucking up to Frobisher is too great. I giggle to myself and turn up the volume very slightly and put my ear close to the speaker.

"Geoffrey Turner is no threat, I'll see to that. He's a bumbling fool," says Frobisher.

"What about the Lovett woman? She's not what I was expecting. I was told she was fat and had a gob like the Mersey Tunnel," says Thackeray.

I reel back for a moment. My mischievous good humour now replaced by intense curiosity as I realise that there is more to Frobisher and Thackeray's relationship than mere chairman and prospective candidate. What's more, the two of them are discussing me in a very unflattering and inappropriate manner. I lean closer; I'm definitely not going to miss this conversation now.

"Yes. She's an unexpected problem," says Frobisher. "She might notch up sympathy votes from the party members because of her association with Tricia Marshall."

"What's her background? Anything we can use to derail her?"

"Mediocre, to say the least. She has none of Tricia's credentials which were watertight. She works part-time in telesales on the local paper. Before that she was at

Hendersons for six years. Husband is a small-time builder."

"What a joke," says Thackeray. "What's she even entering the race for?"

"Apparently, Tricia suggested it. Personally, I wouldn't even give her a second thought if it wasn't for the fact that Tricia spoke so highly of her. She could be a dark horse."

"Can we raise the issue of her unsuitability?"

"I can't do it in the literature. I have to make her sound a worthy candidate, or it would look crass and raise suspicion."

"Perhaps word of mouth would do the trick?" says Thackeray. "I think I know just the person to get the ball rolling."

I make a small gasp as it dawns on me that Thackeray is not only content to lie to ruin my relationship with Ethel, but he plans to use her to start a slanderous campaign against me. This makes the silly digs and petty rivalry between Mason and me seem like kids' stuff. I hadn't anticipated anything like this would happen in the offices of a political party. No wonder Tricia had said she needed people she trusted to help her.

"Drop in a mention of her lack of qualifications a well. She's not even got a degree," says Frobisher. "Her highest attainment is a secretarial course at a polytechnic."

"Impressive," says Thackeray, derisively.

My eyes blur with tears. I've never considered myself an academic, but I'm not stupid. Yet Thackeray and Frobisher would dismiss my abilities on the basis that I don't have some fancy bit of paper. What about all the years I've done slogging it out in business and raising a family? Does that count for nothing?

"When will the goods come in?" says Frobisher.

"Next week," replies Thackeray.

"Good. I have a few interested parties and I'll probably make a nice little earner out of it. Maybe even some donations for the party too."

"Always good to look willing in the eyes of the party," says Thackeray.

My heart begins to thump as I realise the enormity of what I'm doing and what I'm hearing. There's no sign of Ethel but I'm now acutely aware I'm eavesdropping - and that I could get caught at any minute.

"It's amazing what can be overlooked so long as the money keeps rolling in," says Thackeray.

"How are you off for stationery at the moment?" says Frobisher.

I can't believe what I've just heard. This is more than just an attempt to influence the party election process in a dubious manner, which in itself is bad enough, it's corruption. I turn off the speaker and return to the water fountain and fill up my cup and ponder the fact that Thackeray and Frobisher are on the fiddle. I've spent a lifetime in retail and I know what dirty practices can go on. But this isn't just business; it's the bottom rung of politics. It shouldn't be this way. I realise I may not have had the resolve to follow fully in Tricia's footsteps before, but now everything seems crystal clear; I am going to do everything I can to stop Thackeray getting into power and prevent him abusing his position at a higher level.

I sip my water and gaze out the window and mull over what is the best course of action. By the time Ethel returns all I've managed to conclude is that Thackeray and Frobisher have already pretty much stitched me up within the confines of the party. Ethel gives me a quizzical look when she sees I'm not where she left me. She unloads several reams of paper onto her desk before filling up the photocopier.

"A big job?" I say, taking another sip of my water and trying to look blasé.

"Yes," says Ethel.

"You must use a lot of stationery."

"Yes," says Ethel, whose monosyllabic answers indicate she doesn't want to engage with me.

"Better keep an eye on that then," I say. "Stationery is always the first in the queue for theft in an office."

"We don't have that sort of thing going on around here," says Ethel, sharply.

"No, no, of course not," I apologise, knowing that's all I can do at the present. I've met Ethel's type before in the workplace. I'm pretty sure she's a stickler for dogma and procedure and, now that I've sown the seeds of doubt about immoral practices taking place she'll be compelled to stocktake and double check invoices to prove in her own mind that I'm wrong. With any luck, her dogged persistence will result in the discovery of something untoward and her strong sense of righteousness will force her to expose it. It's a long shot but it's a start. In the meantime, I need to do something far more drastic if I'm to beat Thackeray at his own game.

Frobisher and Thackeray stroll into the outer office.

"I'm sorry to keep you waiting, Mrs Lovett," says Frobisher. "Mr Thackeray had an urgent query."

"Not to worry," I say, coming to a dramatic decision. "Anyway, I only need a minute of your time."

"But I thought we were going over your application this morning? Make sure we have it all up to scratch before you go before the committee?"

"There's no need," I say "I've decided to withdraw."

There's a moment's pause as Thackeray and Frobisher take in what I've said.

"Are you sure?" says Frobisher, as Thackeray emits a winning smile.

"Quite sure," I say. "I felt duty bound to put my name forward because of my relationship with Tricia Marshall. But now I realise I'm not ideally suited to the party."

"A sensible decision, if I might say so," says Thackeray. "One must be fully committed to politics if one is to succeed."

"Oh, I am fully committed," I say, "but not to the party. I've decided to run as an independent candidate."

Thackeray and Frobisher are stunned.

"I think it will make it a more interesting contest, don't you?" I say and walk towards the exit.

"I look forward to it," Thackeray calls after me. "May the best man win."

I turn back and see Thackeray gloating as if he has already beaten me.

"Or woman," I say and close the door on him.

25

"I'm so glad you've decided to run for election," says Tricia's mum as I open my front door. "Tricia would be thrilled. Even if it's not for the party."

"Hello, Mrs Reynolds," I say, taken aback by her rapid launch into conversation.

"Anyway, now I can give you these."

Tricia's mum shoves three A4 box files at me. I grab hold of them before they drop onto the doorstep.

"Tricia said I was to give them to you if you were selected to run. They're all her notes. She was very thorough, you know."

"Would you like to come in for a cup of tea?" I ask, clutching the files. "Tina's here too. We're drafting some letters."

"I'm afraid not. There are more files for you in my car and then I must be off. I have such a lot to do before I pick up Oliver from school. Eddie and I have decided to stay in the UK so we can help out."

"That's very good of you."

"It's Oliver who's important now. I'll have to put up with our miserable British weather again," says Mrs Reynolds with a defeated smile. "Can you and Tina give me a hand with these files?"

Fifteen minutes later, Tina and I stare in awe at the enormous piles of files stacked on my dining room table.

"When Mrs Reynolds said Tricia was thorough, she meant it," I say.

"They're all labelled," says Tina picking up the nearest file. "This one says Labour/Tory/Lib Dem/Green/UKIP manifestos and this one says "Labour fiscal policy 1997-2010."

"I don't know where to begin," I say.

"Try this one," says Tina handing me a red box file, a bit like the budget box. It says "Introduction" on it.

I open the file and, sitting on top of the papers inside is a buff envelope with my name on it.

"There's a letter for me," I say, nervously.

"Read it then," says Tina.

I sit down on one of the dining room chairs, pull a sheet of paper covered in Tricia's neat italic writing out of the envelope and begin to read.

Dear Sandy,

Here I am from beyond the grave. I know you are only reading this because you have been selected to run in the election. So firstly, my congratulations for beating Trewin Thackeray. I could not be more delighted that you have managed to oust him. But you must be careful now - he is a truly spiteful man. In fact, I am sure he is up to no good but I have yet to prove it.

I look up at Tina and we silently acknowledge what we already know. My war with Thackeray is only just beginning and is going to be a lot dirtier than Tricia could have imagined. What's more, Thackeray has already won the first round.

In these files, you will find everything you need to know to bring your knowledge up to scratch. Much of it is factual but all my analysis and ideas are there too. Use them as you will. You have always been your own woman and I know that whatever you do with this information you will use it with the best of intentions and follow whatever is the right path. Use your intuition and have faith in what you believe. It is time for change in this country. I hope that you will be part of it.

So this is your journey now, Sandy, not mine. Life is precious; we must make the most of every minute, every hour. Use your life well, my friend, it can be all too short.

God bless,

Tricia.

I choke on the last words and when I look up tears are running down Tina's cheeks.

"Well then," I say eventually, "There's no turning back now. Let's get these files organised and get to work."

* * * * *

Frau Engel greets me at the front doors of The Orchards and ushers me inside.

"It is lovely to see you, Mrs Lovett. This is an unexpected pleasure. I trust all is gut?"

"Yes, everything is well, Frau Engel."

"The residents are missing your mother and her skill at cards. She was an expert player. I am sure they would be delighted to see you and, if you have time, perhaps play a hand or two?"

"To tell the truth, Frau Engel, I've come to see both you and the residents. So that would be ideal - so long as no one minds a bit of chatter. I'm on a fact-finding mission."

"What facts are you hoping to find, Mrs Lovett?"

"I want to know everything about care homes, retirement, pensions. I want to hear personal experiences and opinions. I want to know what it feels like to be old."

"I think much of this you already know, Mrs Lovett. Is this research for your new role that I have read about in the paper? Then we will help and we will do the best we can."

Four hours later, I leave The Orchards with a pile of notes. I put them on top of the ones I took at the local nursery school yesterday. I have time for one more stop. I pull up outside the park and walk to the large open playing space. As I had hoped, there is a crowd of youths playing football. I try to get their attention but they are too absorbed to bother with me. Eventually, the ball comes my way so I stop it and keep it under my foot.

"Hey, give that back!" cries one of the lads.

"I want to speak to you," I say.

"Sod off," says another of the lads with spiky hair and jeans hanging around his bum. "We don't want no trouble. Give us our ball back."

Several of the boys begin to walk towards me. For a moment, I think about running away but I know I must stand my ground. These lads aren't criminals.

"Hey, aren't you that woman with the nutty lady in the wheelchair?" says a lad I recognise.

"Yes, I am," I smile with relief.

"How is she?"

"I'm afraid she died not long afterwards."

"Oh. I'm sorry," says the lad, putting his head down.

"Thanks," I say, touched at the boy's spontaneous sympathy.

"Has your husband got some jobs?" says another familiar lad.

"I'm sorry. Not yet," I reply. "But we have some contracts in negotiation. If we pull them off we could need another two or three pairs of hands."

"Watcha here for then?" says the lad with the spiky hair.

"I need your help."

"Yeah, right," says the lad with a sarcastic snort.

"I need you to tell me everything about being unemployed," I continue. "I want to know about your experiences at school, in the job centre, on youth schemes.

I want to know about your hopes and beliefs and your expectations for the future."

The lads look at each other with disbelief.

"Are you taking the piss?" says the spiky haired lad.

"Nah, she ain't," says the boy from my first encounter. "I saw her in the paper. She's standing as an independent candidate in the next election."

"Knowledge is power," I say.

The lads look at each other for approval. I decide to take the initiative. I take my pen and notepad out of my bag and sit down on the grass. "Now, who left school at sixteen?" I say.

* * * * *

Dave pulls the cork out of a bottle of wine with a healthy pop.

"That sounds good," I say.

"After a long day, it will taste even better than it sounds," grins Dave. "Did you get a lot done?"

"Yes, loads. I'm filling in Tricia's facts with personal stories and details," I say, resting my arm lazily on the breakfast bar. "It's far easier to relate to people if you understand their problems and draw upon their experiences than by merely quoting facts. I'm beginning to put the information Tricia's collated and all her ideas into context now."

"You've done well, love. I'm proud of you. All the lads say they are going to vote for you."

"They're not reneging on their drunken promises then?" I say.

"Not yet, love. So long as you don't file any dodgy expense claims."

I laugh as the door opens, crashes against the wall, and Tabby appears, her face flushed and eyes shining with excitement. "Mum, Dad, come and look at the telly!" she squeals before disappearing in a whirlwind like the Tasmanian Devil.

Dave and I go into the lounge, where Andy, Max and Tabby are fixated by the television. The screen shows a close up of the Prime Minister.

"Parliament is dissolved. There's been a vote of no confidence," says Andy.

"That's less time to prepare, Mum," says Max. "I'll go and finish that poster I was designing."

Dave and I look at each other.

"Not to worry, love," says Dave. "I still reckon you'll make an Honourable Mrs Lovett yet."

26

"What good is an independent candidate?" yells a man from the back of the hall. "You'll have no power to do anything."

"Exactly my point," says Trewin Thackeray with a satisfied smirk. "It's a wasted vote."

"If you mean my vote in Parliament may have less effect, then you may be proved right," I reply to the man in the audience, ignoring Thackeray's snide remark. "But the political landscape of the country is changing and, whilst I personally can make no promises of change for the better, neither will my promises be false or be reneged upon."

"What can you promise then?" yells the man.

"I promise that if you place your trust in me, I will speak loud and clear on the issues that affect this community and the wider community. And I will seek to expose the corruption, lies and manipulation that dominate Westminster."

I shoot a glance at Thackeray to test his reaction; the narrow slits of his eyes are those of a stalking predator. I turn back and address the audience with even more conviction.

"If you vote for me, you vote for a voice born in this constituency, raised in this constituency and that knows and loves the people of this constituency. My voice will be your voice. Together, we will fight for justice, peace and prosperity."

There is a loud burst of applause which reverberates around the hall. In the front row, Deidre gives me a big thumbs up, whilst Morna joins the others, clapping enthusiastically.

Thackeray gives me another dirty look as the chair of the meeting wraps up the event on my high note. He's unable to get the last word which, no doubt, would have been subtly derogative. My lack of education, and non-existent big executive career, is high on his agenda at the moment. Over the last week or two, now I am the official opposition, he has been cunningly dropping in my "failings" at almost every opportunity.

"Well done," says Morna, as I step down from the podium and the crowd filters out into the reception area and onto the street. "That showed Thackeray what he's up against."

"That's what I'm worried about," I say, seeing Thackeray and Frobisher with their heads bowed in conversation.

"Don't worry, lassie. You talk well and I've got some speeches up my sleeve that will have the punters clamouring to vote for you. I've not written romantic novels for thirty years without learning a thing or two."

"I look forward to hearing those," says Deidre, playfully. "I hope you've edited out any whimsical descriptions of the Prime Minister?"

"Oh aye. He's the Antichrist now, along with Mr Thackeray. I'm casting our Sandy here as the heroine and saviour."

"Dear God," says Deidre. "You'll be telling us next that Sandy's related to William Wallace."

"Aye, I'd be lying if I said I'd not thought about it. But it dinnae sit too well with my conscience," chuckles Morna.

"Concentrate on what you can and want to do, Sandy, and leave Thackeray to his petty slander," says Deidre. "Hopefully, it'll backfire on him. Now, let's go and get a coffee. My throat is sore with all this whooping and cheering."

"That's a first," I say.

Deidre, Morna and I make our way into the anteroom for coffee and biscuits with the candidates, local councillors and their guests. Deidre and Morna are soon distracted by the opportunity to circulate, whilst I continue to thread my way through the crowd for the much needed burst of caffeine. I add an extra spoonful of sugar to my cup to help alleviate my flagging energy.

"I'd be careful with that or you might get fat again," a voice whispers into my ear.

I turn and meet Thackeray's venomous eyes. "I doubt it," I reply.

"I wouldn't be so sure," says Thackeray. "When you've lost the election, you might want to console yourself with all those delicious goodies you middle-aged hags love to dribble over."

"You're being a bit presumptuous that you're going to win, aren't you?"

"I think I have the right to be," sneers Thackeray. "No one is taking you as serious opposition. The few votes of friends and relatives will count for nothing on the day."

"If I'm no threat, why do you consistently belittle me?" I rebuke. "You know what? I think you're worried I'm going to pip you at the post. You're worried that people can see through your grandiose image of yourself and see you for what you are: a scheming, manipulative liar who doesn't give a damn about the people of this constituency and who only wants to further his own ends."

Thackeray's eyes narrow again. "I'd be careful what you say, Mrs Lovett. You don't want to provoke me."

"Provoke you into what?"

Thackeray leans over and whispers in my ear. "Let's just say I have something you don't really want to share with anyone else."

I step back and scan Thackeray's face for a clue. Perhaps he's found out about my work with The Beaver

Club, but how? I trust Deidre and all the girls implicitly. They would never let me down.

"Panicking, Mrs Lovett?" says Thackeray with a sadistic smile.

"Not at all."

"If I were you, I'd take the first opportunity to bow out of the race before anything "unfortunate" comes to light."

"You're bluffing," I say, wishing I'd somehow got evidence of Thackeray's underhand dealings.

"Oh, but I'm not," says Thackeray.

"Well, I suppose I'll find out what it is I've done in due course," I say. "In the meantime, why don't you go and look in the mirror and take a long hard look at yourself."

I turn away in an attempt to end the conversation with the upper hand, but Thackeray grabs a tight hold of my arm. "Game over, Mrs Lovett. Game over."

I shake off his hand and stride away, trying to look as nonchalant as possible, but inside I feel as if a very big trap is closing in on me.

27

"You're in the running," cries Deidre, throwing down the county newspaper in front of me. "The latest poll says it's neck and neck between you and Thackeray."

A large cheer resounds around the office that Dave and I have hired as my election HQ.

"Speech! Speech!" cries Morna.

"Yes, give us a few words," says Tina.

I stand up and dramatically clear my throat, to the amusement of the ladies of the PTA and The Beaver Club who have been running the campaign. Most of them have been here almost full time, using their many skills which have been lying dormant for years in motherhood, to administer and drive the campaign forward with a momentum I never thought possible.

"Ladies, I want to be honest with you," I say, deciding it's time to be serious when I see their faces full of anticipation. "When we first started out on the campaign, I thought there was very little chance of success. I was a rank outsider and no one saw me as a serious threat. But how things have changed in such a short time. I...*we*...are now on the very edge of victory. I can hardly believe it. It is truly remarkable that we've come so far and I put it down to you all: your commitment, your effort and your absolute determination to see it through."

I look around again at the dozen or more women who have been here all day for weeks: on the phone; collating leaflets; making appointments; emailing. Their faces are full of optimism and hope. Maybe, together, we can actually change things.

"I also know what this campaign means to you all. What it has become. And it's not only about the memory of Trisha, even though she set us on this path, and neither is it about me. It's about "us" –it is about one of "us" being in Parliament and making our voice heard. We are a large part of the silent majority, the backbone of this country, and, as mothers, we are the custodians and carers of the children who will shape the future. But now it is we who must help to shape the future. It is time that we make our voice heard. It is time to speak out on the issues that concern us."

"Hear, hear!" cries Morna, to a chorus of claps and approving looks.

"We are now only a few days away from the election," I continue. "I want you to know that, whatever happens, I am tremendously proud of what we have achieved. And I'm sure that each and every one of us will walk away from this experience having learnt more about ourselves, our values and our role in society. Those are important lessons. But for now, ladies, I want to thank you from the very bottom of my heart for your hard work, your support and your faith in me."

The ladies applaud again. Their smiling faces fill me with encouragement.

"We have just four days left and we need to make every second count in order to convince those undecided voters so…let's sock it to them!" I say, punching the air.

The ladies burst out clapping and whooping.

"Girl Power!" I shout and punch the air again.

"Girl Power!" returns a multitude of voices as a host of fists strike the air.

* * * * *

The office is quiet, the lights dim. It's nine o'clock and there's only me, Morna, Deidre and Mrs M, who arrived after an evening shift at Hendersons, left beavering away.

"Time to wrap up," says Deidre. "You need to get some rest, Sandy, and we all need to be on top form for tomorrow. It's our last day but one to make a difference."

"You're right," I say, as another email pings in on my computer. "I need to wind down and spend some time with Dave." As I start to close the lid of my laptop, I notice the title of the email and my heart begins to palpitate.

"Game Over."

"What, ducks?" says Mrs M, who is sitting next to me.

"I've just had an email. The title reads "Game Over". That's what Thackeray said to me when he threatened me."

Deidre leans over my shoulder and Morna swivels out of her chair and stands behind me over my other shoulder.

"Better take a look," says Deidre. "It's probably another bluff. It's highly unlikely he's found out about The Beaver Club."

I click open the email. There are two lines of type; one is a hyperlink to a YouTube video and the other a sentence.

"You have twenty four hours to withdraw," I read out loud.

I click on the hyperlink. It takes us to a video entitled Sandy Lovett Gets Her Knickers Down.

"Oh my God," I say. "I know what it is."

I click on "play" just to be sure. A blurred image comes up of Dave and I making love on one of the beds at Hendersons. We're both partially dressed but, nevertheless, it is only too apparent what we are doing. I quickly turn it off.

"Thackeray's a complete scumbag," says Deidre after a brief pause. "I can't believe a man would stoop so low or that people are taken in by his false promises."

"The settings are on private at the moment," says Morna. "Do you think he'll carry out his threat?"

"Yes," I say.

"How did he get it?" says Morna.

"Mason. He's the only person who would do that," says Mrs M.

"You're right," I say. "It's not security. I know Derek must have let on about it during some boys' talk because Mr Mason knew about it - but Derek wouldn't do this to me. No way. Mason must have got hold of a tape somehow."

"I agree," says Mrs M. "It's Mason's revenge for you getting that money out of him. I'm sorry, ducks. I should never have involved you."

"You know as well as I do that Mason's antagonism goes back deeper than that," I say to Mrs M. "But I'm still surprised he's taken it this far. I mean, this is more than petty vindictiveness. But the bottom line is, what am I going to do?"

"I don't think everything is lost," says Deidre, straightening her back. "It's a video of a married man and his wife having sex in what they thought was a private moment. What's the news about that? I think you should brave the storm. The video isn't even that clear. It would be hardly recognisable to anyone who doesn't know you well."

"But what about the kids and Dave?" I say. "Imagine the ridicule at school. I don't know how Dave would take it. He's a proud man. It could floor him."

"Dave can hold his own," says Deidre. "But you have a point about the kids."

"Christ, what am I going to do?" I ramble. "Everything we've worked for would be all for nothing if I quit but, if I don't, I risk public humiliation."

"Now's not the time to make any decision, lassie," says Morna, massaging my shoulders. "You're tired. We're all tired. We all need to get a guid night's sleep."

"Yes, I agree," says Deidre. "I suggest you try and get some rest. Talk it through with Dave tomorrow morning, when things are a little clearer. He has to be a party to whatever happens. Then we'll meet at my house to make a final decision. There's a lot at stake. Including the possibility of letting a man get into power who clearly doesn't deserve it."

"I'm going to throttle Mason next time I see him," says Mrs M.

"Not if I cut off his balls first," says Deidre.

28

I waft the smoke from the burnt toast out of the window, pour a fresh cup of tea and try to find the right words to break the news of Thackeray's malicious threat to Dave. It seemed churlish to wake Dave from his heavy sleep. But now, after playing out a hundred different scenarios until the early hours, I still can't even make up my own mind on the right course of action, let alone find the words to tell Dave.

"What's the matter, love? You seem distracted. You've been stirring that tea for ages. I thought you'd be full of excitement and energy today, now you're so close to victory," says Dave, tucking into his breakfast with gusto.

"I…we…have a problem."

"What's Tabby done now?" frowns Dave, reluctantly putting down his knife and fork, whilst keeping an eye on his next mouthful of sausage.

"No, it's not Tabby."

"You're alright, aren't you? You're not ill?"

I sit down at the kitchen table and look into Dave's concerned eyes.

"I'm fine."

"What is it then?"

"You remember that Christmas party at Hendersons about five years ago? The one where we both got drunk and got a little fruity on the divan?"

"Ye…s," says Dave, raising his eyebrows.

"It was caught on video on the CCTV monitors. Someone…I think Mr Mason…has passed it to Thackeray and he's threatened to make it public on YouTube if I don't quit the election."

There's a long pause.

"The nasty little shit," says Dave eventually and picks up his fork and skewers his sausage with vehemence.

"What should we do?" I say. "I don't want the video published, but neither do I want to quit and let that creep win the election without a fight. And I'd be letting everyone down. But then there's the embarrassment for us and the kids. I'm not sure any of us could handle it."

"Is he bluffing?" says Dave.

"I don't think so. He sent me a copy."

"Let's see it then."

I open my laptop and log on to YouTube. I press "play". Dave watches the entire video, whilst I squirm with embarrassment that someone else has watched us in our most intimate moments. The video ends, Dave says nothing and takes a few sips of his black coffee. I can tell he is thinking it over and working through our options.

It's one of the reasons I love him; he's so sensible which sort of counteracts my impetuousness. We're a good team.

"Well, what do you think?" I say.

"I think I have a great arse."

"Dave!"

"Call his bluff," says Dave, resolutely. "Honestly, love, I don't think it's that bad. It's mainly my arse on show. It's nothing compared to the stuff on the Net these days. If he did go with it, he runs the risk of people finding out he's the one who published it and where would that leave his reputation? Everyone would see him as the shit he is. His reputation would be worse than where it would leave ours. The only thing we've done wrong is to be caught in the act. People would soon lose interest."

"But what about the kids? What would they think? They might get bullied."

"Andy and Max will be fine," says Dave, confidently. "If anything, their mates would probably find it funny that their aged parents still have sex. They'd probably get a few free pints and a clap on the back if it went viral."

"But what about Tabby?"

"I suppose she'd be the most vulnerable," grimaces Dave. "But I think you have to call his bluff...and if we have to explain it to Tabby then we have to. She's a smart girl though. If any kid can tough it out, it's her."

"Are you sure?"

"Yes, I'm sure," says Dave. "You have to call his bluff. With any luck he wouldn't go through with it anyway.

He's probably relying on your feminine sensitivities to do the work for him."

"Alright then. I'll ignore his email and pretend I don't know anything about it."

"I think that's the best option. Play it cool," says Dave, standing up and draining his last dregs of coffee.

"Well, I'm off. Catch you later, love. Try not to worry."

"Where are you going? I thought you were taking the day off? Doing those all-important last minute photo shoots with me."

"I'll be there later, love. First, I'm going to Hendersons to see Mason."

"Dave! You can't!" I say, alarmed at the thought of what Dave might do, even though Mason deserves it.

"I can and I will," says Dave with a rare determination. "He crossed the border this time with you, love. I know you two have had your differences but this is a step too far."

Dave pockets his keys and walks to the door whilst I'm stunned that my placid Dave is going to take action into his own hands.

"He won't be there!" I call out as Dave slams the front door behind him.

I run to the kitchen window and watch Dave reverse out of the driveway and speed away. As I listen to his tyres squeal as he accelerates down the road, I realise it's Tuesday. That's Mason's favourite day for visiting stores in our area.

I grab my car keys and head for the door.

29

The tyres screech as I grind to an abrupt halt in the large car park outside Hendersons just in time to see Dave disappear through the front doors. My adrenaline, which is running high, jumps even further as I spot Mason's Mercedes. I leap out of my car and sprint to the entrance, fling open the door and scan the showroom for Dave.

"What's going on?" says Harvey as I run past him. "Your husband stormed through, looking like he was going to kill someone."

"I hope not," I say without stopping.

I thrust open the door to the backrooms and run down the corridor towards the offices from where I can hear raised voices.

"Dave!" I cry, as I turn the corner into Frosty's office. Frosty is standing between Dave and Mason with a hand on each of their chests. The three men turn and look at me.

"Sandy, thank God you're here. These two gentlemen are having a dispute," says Frosty in his understated military way.

"A dispute? You bet it's a dispute," says Dave. "This piece of low life has passed on intimate tapes of my wife and I to Trewin Thackeray who's threatening to put them on the Internet unless Sandy quits the election."

"I didn't know he was going to do that with it," says Mason, backing away.

"So it was you who gave it to him?" says Dave, menacingly. "What sort of scumbag does something like that? I ought to beat you black and blue."

"Dave! Don't do anything silly!" I plead.

"I agree with Sandy," says Frosty trying to mediate. "Don't do anything rash, Mr Lovett. Perhaps we should all sit down and talk like adults?"

"There's nothing to talk about," says Dave. "I want an apology and I want that tape and any copies."

"I'm sorry, I'm sorry," says Mason, desperate to get out of the situation.

"That's not good enough. I want those tapes. Now."

"I can give you the original, but I don't know how many copies there are," say Mason.

"So what are you going to do?" says Dave to Mason. "I hope you're not planning to stand by while that scumbag, Thackeray, humiliates my wife? Let him get away with it?"

"I swear to God, I didn't know he was going to go to the extreme of putting it on the Net!" says Mason.

"What did you think he was going to do with it then?" says Dave. "Or are you two a pair of perverted voyeurs? I should report you to the police."

Mason's complexion turns white at the mention of the police. But before Dave can say anything more, Mason takes flight and sprints towards the door like a desperate animal.

"What the fuck?" says Dave, astonished at Mason's reaction, and taking off after him in pursuit. "Hey, I want those tapes!"

"Mr Lovett, stop!" cries Frosty and chases after Dave.

As their shouting fills the corridor, I break out in a run too and race after Frosty. The four of us chase each other down the corridor, past Mrs M, who is squeezed up against the wall with a look of terror on her face, and into the showroom.

"What's going on?" says Mrs M.

"Male hormones," I say, as I hurtle past.

Mason runs towards the front exit by the fastest route, which is across the bedroom department. He runs like a leaping gazelle, whereas Dave has the powerful stride of a hunting beast. Mason scuttles over a single divan, takes a few more strides, and leaps onto a king size divan. Dave propels himself forward, grabbing Mason's foot before Mason can jump off the other side. Masons falls, clutches the far side of the divan and tries to wriggle free and pull himself forwards at the same time. His trousers begin to slip down his thighs as Dave refuses to give way.

"I've got you now, you slimy bastard," says Dave. "Give me those tapes!"

"Mr Lovett, stop! Mr Mason, stop!" cries Frosty, as he closes in on Dave and Mason sprawled over the bed. "We can resolve this! I have some Earl Grey in the office!"

Dave starts to pull Mason towards him across the bed. "Give. Me. Those. Tapes."

Mason lashes out with his free foot and catches Dave on the nose. Dave is stunned as blood begins to pour from his nose. He releases his grip on Mason, who pulls himself over the edge of the bed and into a heap on the floor, hitches up his trousers and sprints off again.

"You piece of dirt!" says Dave, as he recovers from the shock. He hauls himself off the bed just as Frosty flings himself on it, trying to catch Dave.

Mrs M, Harvey and I and the other staff chase after Dave and Mason, who are now racing across the car park towards Mason's car. Dave is making up ground upon Mason, who isn't as fit as Dave and is rapidly tiring. Before Mason can reach the safety of his car, Dave grabs Mason from behind, pulls him to a halt, spins him around and lands an almighty punch on his chin.

"That's for breaking my nose," says Dave.

Mason staggers back several feet. Dave steps forward and delivers another massive blow. Mason staggers back several more feet so he is splayed against his car, clutching a bloody nose of his own.

"And that's for my upsetting my wife," says Dave.

"Dave," I say. "Enough."

"He started it," says Dave, wiping the blood from his nose. "I just wanted an apology and those tapes. But now…now I think I should finish it."

"I'm sorry, I'm sorry," pleads Mason again. "I had no idea Trewin would take it this far."

"You want me to stop? Then you get me those tapes and you stop Thackeray. What he's doing isn't right, and you know it. This isn't some silly game. This isn't you and Sandy playing silly buggers. It's a general election."

"I know, I know," snivels Mason. "But Trewin's my cousin. He's a law unto himself."

"You'll have to find a way," says Dave, looking more determined than I've ever seen him.

"He won't listen to me," snivels Mason.

"Look, I know everything you've been up to over the years, Mason, including your appalling treatment of Mrs M's daughter and your own child. If those tapes are made public, then I'll see to it that your employers, and the police, know what you've been up to. Then we'll see who's worse off."

"Trewin has no scruples. He'll do whatever he can to win," snivels Mason again.

"Precisely," says Dave. "Do you want a man with no morals in Parliament? A man who would use blackmail to win? You've messed up big time, now's the time to make amends. You'll have to find a way."

"I'm not sure I can," says Mason.

"You'll have to think of something," says Dave stepping closer again. "Or I'll think of it for you."

"Alright, alright," says Mason, hastily. "I'll think of something!"

"You better had," says Dave, gesturing across to the other side of the car park.

A large cement mixer truck revs up, crosses the car park and pulls up alongside Mason's car. Dave holds out his hand and his foreman drops a spade out of the window. Dave catches it and smashes the rear window of Mason's Mercedes.

"What are you doing?" cries Mason.

"I'm giving you a little reminder," says Dave. "Fill her up, lads."

One of Dave's workmen leaps out of the cab and places the chute from the cement mixer through the window of the car.

"Stop!" cries Mason when he realises what's about to happen. "Please stop! Sandy, don't let them do it. It's a company car!"

"Dave. That really is enough now," I say.

Dave and I exchange glances.

"Wait a moment, lads" says Dave, closing in on Mason, who is cowering against his car. "Alright, you've got your chance, Mason. Make sure that this election in run fair and square, or next time we meet I won't be so forgiving. Understand?"

Mason nods.

Dave nods at his workmen, who retrieve the cement chute from the car. Then he turns and takes me by the hand and we walk back towards Hendersons, leaving

Mason wiping blood from his nose with a crumpled handkerchief.

"You wouldn't have taken it any further, would you?" I say.

"Of course I wouldn't have, love," says Dave giving me a wink. "After he broke my nose though, I decided it was necessary to give him a wake-up call. Sometimes, that's the only way with blokes like him. Selfish bastards. Always in it for themselves. I've seen too many of them."

"Do you think he'll press charges?" I say.

"Nope," says Dave. "He landed the first blow and he knows he's in the wrong."

"We'd better get your nose cleaned up," I say. "What are we going to say to the photographers?"

"Accidents happen all the time on building sites," grins Dave. "It'll just make me look even more rugged and handsome. I'll probably pull in some female votes for you."

I slip my arm around Dave's waist and give him a kiss on his cheek. "You're my hero," I say. "What would I do without you?"

30

"You look so different," says the assistant over my shoulder as we admire my reflection in the mirror.

Eighteen months have passed since Mum and I visited Trés Chic and I bought the blue dress. Now here I am, in the sassy new suit, three sizes smaller, that I'm wearing for Election Day tomorrow.

"Your mother would be delighted," says the assistant.

"Yes, she would," I say.

"Do you want to try on the blue dress now? I've taken it in underneath the arms but I've only tapered it a little down to the waist so it will fall a little longer."

"That sounds great," I say, slipping off the suit.

The assistant leaves for a moment as the shop doorbell rings. I step into the blue dress and do up the zip underneath my arm. I cannot believe how good it looks and, with my fat deposits gone and my hair styled, I look completely different. But inside I am the same me. The me I've always been. I'm emerging from twenty years dedicated to motherhood and family and, now my responsibilities are altering, so is my role. I am in the changing room of my life and tomorrow, win or lose, I'll move forward a stronger and wiser woman.

"That looks fabulous," says the assistant, reappearing.

"It's wonderful," I say. "Thank you so much. You've done a fantastic job." I look in the mirror again and have an idea. "Could you pass me that suit jacket, please?"

The assistant passes me the jacket and I slip it on over the dress.

"You know, I rather like the two together," I say.

* * * * *

My nerves have got the better of me. I slip out of the cubicle and wash my hands after a third trip to the Ladies in less than an hour. I straighten my jacket over the top of my blue dress and check my lipstick in the mirror one last time. Outside, the throb of excited chatter is reaching a crescendo. In a few minutes, the returning officer will announce the results.

"Mrs Lovett?"

I glance to my side. I'm surprised to see Ethel, the party chairman's secretary.

"Yes?" I say, hoping she isn't going to start involving me in some bitter tit-for-tat.

"I wanted you to know you were right," says Ethel. "But there's more. So much more. I've found out what the chairman's been up to…and who he's been involved with."

I nod slowly, taking in the implication of her words.

"I've been very foolish…and gullible," continues Ethel, her voice beginning to break.

"You're only human," I say, putting my hand on hers as tears begin to form in her eyes. "Don't be too hard on yourself."

"If Thackeray wins, I will try and bring them both down. I'm old, I've nothing to lose. They don't deserve to win."

"Thank you, Ethel," I say. "Thank you."

* * * * *

I stand on the podium as the cheers for Thackeray and his twenty three thousand votes fade away. He sneaks me a malicious grin in anticipation of the victory he still believes belongs to him. My heart thumps loudly in my chest. From the votes cast so far, I know it's definitely between him and me now. I look down into the crowded hall and see the hopeful faces of my family and friends who have supported me on this journey: Dave and the kids; Deidre; Mrs M; Morna; Tina; Frosty and the staff of Hendersons; the ladies of The Beaver Club and the PTA; Dave's employees; Mr and Mrs Jaggi; Frau Engel; and even the jobless lads from the park. I am so grateful for their support and faith in me. Without them, I would not be here. I would not have taken this path. As I look down at their beaming faces, I imagine amongst them the radiant smiles of Mum, Dad, Denise and Tricia, whose lives and influence have shaped me in ways that only those that we have loved and lost can do. I am, and always will be, eternally grateful for their undying love.

"Sandra Lovett, Independent," says the returning officer, his voice echoing through the loud speakers.

A hushed silence descends on the hall.

"Twenty eight thousand, nine hundred and sixty four!"

Dave tosses Tabby into the air; Max jumps up pumping his fist; Mrs M and Morna embrace; Deidre hugs and kisses Andy. I glance at Thackeray's dismayed face. He can't believe what's happened and, to a certain extent, neither can I. But, as the cheers resound, it finally dawns on me that I've beaten Thackeray. I've won. I have actually won.

I step forward from the line, look at my supporters and punch the air in victory. Dave's smiling face beams up at me as a tremendous roar of approval erupts.

I am Sandra Lovett, MP, and this is the beginning of my new life.

Acknowledgements

Firstly, I'd like to thank myself. I know it's not common practice to thank oneself. But hey, it's my book I can do as I please! So thanks to myself for not sinking into an arty-farty depression and drowning my sorrows in drugs and booze on all those occasions when I accidently deleted stuff on my PC, drowned it in various liquids and crashed it whilst undertaking "research." Congratulate yourself Mrs T, you did it! Don't celebrate too soon though - remember how those early weight-loss celebrations back-fired?

Now that I've got that initial self-congratulatory hyperbole out of the way, I should also thank my long-suffering beta readers, Elizabeth Axford and Gary Davison. Poor Elizabeth, I can practically hear her sighing as she receives yet another email from me. Still, apart from her fondness for red wine, she's an absolute saint. As for Gary, he's a Geordie gem. I need to thank him profusely for kicking my butt over the finishing line with my novel and for his superb mentoring. Admittedly, his advice and emails were usually pretty blunt and on the lines of "You haven't written anything today, have you? Get off your arse!" but they definitely did the trick. A word of thanks too for my fellow writer, Phil Simpkin, who made my ears burn when helping me with Sandy's saucy rhyme.

I should also like to thank my editor, Debi Alper who is a true professional. It was a delight to find someone who genuinely understood my objectives for The Changing Room and could help me shape the final manuscript. Thank you, Debi.

My thanks also go to my proof-reader, Miss Eve Merrier who is also the compiler of The Changing Room's book club Q & A section and an ever-helpful advisor. I hate it when people younger than me know more than me - it's incredibly annoying. Needless to say, Eve is a lot younger than me. And knows a lot more about grammar than I do. Damn.

I hope you like the cover to my novel. I love it! It was designed by talented American artist, Gracie Klumpp. It took weeks of searching across the Net for someone who I felt could transform my ideas into illustrations with just the right touch of humour. When I finally stumbled across Gracie's work, I knew she was the one. Thanks, Gracie. You're a star.

My thanks also go to my loyal and patient friend, Jean Bailey, for putting up with my ramblings as have many of my other friends, too many to mention, who have indulged my literary musing over the years without confining me to a broom cupboard. (One or two of them may have come very close though.) Thanks, folks!

Finally, last, but most definitely not least, I must also thank my husband and my three sons for their love and support, for which I am truly grateful.

Author Biography

Jane Turley doesn't take herself too seriously and believes laughter is the best medicine for life's ills. She attributes her sense of humour to her childhood spent gazing out of a Silver Cross pram in the seaside resort of Weston-super-Mare. Her excessive exposure to salty air and seagull poop left Jane with an unfortunate desire to inflict her dubious wit on everyone, including passing strangers, scarecrows and stray dogs. Unsurprisingly, sometimes people think she's odd.

Jane now lives in a village in central England where folks are very kind and give her sympathetic looks when she talks too much.

Book Club Discussion Points

Would you vote for Sandy?

When Sandy tries on the blue dress she has a moment of feeling more like herself. Do you have an item of clothing that has special significance or makes you feel a certain way?

Sandy feels as if she is in 'the changing room of life' and her weight and food are mentioned throughout. What do you think is the significance of this?

How do you feel about Sandy as a narrator?

What do you think of the way Jane dealt with issues such as June's Alzheimer's and Tricia's illness?

To what extent do you think this novel makes political or social points?

Sandy goes through transformative experiences in her professional and personal life. Has this novel inspired you to make any changes?

Sandy chooses to keep her work with The Beaver Club from Dave. Why do you think she does this? Do you think she gains anything from it, besides the extra cash?

Relationships between women are central to this novel. Do you feel it's a feminist book?

Did the ending surprise you?

Author Q & A

Have you always wanted to be a writer?

No. For years I wanted to be an actress and spent much of my youth fluffing around in amateur dramatics. I was still heading towards an acting career after I left college when, soon afterwards, I met my future husband. That changed the course of my life. I've no regrets. I've never been someone with any firm plans and tend to follow whatever doors open to me. I think if you are open-minded about life then disappointments are not so overwhelming and it's easier to move on. Now my family are growing older and I've more time to myself, I'm returning to my artistic roots. Writing has come naturally to me - in a sense it's an extension of the creative process of acting, except for now I'm the writer as well as the actor. I think my love for the theatre is why so much of my writing is dialogue-heavy and contains lots of visual comedy. I imagine how things would look in my head, how the lines would be delivered. I don't think anything would please me more than to see The Changing Room made into a film with an array of wonderful British actresses and actors.

What is your writing day?

I don't have any regular routine. I don't follow instructions in writers' guides about when and how to write and I never have a notebook handy at all times. Some days it's a miracle I manage to put my underwear on in the morning, let alone remember to carry a pen and notebook! I suppose there's a bit of a rebel in me too - I can't help wanting to do the exact opposite of what I'm told to do and, even when I am abiding by the rules, I'm usually fantasising about breaking them. In my mind, I park on double yellow lines and use superfluous adjectives all the time. I'd probably implode if I had to study an academic creative writing course.

What advice would you give to aspiring novelists?

Write to entertain yourself first. If you cannot entertain yourself you will not entertain anyone else. Read, write, read and then write some more. Don't be afraid to break new ground and don't let others stifle your creativity. Write from the heart, what is meaningful to you and what you enjoy most. Only then will your characters come alive and become truly memorable. Find people you trust to give you feedback and keep experimenting. When you've served a decent apprenticeship and found your voice, it'll be time to find a good editor. Give clear instructions about what type of feedback you want. Keep your emotions in check and listen to your editor's advice but have faith too in your vision; you're writing your story, not anyone else's. If I'd listened to half the professional advice I was given early on in my writing career I'd never have written The Changing Room. Of course, other people may not like my novel, they may even think it's rubbish, but I'm happy with that. We are not all the same and have different tastes. Ultimately, I wrote a book I wanted to read and which pleased me. If other people like it - that's great. If they don't, then that's fine too.

How difficult is it to combine humour and pathos in writing?

For me, it's my natural writing style. Like most skills, writing styles can be learnt, at least to some degree, but as I'm inherently silly it probably makes it easier for me than it is for some. I can't write serious drama for more than a few pages before something daft pops into my head so I'll never produce a great literary work. I had high hopes when I first started out of producing a masterpiece of English literature but it only took about a week to realise that was never, ever, going to happen. I think many of the professionals I've come across advise against combining humour and pathos simply because it can go spectacularly wrong. But as any comedian or humourist will tell you, humour is very subjective and, by default, you have to take risks and be prepared to fail in exchange for those moments when it works.

What inspired you to write The Changing Room?

I'm fascinated by the concept of change and how easy/difficult some people find adapting to changing circumstances and how society, in general, reacts to any idea of change. For women, in particular, change can be very difficult as we can become trapped in roles that either we ourselves, or society, have historically predetermined. It's hard trying to find the right balance in life with the demands of modern living but, when you factor in the difficulties of being a carer, as Sandy is, life can become even more complex. Inevitably, some women have to make very tough choices. I wrote The Changing Room because I know that place and I wanted to offer inspiration to women in that position and to let them know, that more often than not, a time does come when you get a second chance at your dreams and aspirations. I also wanted others to appreciate that women, as mothers and carers, make a contribution to society that should not be undervalued. In recent years, I feel we've become too focused on money and celebrity, to the detriment of our humanity. We need to think about what issues really matter. And not just on an individual basis. It's a global society now with international problems and, with issues like climate change and overpopulation to overcome, we can't afford to be selfish anymore, either individually or nationally. I'm not a socialist by any means but when some people have more money than they could ever use and others are begging then, as a society, we have probably got something inherently wrong.

If you were an MP, what policies would you advocate?

That's a tricky question. Politics is very complex and if there were simple solutions to current problems then they would have been put into place by now. I think what's most important, in the first instance, is that we elect to Parliament people who have demonstrated honesty and integrity in their working lives and who are able to make tough, critical decisions. Politicians are always going to have to make some unpopular choices. However, if the electorate know those decisions have been made after careful study, with the long-term welfare of the people at heart, then we can at least respect those decisions, even if we disagree. At the moment, too many people in the UK are disappointed that successive governments have been focused on short-term political agendas whilst lining their own pockets. That needs to change. A lot needs to change.

What would your campaign slogan be?

Compassion is not a crime.

Do you see any of yourself in the characters in The Changing Room? Or are they based on anyone in your real life?

I haven't based any character on any one particular person. But every experience I've had, in an abstract way, has influenced the formation of my characters. I'm not consciously doing it but that's what happens; I take little nuggets of my life and observations about the people I've met and combine them with my imagination to create unique characters and scenarios. So, in a sense, there's a part of me in all the characters. My bottom is pretty similar in size to Sandy's bottom for example. But maybe droopier. I think it's good for a writer to find some point of empathy and establish a connection with a character that's not solely based on imagination. Only by engaging with them and seeing life from their unique perspective can a writer really make a character truly believable.

How good do you reckon you'd be at phone sex?

I don't like to brag. But I have many talents. Although they don't include cooking.

Are you working on anything at the moment? Is Sandy going to get a sequel?

I'm always writing. Even if it's just silly waffle on my blog. As for Sandy, I wrote The Changing Room as a stand-alone novel. However, there's the very real possibility of a sequel - it's rumbling beneath the surface like an unerupted volcano. But I'm not going to force it. I suspect, one day, I'll just sit down and the story will burst forth. I think that'll be when, underneath all the silliness, I have something valuable to say. I love to write short stories for the feel-good factor alone but, for full-length fiction, there has to be more than just the laughs.

Sandy reckons it's Aniston or Jolie if she were to bat for the other team – who would you go for?

That's a cruel question. Am I allowed to say both or is that too kinky? Okay…I'd probably go for Jennifer because she makes me laugh. Other than Jen, I'd probably go for Michelle Obama just so I can hear her pillow talk. Or maybe Joan Rivers so I can grab her by the jowls, shake her, and see if anything falls off.

Sandy often quotes advice from her mum. What's the best advice your mum gave you?

Hmm. I'm not sure my mum ever gave advice in the way that Sandy's mum dispenses her pearls of wisdom. My mum was a very good listener and naturally intuitive; the kind of person who led you to your own conclusions without charging £50 an hour. I miss her a lot. She did once tell me to get a tumble drier though which was invaluable advice. I've never looked back on the laundry front.

What advice do you give your children?

Unlike my mum, I give my kids tons of advice. On everything from diet, exercise and how to drive with the minimum use of obscenities to why it is a good idea to brush their teeth, wash their hair and change their underpants. And especially why it's not a good idea to block the toilet. I'm a regular know-it-all. They'll probably hate me when they're older. At the moment, I think they still love me. Well, I hope so.

I've just realised there's far more of me in Sandy's mum than I thought. Blast.

* * * * *

If you have any questions for Jane, want to contact her or stay updated with Jane's latest writing news you can do so via her blog at www.janeturley.net. In the meantime, if you've enjoyed her novel, Jane would be very appreciative of any reviews.

Thank you for reading
The Changing Room!

6916905R00207

Printed in Great Britain
by Amazon.co.uk, Ltd.,
Marston Gate.